Edible Jazz For The Mystical Junkie

Astro-Fiction

By Michael Bannister

"We are living in an age where the very notion of freedom has become shrouded in paradox. We are learning how our ideas become the true form of bondage and that the very thought of freedom actually requires barriers in order to function and express itself properly."

-Anonymous-

-Table Of Contents-

-Thoughts On Astrology-

Let him [the child] know his fairy tale accurately, and have perfect joy or awe in the conception of it as if it were real; thus he will always be exercising his power of grasping realities...

-John Ruskin-

The Six Constants Of Human Observation

1-The law of attraction. –Unity-
2- There is the observed and the observer. –Polarity-
3- Objectivity is seen with subjective lenses. –Relativism-
4- Identification is a concept. –Labels-
5- Change is the only constant. –Paradox-
6- Understand the degree of uncertainty. –Patterns-

Most of societies arguments are kept alive by a failure to acknowledge nuance. We tend to generate false dichotomies and then try to argue one point using two entirely different sets of assumptions.

This being said, opportunity for individual investigation is essential. It is no surprise that people have conjured up countless interpretations as to what the stars really mean. And so definitions occur as mankind struggles to understand what lies beyond, essentially shaping our culture as the years pass.

Astrology and Astronomy were once regarded as the same. With the new era in full motion, there came a desire for predictive knowledge in astronomical observation.

As science gains a better grip on the minds of today, astrology is now considered a pseudoscience or superstition while psychology explains the faith in astrology as a matter of cognitive biases. Better put... it is a system, tradition, and belief. Astrology became an art form while astronomy sided with science.

How could it be that the relative positions of celestial bodies can provide information about personality? How can such massive objects incredibly far away influence human and mundane affairs? How can these placements of planets aid in the interpretation of past, present, and future events?

These are hard questions to answer fully. There will always be a debate of intellect that brings forth the skeptic. If we are able to remember that, the only constant in the world is change, then it will not be long until research exposes serious flaws in the physical arguments scientists have used to debunk astrology.

The scientific method involves formulating explanations on how events happen; testing them thoroughly and adjusting or discarding them based on evidence. It implies that we all have versions of reality running around in our head, but that to must be subjected to investigation and adjustment in order to be more accurate.

As technologies and methodologies improve, research finds that the observable natural world is increasingly showing evidence that reveals a cosmos that is more coherent, connected, and informed in ways previously imagined. Many of the new revelations occurring in the fields of physics, biology and cosmology add fundamental connections to the basic astrological assumptions.

Is it safe to say that science will change its viewpoint on astrology? Of course… that's its function. However, it now becomes a question and study in consciousness. Science should not be limited or exclusive to that which can only be physically measured. Astrology can be the very bridge to this since the objection of science to astrology is theoretical in nature. Because there is no concrete explanation for astrology, it must eventually follow that the facts of astrology will make it necessary for science to revise its theories. Polishing the debate.

Rediscovering the patterns and inconsistencies... pushing us onward.

It is pattern recognition that has led our race where it is today. Astrology taught humans to see life in another way, to find meaning out of something that was once thought of as nothing. The twelve signs of the zodiac are creative outlines, expressing fundamental themes that will be explored within ones lifetime.

From the understanding, philosophical Sagittarius to the analytical worker that is Virgo, the constellations are reminders that everything has its place and timing. Aries is about the ego or what I want, while Libra is about the spouse and partnership, exactly the opposite. When looked at again, Libra has a tendency to be about what one has to do to *themselves* in order to have a partnership while Aries is about how can they better handle *others* in order to get what they desire.

Each sign is connected yet apart. Separate but equal. When viewing an astrological chart it becomes a web of constellations, planets, houses, degrees, retrogrades, nodes and modes, elements and decadents and so on. Pick a region and its culture is sure to have its own ways of interpretation. It is like color in the sky or taste in the sea... many flavors... many vantage points.

When comparing your chart's forward progression to the chart of the present or one partner to another, it becomes even denser with phenomenon. Questions like karma and dharma often come up. The biggest question astrology makes us ask is one of free will and fate. But in order to understand the paradox of paradoxes one must first start at the beginning.

Astrology is based on the individual and their positioning to the stars. This means an investigation within the self then the universe. When studying astrology and the paradoxes that manifest, coincidence happens often. The sense of surprise that's associated with coincidence now looses its lure, as all the important questions in life, for the most part, become only problems of probability.

Astrology can then be recognized as a tool for the soul in seeing what has been conjured up. In simple terms, it is a friend telling you how the clock ticks.

Personality And Retrogrades

It is very easy to see how thoughts shape emotions, only to have our emotion mold our beliefs. It is also easy to see how our beliefs in life shape our emotions, which then generates a list of thoughts on demand. It is a flow of energy. It is the physical mind.

Thoughts = Conscious Awareness
Emotions = Subconscious
Beliefs = Unconscious

Astrology can be seen as reprogramming the belief system with higher functioning software, rediscovering the unconscious behaviors we live out. This is pushing on the doors of fate and will. You become more aware and awake, giving more insight on the matter... literally changing the odds. As far as all of this being quantifiable, time will tell. The phenomenon's that occur in astrology, while being measured by the methods of science, should also be balanced with the methods of the heart. The way we feel our shifts in consciousness is the raw data that needs to be accounted for when quantifying anything.

It is a dynamic play indeed. Looking into astrology really allows us to sit in the seat of the collective unconscious, viewing the agreements and rules of the cosmic game such as gravity and time. As more effort is blended between the physical and non-physical, the basic blueprint for the individual themes one will explore becomes a mirror that does not lie.

We can begin to see a pattern that is growth and transcendence. Through astrology one can work on the tiniest aspect of our self, all the way to the grandest concepts imaginable. The movement between thought, emotion, and belief is widened. The flow of energy becomes about playing the ego behavior to the highest beneficial belief while maintaining lucidity in the higher spheres of the dream world and imagination.

The Higher Mind, that who navigates dimensions of time just as we navigate dimensions of space, is our first glimpse at the non-physical part of ourselves. It is a link in understanding the pipeline of probable events to occur. The Higher Mind constantly guides our conscious thoughts with images and intuition. These are the native eyes of astrology... the window of the individual soul.

Although it takes effort and patience to clearly understand the dynamics of anyone's zodiac, one of the best ways to see our personality is with the sun, the moon and ascendant.

Sun = Conscious Self
Moon = Unconscious Self
Ascendant = Subconscious Self

Sun = How Others See You-What We Emit
Moon = How We See Ourselves-What We Absorb
Ascendant = What Were Moving Towards-How We Move

Sun = How We Think
Moon = How We Feel
Ascendant = How We Physically Act

Constellations = Higher Mind & The Soul
-Celestial Coordinate System-
Planets = Manifestations Of The Physical Mind & Brain
-Subconscious, Unconscious and Thought Patterns-
Houses = Physical Life Experiences
-The Energy In Which The Signs And Planets Function-

These are a few filters to start using when looking at the three strongest aspects of any chart. We can take on the elemental aspects as well. Fire boils water but can be putout by it. Water and air make champagne, bubbly and delightful, while water and earth make mud. Fire and earth is like a volcano while earth and wind are polar opposites, both having good and bad aspects to it. The planets Mercury, Venus, Earth and Mars deal with the inner fabrics of human nature, while Jupiter, Saturn, Uranus, Neptune and Pluto deal with the outer world of our perceptions. Play with this and let your instincts guide you.

Another aspect of any chart to consider is the retrograde process. The best analogy for retrograde planets is like looking at one train traveling eighty miles and hour, while another train traveling one hundred and twenty miles an hour zips below the other train. From the observers' standpoint, the optical illusion will make it look like the eighty-mile hour train is going backwards, due to the second train being faster in motion. It is the same when looking at planets, as they both travel forward, one will seem to be going in reverse.

Everything in the universe has magnetic qualities. Thought itself gravitates towards similar thoughts. When looking at the makeup of any planetary horoscope, some configurations attract while at the same time others repel. The whole world is in a positive and negative paradigm.

A lot of people are "set-up" so they are constantly radiating energy while others will absorb energy. It is how the individual uses and polarizes their planets that will determine the magnetic qualities of any chart.

When a person is experiencing a great deal of energy, it is normal for the planets to act as radiators, becoming a giver of energy to others. Same goes for those who experience less energy than needed, the planets polarize and begin to draw from others the energy that is lacking.

An individual can control his or her own magnetic field from moment to moment. Venus, being an absorber and negatively charged, can show the ability to radiate love to others with poetry and music. The same goes for Mars, being self-centered, can show the ability to energize others. This occurs with all planets day to day.

Astrology tries to teach the individual to use their planets in understanding personal problems, such as relationships, destructive habits, addictions, depression, illusions and delusions. The general idea is for the individuals to familiarize themselves with the zodiac and use their retrograde planets in exactly the same way as if it were in direct motion. A problem that occurs when polarizing is in the threefold retrograde process, being...

1- The individual jumps ahead of himself, trying to live the future in the present.
2- While living out the future, he experiences the feeling that he has already been there.
3- Repeating the first phase in the mind, he actually relives looking forward to a future that has already happened.

In phase one it is almost impossible for a person to use the retrograde planet negatively. They are jumping towards the future now. He radiates outward so he can move towards the people that will bring about the future scenario.

In phase two he is unaware of the first phase that actually brought the phenomenon about. When living this out one experiences a déjà-vu feeling. The person knows they have dealt with the same experiences before, but cannot explain how, when, or why. This is the phase where one becomes misunderstood as apart of himself is trying to radiate his desires while another part of him tries to seek and absorb the understanding of why the experience feels repetitive. It is these mixed ideas that creates a cross vibration with negative and positive energies.

In the third phase one easily repeats looking towards the future that one has already lived. This can throw someone out of synchronization with time and the rest of the world as they try to reabsorb the circumstances that will bring back the past. This is when the individual

9

becomes more of a drain on others, as they are radiating no outward energy.

First we envision what is to be done and we do it; then it is looked at reflected on and we move along. The retrograde process hinders this ability by causing a person to relive all they have already experienced. This traps the mind in an "echo-like" repetition, causing more circumstances that will grow obsessive thoughts and neurotic phobias.

It becomes easy for the retrograde individual to live life in different time sequences than the person without many retrogrades. Depending on what constellation and house qualities the retrograde planet is taking on determines the dimension and density of the time warp one will encounter. Depending on what phase one is in will show the degree in which one is handling his or hers own karma.

Retrogrades give us a glimpse into the past, not only days, weeks or months, but lifetimes as well. These observations can show us how strongly we carry past habits into our present incarnation. These "memories" represent individuals or events meaningful enough to manifest in another life.

The retrograde aspect is a signpost that tells us where to look in order to keep resolving earlier circumstances that appear to be unfinished. With this there comes a tendency for the individual to push their energies onto every individual they communicate with.

Retrograde individuals can easily project thoughts by slipping into the identity of the person they are talking to, while part of him remains in himself, another part of him stays in the other person's psychic space. Essentially the other person gains on the thoughts, desires and wishes of the retrograde person as if they were their own for a short time. If long durations are spent with another thought projector, more time is spent on letting go of these projections.

If there is karma to be dealt with, and there often is, then the retrograde person will see this being fed back to himself through the other person, who has become a mirror. In this process of thought projection it is possible to transfer the awareness one has reached onto the other individuals they encounter. If the karma is good, then it is a most enlightening experience, if the karma is bad than it becomes more of a reflection. Either way it is quite a mystical teaching on subliminal levels.

Retrogrades in different signs and houses will naturally display which retrograde phase a person is most likely to be comfortable living in.

Because Venus is the archetype for female energy, a male who has Venus retrograde will be more content in avoiding females. Females with a Mars retrograde can experience similar difficulties in relating to male energy.

If Mars retrograde is placed in Aries there comes a tendency to reside in the first phase, impulsively and forcibly creating the future before anything is brought about. They live life oblivious to the world around them, jumping to conclusions while at the same time delaying the necessary actions that would otherwise correct the very problems that occur. If the retrograde falls in the tenth house then we add in the conflict of trying to establish the security of ones future, it becomes about crystallizing success in the physical.

Neptune (the illusions and delusions of life) in retrograde can lead someone to fear large bodies of water or get to involved with anything that has unclear outcomes. Pluto Retrograde shows unconscious sexual inhibitions associated with death and fear that can destroy any enjoyment in sexual surrender. Saturn retrograde is not fond of closed-in places, while Jupiter retrograde (being about expansion and knowledge) sometimes exhibits fear of open spaces.

Retrogrades can reveal the role we play in stimulating and perpetuating phobias. What really happens is whatever the individual is thinking in regard to fears and such, is nothing more then a repeating echo of the retrograde process. When this is realized new behavior patterns emerge only to create new experiences that give birth to future echoes.

One can overcome negative ideas and beliefs resulting from the retrograde process just as the addictive smoker can break the habit of reaching towards a cigarette. An individual must refuse to make the "echoes" of life their reality. In time one understands their place and power in controlling their lives. The echoes in life then gradually reside with persistence and perseverance. It is with astrology and the retrograde process that one can ultimately become their own Guru.

Signs	Ruling Planets	Verb	Spiritual Attitude
Aries	Mars + Pluto -	"I am"	Idealism
Taurus	Venus +	"I have"	Rationalism
Gemini	Mercury +	"I think"	Reasoning
Cancer	Moon	"I feel"	Materialism
Leo	Sun	"I will"	Sensualism
Virgo	Mercury -	"I analyze"	Phenomenalism
Libra	Venus -	"I weigh"	Realism
Scorpio	Pluto + Mars -	"I desire"	Dynamism
Sagittarius	Jupiter + Neptune -	"I see"	Monadism
Capricorn	Saturn + Uranus -	"I use"	Spiritualism
Aquarius	Uranus + Saturn -	"I know"	Pneumatism
Pisces	Neptune + Jupiter -	"I believe"	Psychism

Signs	Related Houses
Aries	1st- Body, Self, Personality
Taurus	2nd- Work, Wealth, Possessions
Gemini	3rd- Short Journeys, Communication
Cancer	4th- Mother, Home, Ancestors
Leo	5th- Children, Pleasures, Social Life
Virgo	6th- Health, Work, Service
Libra	7th- Spouse, Partnership, Balance
Scorpio	8th- Death, Regeneration, Sex
Sagittarius	9th- Long Journeys, Religion, Philosophy
Capricorn	10th- Kingdom, Profession, Success
Aquarius	11th- Friends, Hopes, Wishes
Pisces	12th-Prison, Limitations, Self Undoing

Planets	Characteristic	Rules	Falls
Sun	Empiricism	Leo	Aquarius
Moon	Occultism	Cancer	Capricorn
Mercury	Transcendental- ism	Gemini Virgo	Sag Pisces
Venus	Mysticism	Libra Taurus	Aries Scorpio
Mars	Voluntarism	Aries Scorpio	Taurus Libra
Jupiter	Logicism	Sagittarius Pisces	Gemini Virgo
Saturn	Gnosticism	Capricorn Aquarius	Cancer Leo
Uranus	Electricity	Aquarius Capricorn	Leo Cancer
Neptune	Subconscious Mind	Pisces Sagittarius	Gemini Virgo
Pluto	Spirit And Secrecy	Scorpio Aries	Taurus

The Now Of Astrology And Interpretations

If this is how the microcosm works, then how is it being affected by what happens in the outer universe? There is a whole study that relates to ones personal chart and the interpretation of the outside influences. Better put, comparing the chart of the "Now" to the chart of the individual. It is one of the best ways in knowing the astrological weather that is coming.

However, before one gets sucked into the cause and effect that is chart comparison, it is a good idea to look at what the overall theme of the Aquarian Age is. This will help put the individual into the correct perspective when overwhelmed with chart analysis and interpretation.

Aquarius is all about hopes, friends, and wishes. It is the eleventh sign, meaning a great deal of leisure and time to enjoy the hard workings and success of Capricorn. It is living out the dreams one has in life. Aquarius teaches and pushes us forward to group consciousness. The group interests tend to outweigh one's own interests. Even though this sign is about the individual's dreams and wishes, it encompasses the group's priority equally. The group stands first and the individual second.

It becomes easier to see that these elements spell out the word "Service". It shows that the group is the real master in the Aquarian Age. Being interconnected teaches us how to be tolerant while learning oneness. The Aquarian Age is the electricity that fuels the digital age, it is the hope that fuels our idealism and it is sense of knowing that helps us serve society.

When looking at the zodiac and Aquarius, we can see how Uranus also has its rightful spot in helping unfold these global themes and lessons. If Aquarius represents the cosmic viewpoint just explained, then the principles and qualities of Uranus is undoubtedly the planet that links with this viewpoint.

Uranus helps expand and unveil consciousness from matter to spirit. It embodies the principle that is all interpenetrating. It can go deep down within and light up the darkest corners of the psyche. There is no place that it cannot reach. It brings about needed changes to inaugurate the new era through means of uplifting values and destroying false ones.

The planet functions properly in those who can think apart from the brain, those who can push beyond the mercurial energy of logic and reason. It transcends all understanding and intends to operate outside of any rational conclusions, demanding a look at extrasensory perception. Its functioning is electrical, like lightening.

Uranus cannot wait for our brains to understand, it is energy of great velocity. It is not necessary for us to understand right away, it is simply done through us… the understanding comes later. It represents that part of us that is always trying to keep up with ourselves. Flashes and insight occur, the higher mind will make sense of it all then later the lower mind, or physical mind.

Through this aspect or process, the imperceptible becomes perceptible. It is like a professor speaking while at the same time teaching himself, not fully understanding what was said. One can have their own perception of reality, but when speaking through the energy of Uranus, totally different things come through them.

These are called impersonal teachings. It is not speaking from the known— it is speaking from the unknown. The speaker is impressed and the teaching is delivered being fresh and alive. Likewise, there are impersonal writings that attempt to solidify the higher teachings of this energy. Uranus is the higher aspects of intuition and the higher aspect of Mercury. It is the gateway towards wisdom that is deep inside, showing us what to overlook in any circumstance.

This functioning of Uranus enables other manifestations of higher teachings, such as the mathematics and technology of today, accelerating communication, transportation and working methodologies. It can easily shift the emphasis from religion to science.

Uranus is the planet of synthesis. A person of synthesis is at comfort with every other energy system. They co-operate with others as others will long to co-operate with them. This means Uranus can function through all the planets in our solar system without exception. The planets carry seven different dimensions and Uranus has all the dimensions of all the planets, as it is the seventh planet from the sun. Understanding the position and qualities of Uranus in any chart mixed with the cycles of seven is most advised. It is the Grand Alchemist.

There is a seven-year cycle within all humans. We live a seven-day week and regenerate every cell in our body every seven years. Taking into account the twelve signs of the zodiac, we can times them together and have eighty-four. A life lived for eighty-four years is considered to be a full life, a fulfilled life. The twelve cycles of seven can also be seen in its divisions if you break the seven-year scale into monthly periods. The cycles go as follows...

Cycle 1 - (0 to 7 years)
In these years the incarnated soul slowly controls the physical body. It takes about five years for the body senses to follow the mind's command. Here the human body is seen as being ruled by five. It has five senses, body parts or limbs and is made of the five elements. The body is running from the five pulsations of life: inhalation, exhalation, up-thrust, permeation and equilibrium. This process prepares the mind to enter the arena of life.

Cycle 2 - (7 to 14 years)
This is when the child's mind is educated to be constructive and organized. The mind learns better control over body and sense functions. Speech discipline and coordination is practiced in order for clear expressions of ideas. The child learns a rhythm that will insure healthy growth.

Cycle 3 - (14 to 21 years)

This cycle is a period of great work in balancing the body, senses, speech and thinking patterns. Learning to regulate the sexual energies in the body strengthens growth. A sense of aspiration is to be achieved or else it becomes a very hard period for the individual. This is the cycle where we make it or break it, sending us upward or downward.

Cycle 4 - (21 to 28 years)

The fourth cycle is all about how one learns to serve in society. The whole purpose of education is to ensure skills that serve to the group consensus. If their skills are useful, society will take care of them. Economics is the playing ground. In the latter half of these years marriage becomes meaningful and more realistic with a stable basis to build on. It is sound knowledge of skill followed by sound economics that sustains marriages. This is generally seen as the correct way in building a life.

Cycle 5 - (28 to35 years)

This seven-year gap is all about balancing the economic, domestic and social arenas. We better learn to serve society and life begins to show signs of crystallizing. It is in these years that we have our Saturn return, conducting desirable changes in habits and thoughts.

Cycle 6 - (35 to 42 years)

Certain aspects in life can expand or shrink during this time. Aspirations can be progressed as one grows the three arenas of life (Economic, domestic, and social life). Family group will always play a major role. The body's maintenance is kept up in order to crystallize further the patterns and thoughts of the individual. This can also be a tense period in life as one is accumulating responsibilities from family to work. To balance this out it is a good time to dive deeper into the mundane and super mundane aspects in life. Art, music, philosophical and wisdom-oriented topics are tossed around. The key is to stay creative and flush the body with energy.

Cycle 7 - (42 to 49 years)
This is when the body throws some signs of weakness and therefore should be given more attention to. One needs to foresee the logical conclusions of domestic, economic and social duties and prepare for the next cycles in life. By now the individual is completing the 7 cycles of 7 years... becoming truly synthesized. The future depends mostly on the goals and skills acquired thus far.

Cycle 8 - (49 to56 years)
A relaxed approach to life is encouraged. One becomes mature enough to meet the unexpected... to realize the uncertainties of life and stand on their own ground. One finds a sense of detached attachment, learning to be dispassionate in responding to events. One will do this consciously as the passion is more inward and calm. This inner calm is essential for balancing the body system.

Cycle 9 - (56 to 63 years)
This is a time where the activity of family, economics and society gets concluded. Having done the outer obligatory activity of the world, one can now find freedom in relating to subjects that nourish the soul more than the body or personality. By the end of this cycle one should be released of all earthly obligations so the soul can fulfill its purpose.

Cycle 10, 11 and 12 - (63 to 84 years)
These are the years when the late bloomers can finish up on their earthly karma. This is also a time for the early birds to dedicate their time with voluntary service and study, eventually leading towards meditation. Leaving off with meditation allows one to consciously depart from the physical body. Having done this and fulfilled the purpose of life, one can greet death as humble friend.

(Note: The karma of any person can slow or speed up these processes, and at times throw a few aspects from later cycles into earlier ones. The trick is noticing which aspects slip in where they're not regularly, thus revealing karmic lessons and debt… good and bad.)

All one needs to do is understand what cycle they are experiencing, look for other planets in the chart that can be mixing energies with Uranus, then apply those blended energies into a cocktail of insights and interpretations.

Example 1

Lets say someone is going through the 4th cycle and their chart shows Uranus to be in conjunction with Saturn… this will show the lessons of the 4th cycle, (progress one makes towards marriage, knowledge and economics) being pushed through Saturn's seriousness in seeing what can actually manifest in physicality. This means all the effort one does is geared towards success. This can be a beneficial aspect as Saturn rules Capricorn, which is all about status in the kingdoms we build.

If the conjunction lands in the 6th house, one will lean more towards flooding themselves with details about work and health. If the conjunction lands in the 9th house, one will be looking more for a spouse that shares their philosophical viewpoint.

Example 2

Let us say again that someone is still in the 4th cycle and has Uranus in Sagittarius that is in a trine with Venus in Virgo. First the astrologer will understand what role Venus in Virgo has with the individual then do the same with Uranus in Sagittarius. Also accounting for both houses the planets are in the astrologer will make the connection of the two, taking into consideration that it is a trine and not a conjunction or square. Of course the retrograde aspect can be added along with a various amount of other information. Interpretations vary from astrologer to astrologer.

In this case, Uranus falls in the 6th house and Venus in the 3rd. A loose translation would then be, in the search for a spouse one leans towards experiencing love in a manner that communicates health and wellness. The key will be about learning how one applies and defines their love in a relationship.

It is always interesting to note how one looks at a horoscope. With so many systems to account for it almost seems impossible to give an accurate reading without sounding vague or airy. Readings should not be judged by details and aspects alone, but rather from the feeling one gets when hearing or giving the interpretation.

The systems of astrology are really signposts for the intuitive side to take over. The higher symbology of any chart has information embedded within the light that shines onto the astrologer's eyes. Metaphysics at its finest. This means the academics and study of astrological systems is stored in the unconscious and brought in physical form when the talking begins. Interpreting a chart can sometimes feel very similar to impersonal teachings, as one is teaching and learning in the present moment with a sense of curiosity, excitement and awe.

What it means to live in the Aquarian Age is to take the lessons of that sign and adapt them into our lives. Seeing how the energy of Uranus is the forerunner for the Aquarian Age, an intuitive approach is most comforting and embraced. This quality allows us to be more creative, shifting a bit from the strict thought spheres that our logical mind leaves us in

In the end the best way to get results is to keep studying logical and intuitive approaches. A novice astrologer should know how to read a chart as well as they know how to say their name. Studying books and taking workshops is a great start. Sharing information is a must. One should also trace the outline of planetoid events for themselves. This can mean anything from observing mercury retrogrades or keeping track of Venus and Jupiter both on a chart and in the night sky. We can trace the full moons and our swing in emotions or connecting to the energy of Mars with a telescope. Respectfully challenge the systems while fully accepting them as truths.

So, have we come any closer to solving the paradox of paradoxes? Free will vs. fate? Have we found a way to neutralize karma?

This is a question that can only be answered with another question, being… have you moved from a consciousness of cause and effect into a vibration of wholeness?

The largest aspect that will change in the equation is awareness. The dance of duality will always be dancing; it is only a question accepting this, and moving forward. This means playing in paradox, living our lives in total contradiction and seeing how the patterns unfold. It is giving up the sense of control and moving into a path of surrender. Complete trust. Life then becomes more of a surprise, but a willful surprise, as we are still aware of our ability in shifting this depth of surrender.

In essence, paradox becomes the key in shifting our paradigm. Questions like free will vs. fate are no longer seen as a conflict but rather a gateway to universal consciousness. In other words, when the mind separates and defines phenomenon, we no longer become consumed by it… we take in the experience with open arms and remain unshaken. We simply act in full confidence and no longer react to the dramas that cause and effect make us endure.

-The Role Of Mythology-

Let us say physics is A, biology is A+B, psychology is A+B+C, theology is A+B+C+D, and mysticism is A+B+C+D+E. This spells out the path of matter pushing through the body, then the mind and into the subtle aspects of the causal realms. Mysticism is a reflection of the all-encompassing soul.

The legends and folklore of antiquity should not be taken as actual events occurring but rather forms of holding cosmic knowledge and lessons learned throughout the ages. Deciding which part of the legends are real and which parts are embellished is counter intuitive. The stories are meant to feed the soul, reminding us of why we live a life in the first place.

The stars foretold the rise of Jupiter over Saturn. Siddhartha realized his Buddha Nature! Our dharma is constantly spilling into a reservoir of symbology that vibrates consciousness.

With all of this information it is easy to see how carefully planned out our lives can be at times. History essentially becomes his-story... a perspective that expresses itself so willingly, it creates an impression upon the soul.

This phenomenon is persistently blazed across the universe, and I assure you... with the never-ending search to "know thyself" through free will, there are no two stories alike... their history is one of a kind.

These next stories help bridge the gap on how science and art no longer have to be at odds with one another. They are meant to work together in order to improve how knowledge is communicated.

-Edible Jazz-

" Music is the weapon in the war of
unhappiness."
-Jason Mraz-

Static Radio

"Everyone has their own meaning to seek out. I don't think there is a set meaning for everybody, everyday. Everyone seeks in their own small way to find their place in the universe. Some people seem to be doing better than others, but really we are all succeeding everyday we live. Some people are really into religion to show them the way; I believe you should take all the elements of our world and let them show you the way. I definitely wouldn't want to be told the overall meaning of my life. I wouldn't want to feel that insignificant. What makes this planet, our world, is the fact that nobody knows their meaning and that we're all searching together… that's what unifies the human race! Every breath we take, the world succeeds. We are fulfilling our need!"

"Zoe, if I may interrupt. As we live and continually search for this truth to who and what we are doing here, what can we expect along the way?"

"This is all very situational, Alex. The first thing we need is to start accepting change in our life. Change is the only thing that stays the same. Everything changes moment to moment. The way we interact with our environment and process information will inevitably alter our ideals, morals and ethics."

"How exactly?"

"Well let's say we started replacing the concept of ownership with stewardship, doing this will show that we never truly own anything. Now your ego may think you own that car or this property but the land will be there long after you die, just like it was there long before you were born."

"Well said. The point that I'm at right now is what kind of change is the best change? There are a lot of ways someone can change; the transition is not always peaceful. Sometimes people travel down a dark path."

"You are correct. There is no denying the shadow within us all. The question is: how will we use this part of ourselves? We can find the greatest growth when we leap towards the unknown and experience the freshness of creation. The past has already happened, gone, floating off in memory. Sometimes we can recreate the past, but new creation lies in the unknown. Now to answer the second part of your question more fully,"

"The shadow!"

"Yes the shadow. You must know and hopefully all of us come to realize that in any situation, when duality comes in and we judge the situation good or bad, right or wrong... remember that this is your opinion and that's all it is."

"So are you saying if someone commits murder or rapes someone that it's ok to do so, that it's just a judgment and should not amount to some type of consequence?"

"Of course not. We live in a world of right and wrong and I view it wrong to rape someone, but it does not mean that I have to pass judgment onto another and force my viewpoints onto him or her. Two wrongs have never equaled a right."

"I am still having trouble following you. What about justice? What about compensation and balance?"

"Let me ask you this Alex. In a total hypothetical situation, you have sex with a girl who is sixteen. Now you didn't know she was underage and she went along with the sexual affair willingly. Then you find out she is a teenager and word gets around you two had sex, then you get charged with statutory rape!"

"Well ya I guess I would argue and fight in the court, but this is different situation then having sex with someone unwillingly. There are different factors at play."

"Correct, but still, point being, you chose the factors that justified it. You chose to view it the way you wish to see it. Now this is a very extreme scenario we are discussing. If I was to try and have some type of justice out of this scene or any other, it would be that both victim and assailant go through a process of non-violence."

"Do you think locking them up in jail is violent?"

"I believe there are more creative ways to use the potential of a human than just throwing them in a prison of hate, violence and mental torture."

"Building bridges not burning them, as they say."

"Yes exactly Alex. It is essential that we try and give up controlling things. All the knowledge and wisdom we need is inside of our self. The ego only knows a sliver of what our totality experiences. Why tell yourself what something should be when you can find out what it could be. You will discover new things as life tells you what it really is. Then you don't have to go searching around for all the answers. The answers are at your doorstep. The game of life is a game of change, as we find everything we need to manifest what we see fit!"

"So really there is a good reason why all these things happen?"

"Yes, there is a reason why we are all here. This life you live is of the most importance. Everything you say, think or do has its place. Envy and attachment serve us in knowing gratitude and connection. How would you fully know love if you never experienced fear? One actually helps you realize the other. They serve one another for they are a part of each other."

"So there is a purpose for pain and suffering?"

"Of course there is, this is what I have been saying. If you begin to feel the union between all living beings, we begin to ask what is this connection, what is this feeling we get when we start to embrace one another? Can we fully accept someone for who they are or just tolerate that which does not agree with our perspective?"

"What if it is an extreme situation, like the mass genocide and proxy wars around the world… we must surely meet this happening somehow."

"Compassion is your closest ally in these situations. No one person or nation has the right to force another cultural viewpoint upon another. In the end it takes a greater evil to defeat another evil. Showing loving-kindness helps make friends of these so-called enemies. Hopefully with time and effort, they will want to change themselves. Then you find that you assisted someone from within, helping the individuals realize their own light. If we start asking the right questions, we start getting the right answers."

"So taking this information, how would we apply this in certain world issues?"

"Do you refer to the governments abusing their power and the war against so-called terrorism?"

"Yes I do, and the secrecy of what is going on with this reformation of the United Nations, not everyone agrees with the way things are unfolding. No one seems to have the power to speak on the situation without being criticized and labeled as an anti-American or suspected terrorist."

"Indeed these things are affecting the thoughts of many. One thing to keep in mind is take one day at a time. It is easy getting lost in the future of what could be or what should be. There will come a time when the people of Earth will no longer need a government… the government will be more of a governing system if anything. Laws will no longer be enforced but act more as guidelines or reminders. People will look toward themselves for answers and security. The government knows this and just like any organism or organization, it is defending itself from being deleted.

The Government is doing this in such a carefully planned out way that it is hard to see how deep it goes within our very lives. I'm not just talking about the material riches of consumerism that people usually think about, I'm talking about the level of the mind and its conditioning. You see the brain is like an onion; it has many layers from school, environment, television, to whatever it might be. What we should seek to do is remove these layers so we are no longer limited."

"Limited?"

"To think is generally to limit, unless of course you are focusing on not limiting yourself and even then it is hard. You go to college to get a degree, well at some point the list of careers will come to an end. Hence it is limited, but if we can begin to be creative and adopt our own practices that peel the layers, then we find that we will no longer be limited."

"What type of practices can we do to help escape this mental prison you are referring to?"

"For me, meditation and yoga seem to do the trick very well. Everyone is different and not meant to do the same as another, but the end result can be the same. So whether you dance, sing, play sports, play music, have sex or drink your face off, make sure you are doing it with as much awareness and focus as possible. Your intention will lead the way. This single act of conscious living throws you down a path that shreds ignorance. Find what works best for you but treat it as a pathway to your inner balance, for when you have peace… nothing can crumble the foundation you stand upon."

Musically Driven

"It's acceptable to accept-a-bowl! No worries… it's acceptable to accept-a-bowl!" The thick smog of Afghani Kush baked the minds of those who battled the bong.

"So your bro tells me you're looking for Molly?" David inquires.

"Molly. Acid. Shrooms." Loki responds persistently.

"Ok ok, Mr. Cid has left town and Molly isn't answering but I have something elegant for you rate here. It's brand new shit, real proper product if you ask me," David throws the red pills upon oak table.

"What is it?"

"It's the future. People fancy the fuck out of this shit." Loki investigates the pills as pupils dilate, slipping into curiosity.

"Imagine how you feel on Molly but with the visuals of DMT. I can sell you some golden caps that will take you to the moon and back, but this red shit rate here… it's going to take you to mars and leave you there!"

Loki starts negotiations while David laughs, standing still with his seventy-dollar gram offer. Word was spreading about this new drug, this new way of living. It was much more than David made it out to be. It was a way out of the matrix, out of the illusions we call the "real world!" It was an escape, just like any other drug, but for some reason people slowly acted different. Free.

"Let me help you sell some of this stuff," Loki insists with his attention focusing narrowly on money. "If this stuff is as good as you say it is, then you will want help spreading it. Noah and I are going to Sound Wave tonight, it's where all your clientele will be and where you will be able to get rid of it as fast as possible. I know you don't want to be holding on to any illegal shit and I know you like money. It's a win/win situation."

"Damn Noah, your brother is quite the talker. He makes sense, no? So just where is this Sound Wave and when am I going to get my money?" Loki began to speak but was quickly silenced. David made it clear he was talking to me now.

"Did you not listen to a word I said? You be narrating in your head again?" David asks in his British accent.

"Ya man," I reply in a classic stoned voice.

"Ya you're narrating or ya these pills?"

"Ya to both... I got you David. You know I wouldn't screw around with your time and flow. My brother just wants to make some business... you know how it is when you don't want to get a job, spending all your time working, just so you can afford to have a life while ending up with no time to live that very life you worked for. It's ludicrous really. We are going in and getting out. We know at least twenty people who are begging for a new rush, and their friends have friends with loose lips and a bankroll from their parent's trust fund. Their thirst sells itself."

It wasn't long until David felt comfortable lending an old friend and his brother fifty grams of pills.

"Listen, I like you two, both of your auras are glowing with so much orange. You're creative and that's what I need. Too much of the same old shit going on nowadays, we should be smart enough not to screw up."

Just being in the room you could tell that David was obviously playing with his own product. He spoke to us while looking the other way... feeling his chest and hair. I never liked doing work with people who got high on their own supply, because sooner or later the drug usually wins.

Addiction is nectar best served with friends and desire. David could be trusted, of course, but you can never trust a drug; especially a drug that nobody knew what the hell was.

Loki on the other hand always pictured himself as the infamous, Tony Montana and fantasies of the sort. This was a major flaw in today's society; the merging of drugs and dreams based on fragile foundations that crumble under the slightest mental or emotional pressure. The age of destruction gleamed its careless smile, forever pondering the question, "Will they ever learn?"

Going out to the bars was transforming into miniature raves. Clubs like B-Negative or Thirsty Thursdays catered to the so-called "Dark Side." This cocktail usually consisted of drum and bass with a little vampirism. Hooks pierced the skin of mind melting puppets hanging in the air while synthetic blood sprayed the seeds of expression and aggression upon the eager crowd. In a way it was something along the lines of ordered chaos.

The clubs continued to vary. New genres of release sprouted like weeds in a field after monsoon season. From the deepest corners of the soul springs into action the process of co-creation, one of the most creative being the "New Day" event. This was a continuing explosion of music, art, consciousness expansion and of course, sex. It was always moving from city to city, town to town, person to person! It was a world within a world perceived by the spiritual, enhanced with the lyrical, turning the mystical into habitual ritual.

"Amber... Katie."

David insists on Loki and I bringing along his two muses. They walk into the room, slowly soaking in the attention of our jaws dropping... pants tightening.

Amber's lips could make a man lose his marriage, while her hazel eyes drew you in like a tractor beam. Katie's mischievous ambiance was highlighted with white lingerie bouncing off her silk skin. She smelled of roses in autumn, with her Belgium laugh echoing through the ear's touch, sending chills down our spine.

"Ladies, this is Noah and Loki."

"Loki, like the god of mischief?" Katie asks, cutting off David's introduction. Loki nods his head and smiles.

"That's hot," Amber adds, both taking a seat next to their sugar daddy. All David had to do is remotely insist on Amber and Katie going with us and it was already done.

David was usually messed up on anything from cocaine to MDMA but was on top of his shit when it came to knowing the name of the game, aka supply and demand. It also doesn't hurt having two beautiful eye candies on your shoulders when you are trying to sell new product. But there is a reason why he was on top... because once you're on top; you stay on top, and staying on top sometimes means getting your hands dirty. So when you make a deal with David, you best make sure you hold up your end of the bargain.

I knew all about those whose deals had gone south, and let's just say south is where they went: six feet deep! But this was all word of mouth, heard from a friend of a friend who met someone and so on. This being said, it was always second nature to think of an escape plan whenever speaking business. It was my main concern not to screw up, and I never did.

"This is why I like you Noah, you don't fuck up like most people nowadays," David rambles on as he usually does when under multiple substances. "And Loki, Loki, Loki... the apple doesn't fall far from the tree I hope," he continues sinking deeper into the leather love seat.

"You should mob with us," Loki suggests.

"No no my friends, you two take these ladies here and show them a good time, I have business to take care of, so many people messing up, no more honor these days!"

David continues with increased vocals, "Today's generation likes things fast and easy, their music is reflecting it, this womp womp shit, these robot ears have got to go. What ever happened to actual hip hop, rap, good old shit, now it's just the same thing over and over about the same old shit."

You had to give it to him, sometimes when David went off on his tangents, a sliver of knowledge would reveal itself for all to hear. He was an old timer, as smart and reckless as they come, a lethal combination when tested or pushed. David was mostly a good guy, although his visions blended with substance abuse was turning somewhat troublesome.

"Road To Zion"
-Damian Marley-

The brown walls hung movie posters that soaked in laughs and smoke. The throat burned in the best of ways. "If you don't cough you don't get off," was usually the motto.

"This is some good shit no? It's all about the vinyl. The way the needle touches the curves and turns vibration into sound, music into emotion, feelings into inspiration." David's eyes roll up through his skull.
"What's your favorite music Loki?"

"Anything I can dance or rage to pretty much." Katie adds a quick bong toke and exhales while saying, "Reggae, I love reggae." Of course she liked reggae, all girls who smoke weed like reggae.
"Anything I can make love to," Amber whispers.
"That's not surprising," David adds.

"I don't hear you complaining," Amber replies with a certain kind of sass that allowed David to blush, nodding his head in full agreement.

"She sure does like her crazy tribal music. What about you Noah, what tickles your fancy, what gets you hard in the morning?"

"… Live music, for me there is no substitute. Anything else is just trying to come close to what live music has to offer. Somehow in the recording and all, there is a loss of energy. The further down the scale you move from vinyl to CD's to MP3's, there is a lack of essence that can be felt with the highly trained ear."

It has been well known through the history of mankind what music can do to the world around us. Chanting of monks has been said to help cure diseases from tumors to cancer. The sounds of many trumpets have brought down the walls of Jericho. Playing of classical music heightens intelligence in newborn children.

33

Of course these stories come from religion and word of mouth, rarely from some one who actually did their own investigation. Although if you think about it, the cure for cancer or any diseases can be put into the category of "A change in consciousness." Is this not what music does? Is this not why we listen to music in the first place... to change our mood?

Anyone who has had a major comeback from a life-threatening disorder almost always seems to have a one-eighty turn. The smoker no longer smokes, the meat eater becomes a vegan, and the atheist starts studying spirituality. Usually you see this change after something happens to someone, but having this change before something happens helps prevent that very thing from happening, hence music can create this change. Who listens to music and is not affected by it? But I digress.

"Live music you say, that's some shit Noah, who the hell ever heard of that answer. So you play music ya?"
"Just listen to it."

"Ah stop taking a piss, you got to play something, anything, spit it out," David insists.

"He played a bit of guitar back in the day and can write you some lyrics no doubt," Loki interjects with a smile, knowing well enough that I had a slight case of stage fright because what always comes next is...
"Ah very nice, you should play us some music."
"No guitar."
"Well what about singing us something then?"

"They're really poems than songs," I add, hoping he will drop the topic and move along.

"You scared?" David persists. I say nothing, pondering the question.

"Just do it man, does this face look like I give a shit if you're a good singer or not?" David had a good point, but still, when put on the spot it's a little nerve-racking.

"Please sing us a song!" The girl's say in perfect synchronicity like harp strings playing with one another. O they're good at getting what they want or helping David get what he wants.

"You know I'm not too sure I want to spot you these pills if you don't spit something out real quick."

David's typical blackmail routine kicks in, which is all fun and games but at times can seem a bit like pushing thoughts. How else do you think he came to be where he is? Loki looks at me with his "Let's go" look. So I say what I always say in times of great debate. "Fuck it... You like rap, hip hop, turn up some instrumentals."

David laughs in disbelief. He hadn't heard a white boy try and rap since his youth. But to his surprise I wasn't trying to rap. I was just twisting poetic rhythms into something with a beat. Perhaps that's all rap really is anyways... poetry for the 21st century.
"Ya leave it hear, this is nice, nice, nice."

It takes a minute to push everything away. To dive deep within one's self and let the mouth do the talking. The world is our canvas, we but a paintbrush... an instrument... nothing more... nothing less.

Who am I, the one that lies
Under the skies as clouds pass by?
The one that cries and wonders why
We all get sad when loved ones die.

Who am I that observes the mind?
Presses rewind, goes back in time,
Realizing nothing is truly mine.
Not even words that begin to rhyme.

Who am I that's thinking so,
The thoughts we have are hard to let go.
The one who listens, begins to know,
Quieting our mind, we begin to grow.

Who am I that says listen see,
Learn to love and you'll always be
A bird that flies completely free,
Learning of each other, both you and me.

The girls were quiet; Loki's head goes down…
soaking in the essence, one particle at a time.

"That's some deep ass shit mate, but maybe you
should stick to poetry and leave the rapping part to us black
folks," David cracks up at his own joke.

We all laugh and the ice is broken. A few more
rotations of the bong and we began to make our exit. Easier
said than done.

"Where are you blokes going now, you just got
here like an hour ago?"

"We're going to go make you some money and
show these girls a good time."

David likes the answer Loki gives but insists we
dress up for the rave. This might be one of the best parts
about a rave (Radical Audio Visual Experience), you can
dress up and be who ever you want.

We go through David's wardrobe collection, and
let me tell you this collection was thirty years of
Halloween, New Years, and rave paraphernalia. Of course
Loki picks out the white pinstripe suit, with matching
handkerchief, cane, hat and all. The inner pimp is revealed.
I naturally choose Jedi costume. Robe and light saber
included.

"You would pick that shit. You're no Mace Windu,
that fool was black, you're white as rice, pick a different
character."

"This is a blue light saber, not purple, get your
facts straight."

"So you're Obi Wan then?" David suggests.

"Na man I'm my own Jedi."

"What's your rave name then?" Katie asks.

"Don't have a rave name."

I was never into the whole candy kid scene, the
kid's who have all the bracelets around their arms spelling

out PLUR (Peace, Love, Unity, Respect), while they come up to you touching your hair and body, giving you lightshows from their fingertips.

"No one has given you a rave name?"

"I guess not, never knew I had to be given one."

"Same thing with you to Loki?" Katie says with a dumbfounded look on her face.

"Ya I don't get into that stuff, Loki is the name I gave myself, I stick to it."

"But you can be anybody you want to be, it's a right of passage Loki. You don't have a say in it," Katie replies as her right hand locks with his left. Katie takes one of her dozens of bracelets from the arm and transfers it to his.

"White Shadow... your rave name is White Shadow."

Katie insists Loki embrace the name; introducing himself accordingly when amongst raves. Amber walks towards me... glow paint and all. She stares into my eyes for some time, endlessly gazing until her heart felt mine. Amber's face begins to shine; her hand locks with mine and with the slip of a bracelet she whispers gently...

"MAHA!"

"What the hell is a Maha?" I blurt out loud, somewhat confused.

"Show some respect. Maha is a grand name meaning huge, mighty, great and powerful... depending on your translation of the Sanskrit word. It's usually said when talking about any god or goddess in Hindu religion."

"Well that's good, I can roll with that," I utter after she explains this so passionately.

"Follow the hummingbird!"

"What?"

"I just saw a hummingbird fly by your head, that's a good omen," David stares beyond. Was he really tripping that hard, seeing shit fly around while being able to talk to us on a semi-functional basis?

"I'm not tripping man, you are!" David's focus shifts ever so slightly and delivers me a wink.

"Never said you where tripping," I reply with a curious observation. I had thought he was tripping of course, but how the hell did he know that?

While Loki grabbed the pills heading towards the car, David was still following the ghost bird humming around my head. For a moment there, it seemed I could hear fluttering between the pauses of thoughts and words. With this, we left.

Amongst bumpin' vibes and patient anticipation... we enter Sound Wave. The music crashes into the lives of many with digital synthesizers controlling the robotic crowd.

Mist and fog covered the floors like a snake thirsty for pleasure. Glow-sticks light patches of smoke, reflecting the tempo and pace of the manipulating DJ. Horny teens and failed seekers grind together, moaning in an indulgence of what we call lusting impulses.

So every rave has its theme and this one was simple...

"Eternity"
-Titan-

Time is money and money is time, so we waste none and get straight to selling like clockwork. Problem was no one wanted to buy something with no name. Now I'm not one for lying but when it comes to saving my own ass, I'll say anything.

"It's pure molly, better than molly, it's DMT... highly concentrated shit, I'm tripping balls man, I only got a little bit left, this shit's selling fast."

The system was, I talk and get the money while Loki held the pills, that way you don't have pills and money on you at the same time if you get caught. But with Loki having two girls on his arms we split the product between each other to cover more ground.

With four stages and three relaxing lounges we needed to work fast because sooner or later it becomes hard to sell anything, for everyone is already rolling. Of course you have those late arrivals and kids who are pissed off at the fifty-dollar gram that never kicked in.

Honestly it's hard being at a rave when not under any influence and even harder to sell pills while making a profit when your clientele didn't bring enough cash. These unforeseen factors put a little pressure on the mind to say the least.

In the end it works out. Loki's muses pay off and he sells more than I do. I give him the remaining nine pills while he slowly puts two in his mouth, two in Katie's mouth and another in Amber's. Loki doesn't say anything, putting three into mine. They taste like shit but I chew them up to digest better. Loki gives me back the remaining pill saying, "Save it for the hummingbird."
"Ah great you're seeing them too, now?"

Loki nods his head with the beat of the bass, stealthily fading away into the crowd on overdrive. I float around as usual when waiting for drugs to kick in, but it doesn't take long for the effects to spray across the body. David was right… this shit was the future. It's quite hard explaining a drug with our limited usage of words. Magic as words may be… it's something that needs to be experienced and not just spoken about.

In an attempt to explain the phenomenon that is this substance, I will say the improbable became probable, the impossible became possible, and fantasy become reality. I could look up and watch the stars move into geometric shapes. The music became heard from within the head. People didn't know the word stop, only yes and go with the occasional grip of the hip and a kiss. Sex-filled egos bounced off each other like ping-pong balls in a dryer.

At times it's unbearable to hold composure. The drug's wave came back and forth intensely. When looking in the reflected mirror of space-time, all becomes one… connected… feeding off each other… feeding for each other. Then came the over whelming feeling to see the inner self, an inner sage upon the digital age flipping through the night, page by page.

Fighting any drug is a waste of time, so I fully submerge in the moment. My awareness splits in two, the soul begins to view the ego from above… astral projection presumably. The lights became dim; the sound became grim.

From darkness emerged the cloaked menace. Need not think in times like these. His actions told more than words ever could. The menace lifts his hood revealing red saber. Screaming to play, the dark apprentice smiled his stained teeth. In moments time my saber was already out.

The menace weaved within the crowd using shadows and dancing flesh as camouflage, waiting to strike in the blink of an eye. I stand patiently, anticipating his attack. Awareness is my defense now.

Don't think just feel. When the music dropped, the dance began. He came at me with more than vengeance; pure rage was his only ally. Block, block, strike, stand back, and gain composure.

This dark force came wave after wave. I played defense. Let the enemy wear themselves out and then strike accordingly. It was all fun and games until things got serious. The strikes became harder, bolder, faster, without any thought of harm. His wooden saber began crushing my plastic one apart.

He struck brutally until my saber finally broke but this didn't stop him. Being forced to play offense, I take a hit to the arm on purpose in order to throw him off guard. I went straight for his chest with my foot. Flying backwards, hitting the ground, he gets up without hesitation.

"What the hell," I scream towards this unknown samurai. He stands up, takes pose and yells, "AGAIN!"

He was a failed experiment. Somewhere down the line drugs had taken control of this foolish being. With a deep breath, I take stance as hatred rushes towards me. Saber up high, ready to strike, his screams echo across the void as we run towards each other.

Jumping in the air with a right leg to the face, I strike. He hits my left arm, falling simultaneously to the filthy ground. Both stunned, we reach for the wooden saber now broken in two, but I was too slow.

The dark apprentice stood up with half sword in hand... ready to slay waste to my face. His arms rise ready for the kill.

"DIE," I yell with my fist going straight into his balls. Down he drops to the knees like acorns from old oak trees. Things never got this serious before. I make my way out of the stage before he can regain composure.

Time to search for a more relaxing area. This is why I hated the so-called "Dark Side." People just don't give a fuck anymore. Instead of slam dancing at metal shows, they had sticks now, fueled by a mixture of uppers and booze.

Bodies begin to merge back together. No longer did I look upon the scene from above. Thank God, for a second there I might have lost it, out-of-body experience and all. Keeping my eyes peeled for Loki and the girls, they are nowhere in sight.

This little hobbit man was standing next to my side, with a gentle voice he speaks...

"You know you're only hurting yourself!"

"What?"

"You're fighting, lying to yourself."

"And you might be?"

"A friend."

"Friend of whose?"

"Yours of course."

"I'm sorry but I don't know you."

"Yes you do, you have just forgotten."

I was still rolling hard and just speaking on a low level of intelligence was difficult enough. Putting words together was just too much effort. Who the hell was this guy, what did he want, why was he so small and why was he wearing nothing but a cloth around his pelvis with golden garments that highlighted his bronze tan?

"The name's Hermes Trismegistus if you're wondering, and yours is Maha if I'm not mistaken."

"No my name's Noah... well actually its Maha I guess."

"Have you been gone so long you've forgotten your own name? The quickening must have had some side effects."

"What?" This midget wasn't making much sense. "Do you know me or something?"

"I should hope so," Hermes answers, playing with his beard.

"We met on the other side long ago."

"Other side of what?"

"Of life," he replies with a quiet tone and serious manner.

"I've come here to see you. You're quite a hard man to find you know."

"No not really and why me? You need some fixing?"

"No old friend, you are the one who needs fixing."

"You know you talk like you know everything!"

"You know you act like you've done everything!"

Hermes leans towards me gesturing his hand to come down and lend him an ear. I sit on the floor of the second level terrace over looking the third stage's lightshow flowing to alternative electronica.

Hermes begins closing his eyes while nodding his head. The beads around his neck begin to make noise, touching them one by one in sequential order. The feather tattoos on his back start to move, gliding within the psychedelic wind.

"It is not who am I, or what am I... it is who are you, what are you? Know your unmanifested potential coming in here like this. Only those who truly wish to feel the truth are allowed to dwell in these realms like this. Individually and collectively we can raise the consciousness of the people on Earth, so that each of us will be viewed as members of the same family who have come here to claim their birthright of unconditional love and harmony.

Your voyage of self-discovery takes a curve this night. You now begin steps towards new chapters. The ending of such phases in life can be quite turbulent. It's not whether the decisions you make are wrong or right but that you fully realize what is being learned at the moment. You and I shared common ground once, but the road splits and one must choose to stay or go. This density is terribly rough and emotions run high in the souls of many. It is no wonder you have forgotten so much, so fast. But worry you shall not my friend, I am here to honor my end of the karma. All you have to do is listen to the beat of your own heart."

My mind was out of my head. I had no mind; I didn't know what to think. I didn't know how to think. I laughed for what seemed hours on end. I laughed and laughed with him until I couldn't hold my sides any longer.

I looked upwards, viewing spirals of glittering colors coming down, unwinding into different colors, vivid colors, colors that are indescribable. I've never seen colors like these before.

The sounds in my head moved with the transition of thoughts that occurred. We commented and joked at men getting rejected by women in the crowd. Kind of messed up if you think about it, laughing at someone else's disappointment, but their loss is our gain, in one way or another. We spoke very little to each other but rolled in the same thought spheres.

"It has been good catching up with you Maha, I am grateful you can actually see me this time."
"This time?"

"I mean the illusions of fear and denial are fading away for you to see what has been here all along."
"Ok then."

What else is there to say when someone speaks in riddles? Sometimes it's best to say very little or nothing at all. Hermes had turned out to be someone far more intriguing than most met before. Getting up seemed to be an intense workout but I manage to stand firm on the ground.

"Salutations to you Herme—" before I could finish the sentence he was gone. Vanished in thin air, vaporized by oncoming candy kids making their rounds of body massages. I remain still, calm, cool and collective. Even this was a challenge at times with my breath beginning to taste like Vicks VapoRub.

Then it happened. I saw her... the girl who changed everything. She was in her own element, dancing with her eyes closed. Her dark hair twirled around like a tornado of desire. My eyes were glued, fixed upon her glowing beauty.

Time stood still. Her black and red outfit revealed paisley textured spandex, shaping her curves like an hourglass. Her eyes, like embers, immediately walk upon the gates of my soul. She hardly blinked. I follow her through the sea of puppets... It's quite remarkable what a woman can do to a man without saying a word.

I keep composure while all I could do was drool like a dog on the inside. My stillness seems to pay off in the end. She came closer in the softest of ways. She dances around me like a goddess in the digital age.

One song after the other I watch her elegance. Every moment gets more sexual, more desirable until finally we can't keep our hands off each other. We come closer together with a kiss. Universally divine with a lift to the sublime we create our own space and time.

She pushed me to the wall, locking her legs around mine. Arms wrap the head... fingers rush through my hair. Lips are but magnets. She uses her tongue in a manner that placed her on the border of slut and prude, an unusual yet addicting style to say the least.

"Euphoria"
-Monty-

She eventually takes my hand, leading the way through the sex-filled NC17 venue. We find ourselves behind the first stage, under a tree in a field of grass. She pushes me down with my back hitting the trunk.
"Who are you?" I ask on pure impulse.

"I am a bird searching for its reflection!" She whispers gently into the ear.

Goddamn, her words could leave anyone in a trance of curiosity. She took little headphones and an Ipod out of her bra, slowly slipping one bud into my ear. I grab the remaining pill. An equal offering I assume. A little spice adding to the flavor of love never hurt.
"What is it?" She asks.

I didn't want to lie to her, didn't want to say some bullshit like I told everyone else. Then it came like a meteor from space... "It's Mind Glow! It's like nothing I've ever done before."

She takes the little red pill, swallowing it with delight. Her warmth slides around my member. Juice dripped from her lips as she glides, locking me in her web of ecstasy. Her breasts are nurturing, smell arousing, essence untouchable, her beauty unfathomable. She begins to moan and scream...loudly.

"RIGHT THERE, RIGHT THERE, DON'T STOP!" My body goes numb from my crown down. Vibrations heighten. Energies blend.
"Now push it here," she places her hand on my heart.
"Focus here... be with me."

When a girl like that tells you to do something new, intriguing, something that makes your entire being feel more than the ordinary, well it's hard not to play along. I released myself into the unknown. One slight move by her made all the difference. She tightens her pussy and rides harder. This sends me in an uproar of pleasure. Slowly but surely I begin to lose control, approaching the point of no return. She stops suddenly.
"Don't cum, push it up, all the way up!"

Quite intimidating, having a woman in the art of union tell you what to do. On the other hand, it is what every guy dreams of, at some point in his life anyhow. A girl that's great in bed is at the top of every guy's list, except it's not written down anywhere that side effects may include: bruising the ego, lowering self confidence, attachment, and afterwards a slight case of superiority.

Why this case of superiority? Hell if I know, perhaps it's a way the ego defends itself or the mind playing tricks. In any case she begins to ride with force driven by a ticket to nirvana.

I focus on moving energy upward. My spine became straight with hands grasping her plum-like bum. How tender her dark skin is. Keeping focus was hard enough. Drifting back to her eyes she points to my forehead, pushing it to the tree behind. As her fingers pealed away like silent Velcro, our chests came together.

Wider and wider everything gets. Smell, touch, become bottomless pits. Thousand pieces my awareness splits. Down my consciousness everything hits. Life experiences chewed to bits. Stillness. Oneness. All that sticks. Soul commits to the truth that fits… with the help of a playlist she forever omits.

Attachment was at an all-time high. All concept of time was left in the past. We were one, for a moment, until of course we had to split ways. I hate goodbyes. Arrivals are so much happier than departures. Although departing somewhere while being in a constant state of arrival has its advantages, so I use this to help the process.

"I need to go," she whispers softly while playing my fingers like a piano… a love song for the lyrically blind.

She begins to get up but falls victim to the subconscious attraction that leads me into situations like these. She listens to my heartbeat. She says nothing. Lounge vibes started to kick in as new DJs made their sets known. I slip deep into her presence. Contentment found!

There is no gap between thought and action. Everything just is. Everything is instantaneous. I rise higher, stretching into the sky until the people at Sound Wave looked like tiny ants, running around franticly. I can feel every heartbeat extend outward while floating in thin air. Taking off faster than thought, visiting everywhere within the blink of an eye, each place holds such stillness, such serenity that escapes worry.

I view all places simultaneously, like photographs looked upon again and again. The pursuit of adventure lays before my doorstep as a gift under tree on the twenty-fifth. Forever young, emotions overthrow logic and everything merges together, completing the puzzle that radiates bliss.

Pushing the limits I extend into the starlit cosmos. The planets are teachers, speaking of the eternal laws that help create life.

Jupiter is actually mellow yellow and quite a nice fellow. He is brother of the Sun, guardian of the sister planets and holds such abundance of knowledge. He speaks how our brains are but keys ready to unlock the doors of limitation that stand before us.

Mother Earth was actually green and loved everything in between. She was a new parent with a collection of nutrients to share with all. She took in every creature to nurture and provide a safe haven so future generations would have a place to call home. Unconditional love was her song.

Her younger sister Mars was once orange and filled with passion, yet was consumed by hatred and fear from within... forever showing the rest what would become of them if they did not hold true to the eternal law of relationships. She went to war with herself, becoming her own martyr who now glows red... never to be forgotten or missed.

Venus and Mercury were the first twins. Venus was more adventurous than her twin and came closer to the new mother, whispering words of poetry and philosophy for Earth's children to hear. Angels called this planet home. The sunshine reflected off the clouds so brightly; the planet became a beacon of purity.

Mercury stayed close and warm next to the source of light, being protected from the chilling depths of what laid beyond. Mercury was born an innocent and would be a sign to others that no matter how old they are, you must look on everyone as an innocent, and so there she remained.

Saturn was an obtainer of wealth and acquired golden rings to compliment her silver gassy skin. This was just a projection she created to protect her iced hollowness within. Through her material wealth of rings made from the finest minerals the cosmos had to offer, she taught others not to make the same mistake she made. She had not listened to her brother next door about the ways of spirit and that someone who was truly rich was poor in desire. If you're smart you will learn from your mistakes, but if you're wise you will learn from others, the choice is yours alone.

Now Uranus was a very shy woman and would whisper a hello and goodbye just not to be rude. She created a mirror around herself so anyone who looked upon her would look upon themselves. Why she did this is a mystery. Some say she thought that the highest truth could not be put in words; therefore the greatest teacher had nothing to say; thus the answers lay inside us all along. Another translation was if you had anything to ask somebody, you must first ask yourself the same question. Simply saying if you cannot look to yourself for answers, whom else could you look to?

Neptune was a curious one to say the least. She was actually purple but when source shined light on her, she turned blue. She had an icy center that was forever thirsty for knowledge in breaking illusions. She loved hearing new theories and would usually agree that everything is true, even the false. It's all illusion anyways. She was so curious all the time because she loved the variety that the universe offered. She was once very close to Jupiter, listening to all he had to say. Always yearning for more she reached out farther than any other planet before.

Becoming so curious, she wanted to leave her brothers and sisters, venturing off into the depths of space. But she loved her family too much to go, so she took a piece of herself and created a traveler named Pluto (if you but gaze upon Neptune, the dark spot on the lower hemisphere is a scar from the birth of Pluto).

So Pluto surfed throughout the garden that is our galaxy, learning everything possible until he finally ventured off to distant remote families. He met fellow travelers, guiding them back to his home tree where they would learn from his brothers and sisters just as he had.

One after another the Moons and Asteroids found a place to call home. Pluto always came back to tell Neptune what was experienced and learned. He was a guide to everyone, always reminding his family that we are all branches of the same tree, forever growing, spreading out farther than the eye can see... over and over again. Transformation was the key.

Drifting into the emptiness, the vacuum that is deep space, I fix my attention on darkness. Just like that, I see an eye open and look at me. I'm startled yet intrigued that the emptiness of void had the same reaction as me. Even space, I suppose, had some sort of awareness and consciousness of itself. "NOAH... NOAH... WAKE UP!"

Dazed and hazed, eyes open... the mind quickly followed. Loki hovers over me asking if I'm ok. I say nothing. All I can think about was her... the one that got away. I didn't even get a name, a number or even a goodbye. Dusting myself off, regaining balance, I begin to look for her as people thin out. Of course she is nowhere to be found, "Damn!"

Amber and Katie go on about how amazing the night was and how much they loved the new drug.

"It makes your mind light up, it shows you things that make you smile and glow," Amber goes on.
"It's Mind Glow," I say.
"Yah, yah it kind of is. I like that name," Katie persists.

We make our way out of the venue. Approaching David's, we drop off the girls and money. He is more than happy to get his cash so quickly as we are more than happy to get rid of it for him. Loki is a bit upset in not making much profit, but I assure him that it was more of a test on David's behalf to see how Loki would do.
"What do you mean?" Loki asks.

"Well I mean David wanted to see if you were in it only for the money or for the business. Trust is earned and gained, not just given away. If you're in it for the money then that's what you will get. If you're in it for more than money, if you can show him you're trustworthy then you'll have a chance to progress. A simple test, one I unknowing did years back."

"Well if you did it why didn't he hook you up with the price then?"

"Well that's simple, I wasn't the one who was persisting we could get rid of it… you were."

We leave David's and head towards Loki's for much-needed rest! But first… Mexican food with extra hot sauce and chips always helps after a night of sensory overload. Don't forget ice-cold water to wash down the spices of course. I noticed myself still wearing the Jedi costume. O yes the saber was gone, broken in the heat of battle. Flashbacks started to come of a night gone adrift.

I had forgotten all about the royal rumble that left my arm bruised. That's when I found it. In the right pocket of the robe was Her Ipod. It was an older one, the one with the circle turn-dial. Surprising, all they sold anymore were the touch versions. It was red and had the letter K carved on the back. At least I had a link, a clue, a hope at finding Her again. I scroll up to shuffle and press play… away I listen.

"Haiti"
-Arcade Fire-

"We live in a world where we have to hide to make love, while violence is practiced in broad daylight."
–John Lennon–

Static Radio

"We are the product of a billion-year lineage of one enduring stardust. We, all of us, are what happens when a primordial mixture of hydrogen and helium evolves for so long it begins to ask where it came from! We are coming to a point in this particular leap in consciousness where we are beginning to become aware and take action in responsible freedom of self-determination. Becoming truly self-confident and free without being coerced to accept some higher authority. Self-sufficiency and self-preservation are upon us. It is not a matter of, if it will happen, but only when!"

"This is very up lifting to hear Alan, in some ways it makes us look forward to the future with hope instead of fearing it like a war."

"This is the thing Alex, getting rid of the fear that has been imbedded in us for God knows how long, and I'm not just talking about this lifetime, if you believe in reincarnation that is."

"So how can we get rid of this fear?"

"By marrying it with joy of course. Now this may seem very strange at first but if given a minute to contemplate on and a lifetime to try out, you will see wonderful results."

"So you're saying I should be happy when I am feeling afraid of something?"

"No, you should be filled with joy in knowing what exactly it is teaching you. For one, it is teaching you that you do not want that vibration with you, no body wants to feel fear yet we feel it everyday in some small way, unconsciously mostly. If you ask people what religion they believe in they say this one or that one. If you ask them why they believe in it, depending on the religion and person... a majority of them would say some type of answer that insures them they are on the right path and will be in heaven, or escape the wheel of life, death, and rebirth. This answer has roots in fear if you dig deep enough. They are being blinded... it is everyone's birthright to return home from whence they came, regardless of belief."

"I catch your drift to some extent. I am very practical, a bit of a realist at times. But to understand you fully, are you saying that everyone believes and does what they do mostly out of fear? If this is so, then I would have to disagree with you on this."

"I am not saying everyone is like that but I am saying the society we live in projects this on a big level. You take the concept of original sin... this is ludicrous to think something as natural and beautiful as sex can be a sin, but people believe in it anyway. A lot of people stick to religion as a security blanket, so they don't have to deal with issues themselves. They begin trusting in a higher power to do the work for them! Ladies and gentlemen, we must meet this higher essence halfway if we are to ever unravel the veil of fear that seems to be choking humanity."

"So really, as in all things, we must make our own way through life. When you start talking about subjects like these, there begins an unraveling in the layers of conditioning that we or society has painted."

"You're absolutely right."

"But how can we best shed this fear? Yes I understand the joy aspect, but practically is it through courage, ambition, should we start support groups like A.A. meetings or just surrender to reason and logic?"

"Yes you have very good ideas. For one, courage is the mastery of fear, not the absence of it, so this would be a good first step. What has worked best for me is in knowing that the love you withhold is the pain you carry, lifetime after lifetime. There is not a day that goes by where I don't remind myself or think about that. It has helped me reevaluate all the decisions that I've made in my life. These are some of the things I speak about in my new book: how we can begin taking ourselves apart and look at all the pieces of our personality, what our belief systems are, what we think is true and what we think is true through experience. It takes a long time and is still a process that I am going through today."

"Wow, you are correct in how we are constantly redoing ourselves in some way, reevaluating our belief systems. Our reality here on Earth is nothing but a huge belief system, for the most part. It seems that the shit has hit the fan; I mean ever since 2000 we have had major global disasters at a more alarming rate, from record-breaking earthquakes, massive floods, tsunamis, frigid temperatures to extreme heat that is killing off our agriculture at a frantic rate."

"This is the earth releasing fear that has been built up over generations of tyranny."

"So you're saying the earth knows what fear is?"

"Of course."

"Fear is an emotion, right? So you're saying the earth can feel emotions?"

"The earth is alive, just as we are Alex. You see the issue with fear is that it always needs to feed. Fear does not create itself. It devours us of our focus and original intent. To have fear is to lack clear understanding of most situations. Without focus we become confused. This is what's going on in our world right now.

"No doubt, everyone does seem to have some fear, but what if we need that fear to help us, sometimes fear of something can help protect us in the right situations. I was afraid to touch a snake in the jungle so I didn't, but it saved me from a venomous bite. This overall helped me."

"You see fear withholds love. How can we understanding love when so many of us withhold it from ourselves! That part in us that felt compelled to touch that snake, which is love, and then the fear kicked in. What if it bites me! Just try and feel the words that come out. Was the first feeling of you touching the snake a connection in love? If so why would you not want to follow that?"

"Well yes, the fear does kick in after that thought. But what if you didn't think of that fearful state right away?"

"Withholding love only creates a never-ending disintegration. I've said it before, if you withhold from love, you are drained of the life force behind your original intent. It implodes and destroys the very thing you are trying to create. Whether the creations come on the physical, emotion, or mental level, it doesn't matter."

"What are some ways to recognizes this fear then?"

"Well most of the time the first projection of fear comes in the form of denial, an emotion with powerful restriction. With this combination the very thing you don't want to happen, will happen. You are still attracting it by being afraid of it. Fear is in relation to our perspective, a point of view that becomes misunderstood of the value on one's own worth and security."

"How do you mean?"

"Well take a look at religion. Some beliefs have made people think that they are sinful in nature, original sin, the Ten Commandments… Now I was raised Christian, so I'm just picking on it, that's my nurturing. But it doesn't change the fact that it's not helping the process of love in an enlightened way. Did you know that the word sin can be traced back as far as the Sumerian civilization, meaning genetic defect. See how long it's been in the spoken language! Our culture!

You see Alex; all we have is our free will. It's the only true sovereignty in this world. You are because you choose to be, that simple. And if you choose not to be, then you can do that too, but it's your choice. Do not fear or blindly obey a power that is written in a book saying God is all-loving and forgiving, but do not sin or you will be thrown in an eternal abyss. Is this not confusing and a bit dysfunctional? This is the fear of insecurity and unworthiness being created."

"Wow. So can you say that you have overcome fear yourself?"

"Now that's the real question Alex… No I have not!"

"Then with everything you write in your book, how can you fully say we don't need fear, if you have never maintained a state without it yourself?"

"I have fear in my being because I am a victim to your fear, just as you are a victim to my love. It's the price paid in being able to help others, to spread the message that all beings belong to each other and to embrace growth within. It's a working process, like everything else in this world."

"… Amazing… Alan Green everyone, sharing insights from his new book, Awakened, a chronicle and tool on how we can change our lives; one step at a time. We'll be back after these sponsors."

Musically Driven

"Summertime Sadness"
-Lana Del Rey-

Again she consumes my thoughts. Everything leads right back to Her. From fantasy to daydreaming, drifting off, focusing, even tried meditating and again she was there. Shifting to the past, only five days ago, I am still tormented by Her mysterious disappearing act. Not even a goodbye! Ice-cold if you ask me, but this might be adding onto the list of things I was attracted to Her by. As weird as it may sound, I'll put that thought in the neutral category.

The most amazing aspect about this woman was Her music. Her Ipod had the best kind of tasty nuggets. First was the playlist called "Enjoy." I must have listened to that playlist on repeat for an entire day. The second was more instrumental with the list named purely "Insidemental." This was my jam. No lyrics just the beat of the drum with a little mix of acid jazz and trip hop to fill the glass.

The third day I found the playlist named "November." This is when I went through the phase of being a bit melancholy. Azure Ray, Bon Iver, Billie Holiday, Sigur Ros, Bright Eyes, and The Postal Service made out to be one hell of a lethal concoction for lust to stick on tight.

By day four I was kicking it old school with "Woodstock." I'll let that playlist speak for itself. And by day five I was already in the process at looking forward to other flavors in the sea. Perhaps this was the best way to handle the devastation that was the mystery of my music goddess. As for the new playlist at the moment, I choose "Days Go By."

I parked what little belongings I had at Logan's house for the time being. Now Logan was what you call a professional burnout. Too many drugs in a short time does that to kids in their early twenties. He was a couch potato.

And when he got up, it was because he was eating, shitting or maintaining the grow operation him and his aunt had.

A mighty operation it was. Forty-eight fine looking females lined up in rows according to their ethnicity, with a whole upstairs dedicated to the nursery of clones.

Logan cared for an incredible selection of plants ranging from classics of the Kush family to the lucrative Tangerine Dream branch off. Bubble Gumdrop, Mother Ship, G13, Fruity Duty, Heavy Fruity Duty, Blue Dream, Grimm Reaper and Madhi.

"Yes thee Purple Haze, she's smelling great in the mornings... So my aunt says you're sleeping here for a while," Logan speaks while spraying the plants with mist.

"Ya man, my girl flipped and kicked me out with nothing but my backpack and some money to the name."

"What the hell man... that sucks," Logan says, trying not to laugh.

"Ya ya laugh it up."

"Ah come on Noah, there's got to be a reason why she kicked you out?"

"Ya. She found out about me cheating on her."

Logan sighs shaking his head, knowing I was in the wrong.

"But I did this after I found out she was cheating on me," I quickly add.

"Two wrongs don't make a right," Logan spills out, mixing words with marijuana smoke...

It was mostly denial. Denial of something I did that made her want to cheat on me in the first place. I did the same thing as her, to her, making myself no more than an equal in the matter.

"So who'd you hook up with?" Logan just had to ask.

My heart stopped a few beats. I had in fact hooked up with his aunt Janelle, but there was no way I was telling him this. She had been hitting on me for months. I helped her watch over the place while she made her delivery rounds... then she would get horny so we rounded home base a few times.

"She made all the moves on me, if I remember correctly."

"Who's she?" Logan persistently asks.

"Ah this girl I hooked up with at a rave the other night…" I wasn't lying completely. I couldn't stop thinking about Her.

"Was she fine?"

"She was more than that… she was perfect.

"So what's Her name man, stop holding out!"

"No idea. All I know is she loves good music and she rocked my world!"

I occasionally drifted off, thinking about future events with Her, such as our next encounter. Give Her the Ipod and hold Her again. We could talk about what band in history she would be a groupie in and what musician I would be, picking Her out in the audience to come back stage.

We could make love to vinyl spinning in the background. Led Zeppelin III if you must know. We could puff blunts and philosophize, bouncing from one smoke cloud to another in hopes of finding truth and fulfilling purpose. Her soft hair was my pillow upon chest, Her breath the lullaby… Jesus Christ, I was almost living the moment.

"This stuff rate here man, this nugget of choice is hands down, best shit I've hit."

His girl at least had a name… Mary Jane. We roll joints, light them up, inhale and exhale. O how the ritual and reward go hand in hand. I help Logan check the pH levels in the reservoirs, clean the dust off of the fans, blow smoke around the plants, listen to Cypress Hill while maintaining a margin of 1.2 temperature change.

Growing buds is an art form. Let me tell you. You are a parent to those young ones. This is why Janelle asked me to help her with growing these beauties. I knew what I was doing, dependable, and apparently she wanted my nuts. This has been known to get me in trouble at times. Sleeping at a woman's place means she has pussy power. A much-embraced quality that women know is men's kryptonite in the hardest of times.

My spider senses starts tingling with an overwhelming urge to call Loki. It had been almost a week since we last talked. I'm sure my brother was convinced Janelle had me hostage by now.

"How much is the ransom?"

"Loki, what's good?"

"Bitch hasn't kidnapped you yet?"

"Not yet."

"Why you ant answering your phone? Thought you might be in love again with another one of your fairytales."

"Ah…"

"So it's true then, always getting to involved brotha." Loki heard the truth in my voice.

"Alright alright. There is this one girl who's been floating around lately."

"Just another fish my friend. Go jerk off to her in the shower real fancy like and if you're still thinking about her five minutes later… then call her. Trust me, you won't be thinking about no girl after that, and if you do then at least you rubbed one out."

"Did you say, real fancy like? You've been hanging around David much?"

"Ya, been doing some real good business. People been talking about that shit we had at Sound Wave. The red stuff."

"Ya, Mind Glow."

"Ya… Mind Glow... That was out of control."

"It's actually some real heavy shit. It's like I can feel some of it in me still."

"You just high as shit."

Loki laughs, hinting towards smoking some herb and most likely plan our next payday. He was always talking about profit, gaining anything, selling everything. After awhile it became hard talking to him on a down-to-earth level.

Anything that gave him adrenaline, he was on it. Skydiving and sex being the two tied for first place. The runner-up in second place was, you guessed it, drugs. Third of course was money, although money took drugs for a spin a few times.

"I can't meet up right now but I'll hit you up after I do some stuff."

"Chill out Noah, I'm just gunna come stop by and show you something!"

"You don't know where I'm at, Janelle doesn't like people at her house when she's gone."

"It's cool bro, I got you on Friend Tracker. You're ten miles away, see you in a bit." CLICK.

Technology bites us in the ass. Damn Iphone apps. No privacy anymore. Everyone's becoming plugged into the grid. I had kept the fact of Janelle growing weed out of the picture from Loki. He had enough to handle and it was better he didn't know. It wasn't even my operation to be allowing the spreading of words about crops this dank anyways. That's how people got caught.

"Logan, I need you to stay in the room and watch over the plants," I say with force like a father would to his son, looking Logan in the eyes.
"Don't leave this room, make sure these plants don't die."
"What's the problem?"

"Nothing. I need to do important business. Need to make phone calls. Long distance, very important. Make sure these plants don't have bugs."

Wow it's hard lying when you're high. Everything gets very awkward. You feel the other person looking through your bullshit. Turning up the music upon leaving, I make that last smile. The kind of awkward smile you give when you have nothing to say to someone, but they are still looking at you.

Of course Loki was there within fifteen minutes. If Janelle walked in right now, well, it's just best not to go down that thought.

Loki's Mustang rolls up with the bass rattling the windows. I open the door in a clutch performance not to have him ring the doorbell. We take a seat and begin the usually ritual. Grinder, herb, Gandalf pipe, flame and a plan, following along with some beats of course! Notorious B.I.G, Nas, Deltron 3030, UGK, anything along those lines seemed most appropriate.

"Bro, you need to take a look at this," Loki spits out while flopping on the couch, looking around, taking notes momentarily on the new place.

Loki pulls out a zip lock bag of red pills. Mind Glow! Temptation sinks in. I say nothing and force a smile to recede, all while trying to keep my poker face.

"I knew you would be down. Let's do some of this shit and celebrate."

"Hold on man, this is from David and you're still holding this weight just to break even?"

"Shit, I'm making double that. I'm charging two hundred for these pills." Loki smiles.

"You really think people are going to pay two hundred for a pill they don't know about?"

"I don't think they will, I know they will. They already are. People are buying this stuff like clockwork. Mind glow, I like it. I'll start using that. It's catchy ya."

"Wait a minute how many pills have you been selling? And to who?"

Loki lays it down. And I must say, he had done it smarter than assumed, yet a bit more careless than I would care to partake in. Loki got what he needed from David, always paying upfront to make business more of a deal rather than an, "I owe you."

Loki had the people's thirst for drugs on his side. In a world of little virtues and golden vices, he took full advantage. Loki went to every club and rave he could attend, and if two raves were going on, he had someone else at the other venue representing his interest.

Loki picked this candy kid named Perkulator. Well that was his rave name. I told him that was a retarded idea and you needed someone you could trust, no candy kids. But it didn't matter, for now it was working.

He sold most of his product in a few hours and was done with it. He didn't go by any schedule other than the customer's schedule. Which consisted of raves and local middlemen who sold to the hungry youth of weekend keg standers.

"So that's how it works roughly… and I'm expanding very fast. I need your help brother, make some cash with me. I need someone I can trust, like you said."

"I meant find someone else you can trust man, I sold those pills with you to help out and make some quick cash. Now it looks like you're all good on your own."

"But this is a goldmine we are sitting on Noah. Soon they will take this stuff and start cutting it with God knows what… then it will be called something different, feel different, the trip will be diluted. This is some pure shit rate here. This is only going to last for so long. Make some money with me then get out. You would have enough cash for your own pad at least. Not having to stay over at a muse's place under every sexual demand."

"It's not like that."

"Ya not yet, but it always turns out that way. Trust me."

It got quiet for a moment, what he said sank in. Then we heard Logan scream and yell, "AHHHH FHAAAAAKKKK."

Logan kicks the door open, running out to the kitchen. The rays of high-pressure sodium light bulbs shine their radiance across the living room. Logan begins pouring water down his pants.

"What the hell is this? Goddamn Noah, you been telling me not to hang with candy kids and you got yourself one locked in a room," Loki says, walking over to see Logan's situation.

The light makes everything more dramatic when listening to the explanation Logan gave. Apparently he had been smoking a blunt to his dome and passed out. The ember fell on his lap and burned a hole through his basketball shorts onto the tip of his dick.

"Damn bro, why you been holding out on me this whole time, growing crops and shit."

"Seriously Loki, you can't tell anyone. I mean nobody."

"Ya ya just like you didn't tell your own brother!"

"It's not like that. I've been helping her out for a few months and she gave me some cash. Then she started hitting on me when things between Ashley and I started going sour."

"O ya, what happened with that lunch that made you guys break up? That was like a week ago ya?"

" Six or seven days; it doesn't matter, water under the bridge."

"You're always holding out, Loki says while sparking a joint, beginning to look around the grow room, smelling and observing, taking notes as usual. So I tell him the story, in detail cause that's what he likes, always attention to detail.

We met up at a neutral place in case things got intense the explosive drama part would be limited, not making a big scene in public.

Jason's Deli was a fine choice. Spread wide out, open and clear with amazing sandwiches. Ashley came dressed fine as hell, always adding to the sexual attraction. She talked about how I had changed and became distant. I explained she was doing the same. Ashley had no longer been the same girl I once knew.

She said, "That's the thing, I still am the same person." Or my favorite was, "You can't just be with one person, you're always flirting with other girls."

It always came back to some jealousy. In retrospect, a lot of the time people confuse kindness with flirting. I saw her point of view, however it was dramatized with clouded vision… somewhat.

"What did you expect to happen between us, we started seeing each other when you were still seeing that Russian guy."

"So you're saying you never saw us being anything more than a fling?"

The mind weighs heavy in situations like these. So much to compute that the longer it takes you to answer, the worse it becomes because you actually had to think about it.

Long story short I said yes. Afterwards she stood up, splashed lemonade in my face saying,

"Making a girl think she can have something and knowing you don't want to give her is beyond fucked up." Ashley storms off yelling, "FUCKING PRICK!"

"No she didn't," Loki inhales and laughs even more. "What was she wearing?"

"I don't know man it was this cute, just-got-done-doing-yoga outfit, with her hair all tied up and tight spandex. The kind that forms girls' apple bums into cherry blossoms."

"Was she wearing a v-cut shirt?"

"Dude, it doesn't matter, point is that it's done. Story over. Now is not a good time to be thinking about her, too much collateral damage."

It only pissed me off more that most of my stuff was at her place… and the fact that she was correct in the argument.

"It is kind of fucked up if you think about it though. You know, screwing around with girl's minds."

I ignore my brother's attempt to fuel the fire. He was just cracking balls because every time he got himself in a similar situation, it ended up far worse. Loki continues onward about the pills.

"Come on bro, I need your help," was the first and usual opener.

"You're smarter with these things, I need your brain," was my favorite.

"I just want to make some business with my brother from another mother, I just wanna help you out," ended up being the closer.

I pick up a pill and stare into its pixilated maze. It really was amazing stuff. Curiosity kills the cat only one out of ten times, right? "Fuck it," I express out loud.

If things got too intense I could just dip out like I've come accustomed to. This is the single most ridiculous idea I could tell myself, or the greatest of all self-suggestions.

We both popped a pill and washed it down smoothly with some White Russians. We were generous and gave Logan two pills. After all he did burn his dick... and it's never a good idea to be doing psychedelics with someone who isn't on the same level as you are.

Loki calls up Amber and Katie, another essential ingredient, the opposite sex. I mean it's not a necessary thing, but it tends to have its advantages in more ways than one. Polarity, yin-yang... or my yang in her yin as Loki loved to put it.

Now, I've done my fair share of drugs, I'm not proud of it, or ashamed. It's more of a background thing in my life. It is there just like everything else is just here or there. I have built a pretty good tolerance to most of the goods on the street. But this Mind Glow stuff was out of control.

O you could control it, or more like curve the effects. It was interesting watching myself do things, watching how I react to a situation. It was far denser than the occasional out-of-body episode; the experience was like watching your life on a 4-D television screen.

Somehow it seemed to highlight people's positives or expand their shadows. And if their positive was their shadow, then this drug wasn't for you. Something very different happened. I mean Loki turned into his usual self but just on crack. Typical Scorpio was all over the girls, who had come in fashion with glow-sticks, vapor rub, lingerie and friends.

I seemed to be riding the drug out ok, other than the walls shining florescent purple waves. The laughs of young candy girls hitting the slopes was going straight through my head. I was still worrying how Janelle could come home any moment and rip my head off for abusing her trust. But that's what was different; I was ok with worrying in some odd way. Feeling the anxiety was a rush all of its own.

"Janelle is out all night, she don't get back till the morning."

Logan had changed as well. He seemed a bit more telepathic to me… much smarter, classier, informative, like a professor at a university that taught philosophy or metaphysics. Logan gave me a look while putting pipe in mouth, puffing away like a train heading into the grow room. My concentration was in a state of wind, so I follow.

Upon entering the golden lights of Eden, I am greeted with applause and glory. The plants were indeed alive, beautiful princesses with all their lovely perfumes making the nose short circuit. Little giggles with whispering secrets made you feel somewhat admired and welcomed, a strange concoction indeed.

I continued to hear the plants whisper to each other. In a state of cluelessness I simply observe these talking plants. Such wonder. Logan seemed quite fine handling himself, greeting the ladies with a gentle touch or two. I again follow his lead and bow my head, like a shy child. The lights became a vortex of shining particles too intense to reside in, so I slap on the shades and turn on the tunes.

"Los Angeles Daze & Acid Raindrops"
-People Under The Stairs-

"Here's a theory… the Men In Black are real. They're called the NSA or blah blah this and that agenda, and hybrid aliens are living among us just as much as the robotic avatars are. Now this automatically gets thrown in as conspiracy. Ok then. But as we move along from judgment towards sensing, you can clearly see how astonishing things have become.

I mean it was only two thousand years ago that revolutionary steps were taken in China towards a new system of health, which would make today's health care look like anarchy and corruption. It was so simple; the patient only paid the doctor as long as one remained healthy. If the patient became ill then the doctor was not paid.

Now this way of health care seems strange at first glance, but if we look at how it is run today, just the opposite, then you can see we are making the doctor dependent on our sickness. The illness then becomes the doctor's interest. This of course is highly influenced by capitalism and consumerism. These major governing systems of our social order hardly get questioned and are blindly accepted by the population at large.

To be all fair and honest it's reaching the borders of slavery of the mind. The system, dare I say the matrix, has us at our throats and doesn't seem to be letting go.

To release this bondage that is rooted in our unconscious will consist of a journey without and within. In this awareness we gain freedom in knowing nobody can make you unfree, other then yourself of course.

The sum total analysis comes down to the desire to be unfree. It is the desire to be dependent or independent, that makes us unfree. To revolt is to be controlled by a desire that automatically blinds us from the truth of becoming interdependent.

Life cannot become without death. Joy and sadness are a part of the same stream. This is the very nature. This is the Tao of things.

But you see… you have to understand that there are a lot of people who are not ready for this system to collapse. And many of them are so sure, so hopelessly a part of the system that they will fight to protect it. It is their way of life. Can we expect anything different?

Hence you are confronted with distress, tension, anger, and conflict. This shows how it is a time of harvest, ascension and service. The greatest souls are awakened out of suffering. The most impressive personalities endure many scars.

Remain humble and remember; you are not here to change the world…right now… the world is here to change you!

This talk really boils down to consciousness and creativity in the brain. If you have a golf ball size consciousness, when you read a book, you will have a golf ball understanding. You wake up in morning, golf ball size wakefulness.

But if you can expand this consciousness, then you look out the window with more awareness, wake up with more wakefulness. It's the source energy, of all illusionary matter.

We are learning that all matter originates and exists only by virtue of a force that brings the particle of an atom to vibration and holds this most minute solar system together.

We must assume behind this force is the existence of a conscious and intelligent mind. This mind is the matrix of all occurrences.

Matter seems like a good place to begin. It's a fixed point you can see and touch. All of this is a result of a frequency. Which means if you amplify that frequency, the structure of the matter will change.

Everything owes its existence solely and completely to sound. In the beginning there was the word and the word created form, sending it into the great voids of space and time, thus all matter took shape.

Quantum physics is revealing what ancient masters have known. Matter does not exist. The modern concept of matter came from Aristotle and from that concept came science's conception of matter. The fact is that the substance of the universe is consciousness.

Belief in the fact the universe is made out of matter can be related to a fear/greed dichotomy. As people sit in their quiet desperation, trying to accumulate as many possessions as possible, eventually suffocating themselves. The substance is consciousness; therefore it is behavior that is important.

Our true consciousness doesn't exist in the brain or body. This illusion along with the misinformation about our ancestry has projected the idea that we all think independently from one another. With this misunderstanding it would be hard to explain telepathy, clairvoyance, spiritual mediums and other phenomenon dealing with the communication of information between sources by means of non-physicality.

But when you understand that there is a common spiritual bond that links us together, that we are all a part of the one Divine intelligence, you will see no phenomenon is unexplainable.

The blank matter within the most fathomable spaces of perceiving existence is malleable, therefore molded by emotion and intent. Consciousness shapes our reality.

Every male and female within themselves has male and female qualities, duality at its finest, both vital to spiritual and physical health. The intangible of our existence, such as emotion, is the true reality of our higher consciousness.

What most people think is emotion, is not the true emotion, it is just a manifestation. Emotion has frequency and speaking in duality there are only really two, fear and love. All other emotions branch from these two. Fear has a low slow vibration as love moves fast and rapid.

There are 64 codes of amino acids that are found within our DNA made from four elements: carbon, oxygen, hydrogen and nitrogen. By any means of commonsense we should have all codes activated. But we only have 20 active codes.

There is a switch that turns on and off those coding sites and the switch for turning them is emotion. It is linked all the way down to the physical. Now when an individual lives in fear they are limited. Love is a higher frequency, many more occurrences happen on the genetic code for linking and accessing coding sites along the genetic pattern.

Tiny particles of light or photons remain aligned along these accesses of the DNA. As science bridges the gap with the phantom DNA (physical and ethereal), studies show emotions directly affect the structure of our DNA. This is a hard digital link between emotion and genetics that should not be overlooked.

Our DNA is an antenna. It's a receiver of these light particles, taking in the spiritual energy and sending it out for manifestation in a quantum field, the physical matter of the body.

This is the difference between the power of the creator and anything else… you can go into a pitch-black room full of hate and darkness, light a candle and instantly the darkness flees. But you can't do the opposite. Love always overcomes fear. It is its function. Light up the darkness. From above and beyond the stars down to our very structure, we are on the winning side."

When Logan was sober, he was fried. When Logan was high, he was a genius. He continued for hours reasoning about everything with outstanding accuracy. He was a wealth of information and assurance. It was quite remarkable actually. Logan should have been put into a science lab, questioned and probed, a walking biological anomaly. He discussed the wildest spun out theories with a sense of urgency and excitement... too dangerous to live, too rare to die.

"It's the vibration of our body that is being changed with these pills. Allowing us to perceive things at different levels or frequencies. For instance, being able to see other phenomena occurring that were once invisible to our narrow vision within the light spectrum.

The reason for the plants speaking is not a matter of them being able to speak, but a matter of us being able to hear them speak. They speak through electrical waves that we translate it into this word or that word, this feeling or that feeling. You see your brain is a super computer and your mind is the software. An interface to use as we interact with our surroundings."

Logan was beginning to trip me out with his talking. Not that it was wrong or boring, on the contrary, it was remarkably entertaining. Before I had time to think and formulate a question he was already answering it. His software was a bit more advanced at the moment. I felt sad for thinking Logan was a burnout, but then again, he didn't seem to be burnt out anymore. Logan was much more than the fool who had just burned his dick with an ember of weed.

"Who are you man?" I just had to ask.

"I've been asking myself that everyday, still… no answer settles well."

"I mean you're not Logan, I know Logan and you aren't him."

"Ah yes. Well you see this drug is something much more than we realize. It seems to me that on top of being able to show us what's really there or here, it helps us become who we really are, what we see inside of ourselves. That is of course if we know who we want to be."

"What if we don't know who we want to be?"

"Then enjoy the ride of self-discovery my friend."

Every time I asked Logan who he was, the response was the same. Every time he asked me who I was, the investigation pushed forward.

I would say, "I'm Noah," and he would say, "Who's Noah?"

"Noah is the one who experiences this reality."

"Who is the one observing at Noah?"

There was no winning with him. Logan had all the quick comebacks that kept me thinking, who am I? Who ever this twin was, he had this comfortable way about him. It was that type of truthful knowledge embodied in ancient wisdom, well maybe foolish wisdom is a better word… or perhaps, just perhaps, I was the fool.

Even in the midst of tripping in a grow room, having lovely nuggets with purple, orange, and red hairs smelling so sweet and delicious… I was preoccupied. Even when there were four young ladies out in the living room, half naked with Loki, waiting for his wingman, aka me, I was thinking of another. And to top it off here was Logan's knowledgeable side, hardly seen or known about dropping some chaotic simplicity into my life… and all I kept coming back to was Her, the one that got away.

"Why so down?" I hear in the faint distance of my awareness. "You ok Noah?" Logan's voice crystallizes.

"This girl, I can't get Her out of my mind, all day with every song she is there. I think I love Her man." Logan just laughs as usual. This didn't help in any case. "Love and lust turned cold then dust," Logan utters.

"That's some sad shit if I ever heard it. Who would want love to turn into dust?"

"I don't know! Why do you always let relationships end up as dust is the question you should be asking."

Loki made his way in without haste, swinging the door open, leaning on Katie and Amber under his arms. I really didn't want the girls to see the grow room and usually I would be pissed off that Loki just ran in here like that with them. And let's not forget the two other girls whose names were forgotten when introduced to them. All of this came to me in a second and left just as fast.

We played games with the plants, chased the girls around with lighters trying to burn the rest of their clothes off. We sniffed some rails and puffed mad blunts, all a part of the foreplay. Logan was conducting the music perfectly while playing tic-tac-toe with smoke rings and Kush stems.

We were swimming in our own imagination. Co-creation at its finest. Infatuation was at an all-time high. Amber was in her own world, dancing and swirling in a tornado of passion. Katie was by Loki's side and Logan eventually found a comfortable spot between the lips of the two girls whose names still slip the mind.

Life felt like a hiccup, far denser than most. It was a fine blend between dream world and waking life. This is when everything slipped; the memory becomes lazy and distracted with sensory overload. Ability to relay information is a bit foggy. You know you're doing something but can't remember what you are doing while every second is a new experience with no past memory to recall upon.

"Soul & Revolution"
-Asheru-

I am awakened into a world of laughs and the smell of permanent marker.

Loki decided to take full advantage of my infantile state, drawing all over my face. The girls ended up getting the arms; at least they were love hearts. Much better than the pair of boobs on my face with letters spelling out "BITCH TITS."

I take a deep breath in and out. I am more ashamed than mad curiously enough. Only an hour had gone by and they already had plans of humiliation. Vision now sets on Logan, who had fallen deep asleep.

My smile grew like the Grinch… taking the black marker we began to paint a novel of payback upon legs and face. Again Amber and Katie designed a cookie cutter spreadsheet of hearts and stars upon his arms. Revenge is a dish best served with creativity, Logan being our masterpiece!

We make our way to the living room. The plants sing us goodbyes, beginning their nap. I was still tripping, although it was a much more subtle trip, not so much of a body fry but rather that lethargic awareness of physicality. Loki raised his glass up in the air, handing me my own drink.

"To Mind Glow and the massive amounts of loot we are going to make." I slowly raise glass to kiss his and with cheers we drink for good luck.

"Fucking hell Loki what is this stuff?"

"A poor man's Velvet Hammer."

"Consisting of?"

"Gin and vodka on the rocks."

"Why the hell did you make me this?"

"It's all that was left."

I wash my face off to seem a bit more respectable with hammer in hand. We surf the web watching crazy YouTube videos from Ancient Aliens to Sacred Geometry, all half tripping still in that giggly relaxed mood. It was a gradual come down.

I hear the garage open; with this my body froze while the ego comes to grasp the density of the situation.

Loki looked at me with the same look I gave him, the look of terror. The garage door opened and in she came.

Janelle had indeed come home the next morning, but at six a.m. in the morning. This was unexpected. I could feel her thoughts when she walked in, viewing Loki, Amber, Katie and myself half naked in front of a laptop with two other half naked girls fast asleep on the love seat.

I see Loki grab the pills, hiding them under the coffee table. He took a pill and slipped it into his drink with one fluid motion. As my eyes shift to Janelle, all I can do is shrug my shoulders. This is when Loki took a leap and surprised me.

"You must be Janelle," he says while standing up to greet and meet... Janelle said nothing.

"Name's Loki, I'm Noah's brother. I dropped him off here a week ago."

"You're the one with the White '67 Mustang parked out front, yes?" Janelle finally speaks.

"Indeed. Now I don't wish to intrude on anything, I kind of came unannounced hoping Noah might be able to help me out with some business advice, one thing turned to another and we finally came to a good understanding, so it's a celebration," Loki explains, lifting his glass up high then taking a sip.

Logan begins to push the focus onto Janelle herself, asking if she would like a drink. Janelle accepts the offer while we head to the kitchen.
"And you ladies are?"
"Amber."
"And I'm Katie, nice to meet you."

That introduction was supposed to be by me, but of course everything is a bit sticky when you are in awkward situations like these. Most of the time it's really you who is making the situation that much more awkward by putting attention into the awkwardness itself. What a vicious cycle.

We all sit on the high top table eating leftover pizza. Loki slides Janelle a screwdriver saying "My treat."

Logan emerged from the dark cave of ganja, making his way like a zombie to the table. Milk, bowl, spoon and Cocoa Puffs were the usual routines. Logan was back to his usual self again, eating his cereal, giggling at every little comment and gesture we made at him.

After all he was covered in graffiti and artistic expression with mostly sexual and vulgar words. My favorite was the huge red dick on one side of his face running into his mouth with the words "Deep Throat" on the other side of his cheek. Logan had no idea. And none of us had the heart to tell him; we just kept eating and laughed back.

Loki gives me a wink while sliding a baggie of pills my way as the girls thanked Janelle for the breakfast and hospitality.

I make sure Loki doesn't leave the two girls on the love seat, whose names still have no substance to stick in the memory. Mostly when it came to names I was terrible at remembering them. Irony it seems has its way with me when the only name I actually did want to know was becoming seemingly difficult to accomplish. Janelle gets up, saying the words I don't want to hear.

"Can I have a word with you in my room Noah!"

Of course she was mad with me. Following Janelle towards the room, she let me in first, shutting the door behind her. She starts rumbling through music records, putting the needle on black canvas with style and a kiss.

"So we have two options Noah. One, I can tell my brothers about this little situation we had here with your brother and the girls. Which I'm sure they won't be too pleased to hear how their investments in a grow operation are being used for a party house. Or, there is option B."

"What's option B?" I say with a slightly enthusiastic tone while she takes off her dress, revealing navy blue lingerie and a push-up bra, bouncing those C cups up and down.

She rips my shirt off and there on my stomach was the word "CUNT" with an arrow pointing down. I just laugh; any explanation would fall upon deaf ears by now. She gives me a weird look then massages her lips against mine.

Blackmailed for sex has its benefits. I fall easily into Janelle's tractor beam, letting her work magic to the tunes of an appropriate rhythm. Bill Withers' record spun around and around… the song "Use Me" made its symbolic nature known.

Let me tell you… She was a giver. I was a volunteer sex puppet in the depths of exotic ecstasy. Janelle was a cougar pouncing at any moment to reach her desired climax. The things that came out of this woman's mouth were legendary.

"O you know daddy doesn't like it when I fuck the slaves," was by far the strangest.

She was into role-play but this kind of role-play was more in her mind than mine. She was back in time with her words becoming one of Roman tongue.

"Remove cock from ass and fill mouth with seeking pleasures."

Or perhaps it was more of a command than simple request. For a moment it got a little out of control. Janelle insisted I choke her from behind, with slight punches to the ribs. I must say it was way outside any comfort zone but in the lust of infatuation, it's what we have been seeking all these years. You know, the situations that put you outside of the norm and into the extraordinary.

She loved it, so I was ok with hitting a girl a little. And biting was ok but what she wanted me to do was borderline vampirism. Janelle's body shook and quivered while her orgasm dripped down glistening legs of sweat and coconut oil. And with an exhalation on both sides, we fell into the king size bed.

Now there were a handful of side effects Mind Glow had. First being it affected everyone differently. Second being that it brought out the shadow or light side of us on different occasions. Third was you saw the unseen, heard the unheard and felt the unimaginable! The forth was dreaming… it seemed as real as waking life itself. And the more I took Mind Glow the harder it became to distinguish the difference between waking life and the dream state.

Glimpses of the masked menace chased me through the astral. This had more of a feminine feel rather than the lost soul I battled at Sound Wave. All I could hear was the shrieking voices of fear and terror as I ran through cloudy damp streets. It was one of those classic scenarios where no matter how fast I ran the darkness creeping up on me was always faster. Waking up abruptly, relief and realization kicked in… just a dream.

"I need you to do something for me?" Janelle asks in a half awaken state.

"I need you to drop off some herb for me today."

"Why can't you do it?"

"Because my ass hurts. I'm too drunk off cock."

We both laugh like it was a comedy show routine. It seemed I was more alert than she was. Janelle looked like she was coming off of Mind Glow herself, being lethargic beyond reason, so I agreed.

I packed up half a pound of Master Kush and Madhi, rolled a joint, grabbed the keys to her mini van and drove away. Why did she have a mini van? Well that was easy.

"Cops tend to pull over mini vans fewer times than more." She had her angles covered.

I made my way into the foothills. Nice mansions for the wealthy consumer of fashion, status, and privacy. Politicians, lawyers, judges, corporate mongrels, and entrepreneurs alike called this place home. But there was an outcast amongst the thin breed that dwelled upon these hills.

A man by the name of Chris Adams had found his spot up high, overlooking the mirage of city lights. His occupation varied from pornographic videos to tantric yoga classes, among other investments. Chris was a free spirit and whatever he touched turned to gold.

Chris spent his youth on the small mountain village of Bhagsu in Dharmasala, northern India. The son of an outspoken journalist mother and a rationalist hippie father, he learned the ways of tantric meditation very close to the Dalai Lama's palace. In fact Chris was blessed enough to speak a few words to His Holiness in person when a young child, but this conversation has faded into distant memory with the passing years.

I arrived at his mansion of granite pillars and clean cut grass. His guard gave me a stare down then a nice smile.

"I'm here for Chris on behalf of Janelle," I say as he nods his head, opening the door.

Everything was pure white with a smooth calming essence. I could hear my footsteps echo, it was that fancy. Wandering around looking where to go for a few moments only added to the presentation of it all.

Suddenly out of thin air I was tackled down to the cold tiles below. It was Chris, laughing away. Pushing him aside, a bit pissed off and on the offensive, words were spoken.
"What the hell?"

"Welcome Noah, Janelle told me you were stopping by. Let me give you a tour."
"A bit dramatic don't you think? Tackling and such."

"No, it's how I greet all my new friends. It's a right of passage."
"Whatever that means."

"It means if someone can't get tackled with love, then what can they do?"

Chris gave me a tour around his Casa Del Sol. The movie theater, balcony terrace, kitchen with full staff catering to his every need was choice. Seven bedrooms on top of his master bedroom with king size bath, backyard that looked like something out of the pages of Alice in Wonderland... and how could I forget the bushes cut into sex positions... the list goes on.

Chris' basement is where we dwelled now. It was decked out with Rasta colors and Indian posters of Ganesh on top of the ceiling. Ganesh being the Hindu god of new beginnings and the remover of obstacles, it wasn't a bad idea to plaster these kinds of thoughts within the man cave.

Bob Marley's vibes ran through the palace. It was all about peace through music to achieve a state of union.

"Let me get Samadhi?"

"Say what?"

"I need Sum Madhi, can you take me there?"

"What the hell are you talking about?"

"Listen Noah, I like you, but you're not making any sense, I need to get to Samadhi and I need somebody to help me get sum Madhi."

The pills had to still be in my system, what was being said had multiple meanings and unclear intentions; I take a moment to recheck myself. Chris' eyes glance towards my backpack... now things were clicking. He wanted sum Madhi. Weed. Or better put, he wanted to get fixed and sorted out real nice. Chris took all of it, both the Madhi and the Kush. This guy smoked faster than I did, like there was some time limit on how high he could get before the world faded away.

"So what's your story man?"

"Don't really have a story."

"Bullshit, everyone has a story. That's all we have. We do this, I did that, such and such is feeling like this. We are made up of tiny stories that we tell people in order to communicate to each other and satisfy some self need of expression and connection."

"Wow... now that you put it that way... I don't really know where to begin. What's your story?"

"I am that. I am nothing. I am everything trying to reach a state of perfection and awareness, a state of void, of non-duality that humans nowadays call Samadhi, which is really the state of continual concentration within contentment. Everything I do is in some way or another trying to achieve this. All I can conjure up to answer any question is by getting to the source. This eventually comes into reality as a simple question in itself."

"What's the question that appears as answer born of a question then?"

"Who am I?"

"Who am I?"

"Ya."

"You know my friend was just talking about this last night but I haven't completely digested the words yet. It's still lacking something."

"It's simple Noah. Ask yourself who are you. Who is the one that observers the mind? Who is the one that knows you are more than the physical body? When I ask you, 'Do you have any weed?' who is the one that identifies with self as being Noah? Who are you Noah? What are you?"

"I am Noah, pretty much an accumulation of all experiences I guess."

"Go beyond that. Who is beyond the experiences?"

"Um, I honestly don't know, do you?"

"How can I know who you are when you don't even know who you are?"

"I meant do you know who you are?"

"Now this is the question at hand isn't it? It's all about patience and persistence. This is what you might be lacking. I ask myself this kind of stuff every morning, every time I make love, every time I get a silent moment to myself. The only answer that is remotely possible is… I am the pure witness. I am source."

"Source? You mean like heaven?" I reply.

"If you want to call it that. I prefer the word source because it is this eternal presence that we step into and reside within spirit. We are the action of source experiencing itself subjectively! We can choose to experience anything we want. Only in the unknown can we find growth, only there can we express freshness of creation. The known or the past is already experienced. It's gone. Lingering in memory. We recreate the past sometimes, however, new creation lies in the unknown."

"New creation lies in the unknown… I'm listening!"

"Step into the unknown on a regular basis. Serenity of intention… just let go. We can ask our self two things, is this a way to accelerated growth?' and 'Is this the greatest version of the greatest vision I have ever had of myself?'

After that, adjust your thoughts and actions based on the reflection of these inquiries."

Chris takes another toke of his pipe, hands it my way and continues.

"We can discover new things when we stop telling our self what we think it should be. Let life tell you what it really is. Then you don't have to go searching for what it is… all we really have to do is sit back and life will reveal the secrets. You are the source. You are the magic. You are the design of light enabling consciousness to expand forever."

Silence rushed over the room like a calm autumn wind. A few leaves ruffling together were in relation to the tiny thoughts popping in the head.

"So the question remains the same Noah. What's your story?"

Of course I thought of the music goddess that got away, so the story spilled from lips like oil on wood. Painting him perfect scenes of everything felt.

The music was the X factor. Any woman who had better taste in music than I did was an automatic keeper. I mean she didn't waste any space at all. Usually on someone's Ipod there would be songs you skip over in dislike. Not on Hers. Shuffle, playlists, artist, everything was up to par. I found more good bands in a week than I did in a year. Last but not least was the sex; she had shown me something more than just shagging or a simple fuck. This was lovemaking with intentions and techniques foreign to my own.

"Ya man it sounds like she was a tantric."

"How do you know?"

Chris explained how the intention not to ejaculate and focusing on the heart while trying to raise energy indeed had roots in tantric yoga. The transmutation and sublimation of the sexual energy was a tool in getting to Samadhi and universal liberation. Chris was one to know; he had studied tantra since he was a kid, and when he studied tantra he studied everything that is the web of union.

"Rolling In The Deep"
-ADELE-

For Chris, it was all about meditation. But what is meditation really? To go to a state of nothingness, absolute stillness that we identify as being closer to something? Is it the disintegration of our ego or a blending of it with the soul? Was it denying the illusion that is reality or embracing it like humble neighbor? I asked him all these questions and it always came down to one thing. "What do you want out of your meditation?"

"Peace of mind really, I'm always moving, pushing forward to one thing and on with the next. Every time any attempt is made to slow the thoughts down, there is a great wave of resistance in the form of images, feelings, past, future, dos and don'ts, rights and wrongs, truths and lies, illusions and fears, you name it I think it."

"What you need to do Noah is focus your mind on a single object. Baby steps. You may achieve the same results by different methods. This is why there are so many meditations in achieving the same outcome and why there are an infinite amount of methods in achieving multiple perspectives. Everyone works differently."

"So what kinda techniques do you use?" I had to ask.

There was the intention to reach pure void, a state of bliss; in which Chris recommended a tantric sex approach for those who lean towards the playfulness of life. There was the Zen practices for the aesthetically tempered and Tai Chi for the seekers of philosophy through means of martial arts. Some Eckhart Tolle and Mooji for the present moment pick-me-up was always recommended while those who wanted to pursue the way of the Tao... there was no better place than nature.

"It really depends on what I want to achieve Noah, and how. If I instantly want the peace of mind you speak of then I stop trying to live in the future and become friendly with the present moment. I sense the background stillness of the now."

"I guess I meant on a more technical level. What methods do you use? How do you go deep and not just drift off again. It all seems a bit impossible."

"Nothing is impossible, just improbable at times. It begins with morals and ethics. Once you live these out and constantly probe those topics with a discerning mind, then we can begin to support the body through asana practice. Then I push forward with some breathing exercises and gestures of the body. Playing with the coiled snake of Kundalini reveals an endless supply of vital force energy. This path runs up along your spine splitting into thousands of routes throughout our being. Like blood moving through your veins, I play with energy just the same. Where the mind flows, the energy goes."

Chris loads another bowl, continuing to explain.

"Now all of this is in preparation to become content. Then through this absorption of contentment comes the true state of concentration, eventually coming to a state of Dhyana, or meditation. Dhyana is the unbroken flow of thought towards an object. So really you can meditate on philosophy, time, space, breath, anything at all. The key is focus. If you can bring absorption, concentration and meditation together then you have achieved a state of Samyama... the door to Samadhi."

"Then you're enlightened and there's nothing more to do," I crack a slight joke.

"On the contrary. There are many forms of Samadhi, so the yogis and monks write it."

"Ever been there yourself?" I ask.

"Yes and no," Chris smiles, taking another puff.

"Samadhi is achieved by a conscious act of controlling thought waves. With this control we can continue deeper into Samadhi. The mind is in a calm flow, thus mental distractions disappear. The mind becomes one-pointed," Chris adds.

"One-pointed? You mean the thought waves arise without gaps, our concentration perceives it all as one?"

"Yes you're getting it Noah. You are a natural. In this state the changes in gross matter and the organs change in form. The change of time and condition occurs. The attributes are subject to change of the past, present and future. We are literally teleporting to a reality that has the events of our choosing."

"I don't understand."

"Saying you do not understand will put you in a reality where you do not understand. When I mean teleporting to a reality I mean your awareness shifts within hyperspace. By making Samyama on the sound of a word or phrase, one's perception of its meaning and reaction to it can allow you to obtain understanding of all sounds uttered by living beings. Through this one attains knowledge of what is already happening."

"So by making Samyama on forgiveness or compassion, one can develop the powers of these qualities?" I ask.

"Yes, Samyama with the sun will bring knowledge of the cosmic spaces. With the moon one gains knowledge in the arrangement of the stars, and with the polestar one can gain knowledge of the motions in these stars. Samyama of the navel or the throat and chest, one acquires knowledge of the body, its hunger and thirst. Then the individual achieves absolute motionlessness. With this knowledge in controlling the forces which governs Prana, all is possible... but they are only powers in the worldly state and are obstacles to the true highest state of Samadhi, to liberation."

"Wow, that's a lot to take in. You practice this?"

"Hey man you asked. You see, the brain is hardware and the mind is software. Now we have a super computer in our skull. Better than any computer today. So when you meditate you are downloading software upgrades to your interface, thus reality becomes more fluid and precise... more aware."

"Damn, you need to talk with my friend Logan, you two would get along perfect."

"You talking about Janelle's nephew?" Chris asks as I nod my head.

"Ya, Logan used to come around here a lot with Janelle, got into some wild parties, then he became kinda burnt out. Too much man he took too much."

"Too much of what?"

"Too much of everything. He started getting into hard hallucinogens. Started seeking outwardly for his answers, forgetting he had them inside all along."

Chris told me all about Logan's story, and in short, it was about addiction, an all too familiar story amongst the generation of today's youth, myself included. I told Chris how Logan indeed was a burnout but on Mind Glow he was a genius.

One topic led to another with Chris, however he always found a nice way of bringing it all back around with some type of lesson. It was more than just talking and shooting the shit with somebody. It was reasoning.

"It is human nature to envision the future and co-creation. We are a part of the cosmos and hold just as much right as everything else to do anything we want. With power that goes beyond the ordinary there demands a wisdom that exceeds the extraordinary."

"This is most likely why such spiritual accomplishments have not been told to the masses. There seems to be a requirement known as perseverance, and when cultivated, will yield a garden of features farther than the eye can see," I reply intuitively.

"You got it Noah. Reasoning is my favorite meditation."

Next, Chris shows some asana practice to relax the physical body. Surya Namaskar, Padahastasana, Uddiyana Bandha, Nauli Kriya, Dhanurasana, Paschimottanasana, Chakrasana, Ardha Matsyendrasana, Sarvangasana, Sirsasana, Svastikasana, Pranayama. Holding in the full breath, focusing on the direction of energy, breathing out while holding the void retention, the techniques go on.

"Where the mind goes, the energy flows," Chris reminds me. "The focus is on Anahata (the heart) when breathing in. Then visualize, sending it up past Sahasrara (the crown) while breathing out." This was his Tantric Vipassana technique that worked best for long periods of investigation.

Chris was full on with his intensive yogic knowledge, handed down from guru to student. A flash of gratitude uplifted the body while coming out of Shavasana. The bodymind felt more connected than previously realized. Silence overcame us with an overwhelming sense of peace. His yoga class was most insightful.

"I tell you what Noah, this girl of yours has some good taste in music. Why don't you go out looking for Her?" Chris' words spill out, continuing to scroll through the playlists.

"Don't know much about Her, just randomly met one night... I wouldn't even know where to begin."

Chris couldn't accept this. He didn't take no for an answer. Was it any surprise he is where he is today, in a house like this with the world at his fingertips? But to find this mystery woman required a lot of investigation. I mean what was I suppose to do, call everyone that had bought a ticket... meaning I had to dig around and find who were linked to the box office sales.

"You do whatever it takes," Chris said over and again.

"I don't know."

"I mean honestly, I don't know you that well Noah but I know the look that's on your face. This girl is going to drive you crazy stupid. Retarded even. It's the love drug my friend and it's what helps mold us into the creatures we are. Embrace it and do something about it rather than moping around like something is wrong."

Chris really threw it at you hard sometimes, and with that it was time to get moving. Never outstay your welcome and always leave on a thoughtful note. Your lasting impression is one that sticks most with people when you first meet them.

Before making an exit I offered him some Mind Glow. Told him a little more about its highlights and briefly added its side effects, being everyone had different ones of their own.

I'm not too sure why an overwhelming feeling came to share it with Chris. Maybe my subconscious super computer knew he was a good person to get involved with. Chris could make things happen and he knew how to handle himself. Maybe it was the curiosity of what Chris might be like on the stuff.

Call me old fashioned but when introducing a new product to someone, it's always complementary to give out a free sample. It turned out to be a lucrative investment.

It didn't take long for Mind Glow to take effect. Chris smiles, looking straight above my eyes. I tried to leave multiple times, I even gave multiple excuses, but time and time again his persistence prevailed.

Some of Chris' friends came over, making my bankroll look like child's play. They played poker with five thousand dollar buy-ins. They watched basketball, football, and soccer games on high definition projector screens, betting five hundred per free throw or third down. It was a bit sickening how they all treated their cash like monopoly money.

But this sickness soon resided when they all wanted to dive into some Glow. It was expensive, new, effective and fun. New clientele were always welcomed... and so it began. One pill after another was being dropped on glass table, crunched up and snorted. Why did everyone like to sniff it up the nose, I have no idea.

Where there are men with lots of money, drugs, and music… there are girls not far behind. I mean let's face it, it's human nature, why fight it. These ladies had thirsty mouths as most do. Mind Glow set their limitations to limitless, their expectations to anything and their ambition to getting laid and having fun while doing so.

Within a few hours we had most of the girls topless or completely naked with only their G-strings keeping them company. Not that it was hard, all you had to say was, "Let's play strip poker," and the clothes flew off faster than they were put on. A little after that is when things started to get different and I began to know why everything Chris touched turned to gold. It was because he had such good ideas.

We turned the lights off with everyone getting a flashlight of some kind. The music was holding us together while we grooved to the vibes of a sensual kind. There were more women than men, thank God.

We all found our counterpart and some more than one. Chris made sure he showed his guests a good time. It became an all-out orgy. Black lights were turned on with florescent glow paint being tossed around from couple to couple. Some people painted tribal marks, some painted hieroglyphs and others just dumped the paint all over them with no conscious perception intended.

When you were done or someone was done with you, then it was time to move to the next person, respectively of course. And with Mind Glow in the mix it seemed that everyone was fucking everyone else simultaneously. We were one big organism in perpetual flow of energy and sweat, addiction and gasps, orgasms and moans with the occasional laughing and crying. So many flavors; every woman had their highlights.

The dimples in the back just above the buttock, the golden triangle in the middle of their legs, and let's not forget the roughness and tenderness they all explored while riding me like a bull.

It felt like a dream, like one of the fantasies I would create when thinking about Her. Except this felt denser. On top of that, the night moved from clip to clip like some movie montage. This single glitch in my matrix was holding on tight.

The scenes that stand out are a bit fuzzy and made sense only in the end. I was sitting down, white glow paint and warrior stripes across the face, with a beautiful blonde at the depths of my cock. She was basically choking on it to save her life.

So much enthusiasm and joy in her actions. She should be holding class at the local YMCA. Then sits this older man next to me having orange glow paint slicked back in his hair with a couple purple feathers running along his arms. He found himself a redhead to play with that I secretly wanted to have next.

After we were done he introduces himself, "Nathan Peterson," with a firm handshake. He had a familiar face and a catchy charisma. He was the exact opposite of shy and wouldn't shut up about money.

"It's what makes the world go around my friend! Money, beaches, boats and babes, pills and thrills, what doesn't money buy? Am I right or am I right?"

"Ya sure, I guess," I reply in an awkward tone. Talking to a man with orange hair was the last thing I wanted to do when so many beauties were bouncing around.

Nathan had an addiction to power and breaking all the rules. He was on Mind Glow though, so really this could have just been his alter ego talking. Nonetheless when Nathan found out I was the man with the Glow; he treated me like his best friend. How cliché, once people know you have something that benefits them, they act as if they were your closest allies.

Underneath it all he seemed like a good honest man. Nathan's theory was that money was serving its purpose and needed to evolve. If everyone had money, all problems would go away and eventually come to a point where people would give up money all together. There was also the flipside that money was the root of all greed and evil. He knew this but was still a slave to its influence.

"O yes, as long as money exists we are but sheep, cattle for the slaughtering. But if we can somehow overcome the greed and gain compassion in action, then the world will see a new dawn of growth, both spiritually and materially. More a blending of the two if you ask me. But if technology surpasses spirituality then self-destruction is inevitable."

Nathan had an amazing point. He just wanted to live in a world where people could do what they wanted without being judged or criticized, punished or scrutinized. "That's why I joined politics," he says. And then it clicked.

"You're the guy who's running for Senator?"

"That's me. But Shhh quiet, don't tell anybody."

I couldn't believe these were the type of men running our country. Just like everyone else, only human. Born to make mistakes and if grace granted, perhaps learn from them as well. Funny how people can understand their own downfalls then make the same errors again and again. Irony knows no bounds or barriers, choses no side or gives any favors.

"Knocked Up"
-Lykke Li-

Morning's dawn cracked through the curtains. I grab my backpack and keys in order to silently leave and wash myself of this orgy. I run into Chris before making my way out.

"Don't tell everybody about things that go on here, it's better to keep it low key, on an invite basis only. There are a lot of guys last night who have wives and are in positions too important for anything about sex parties leaking out into the ears of many," Chris explains.

"Ya for real, your secret's safe with me. Thanks for the party. Until the next time you need anything, keep it real Chris," I say while shaking his hand in the usual West Coast manner.

"Make sure you find that girl," he yells, greeting the morning's light with delight.

The ride home proved to be most beneficial. Every now and then if you're aware of it, you have a moment where things just click. There is a shift that takes place and you start acting different, a fresh start so to speak. This happens perhaps a dozen times in our life, if lucky enough you can capitalize on every one that takes place.

In my case, it was the exuberating urge to see my dreams come true, specifically with the girl who slipped between my fingers. There is something about riding in cars, having the city rush past you that can take us to a very contemplative state. If that's what works for me right now, then that's what works. Life is the meditation in all its forms and it's best not to waste a single moment of it.

I now looked at the world with a sense of gratitude. So rarely had this come up in my life. But after a night like the last, things started looking different. Nothing really changes it seems but ourselves.

No longer was there an understanding of anything that was not beneficial in achieving my goal. With this, many things came faster than expected. First was doing the dirty work.

Calling everybody in my phone that could have been connected to Sound Wave was a first when connecting the dots, or at least finding them. A few small leads surfaced but this fire was quickly put out by everyone's answer of, "I don't know."

Plan B came to me a day later when trying to copy Her songs to Logan's computer. It was a failed experiment with Her Ipod being an older generation. Any software update would erase the music entirely. But it never occurred to me to look at Her videos until now. Four videos taken and that's four more clues than previously before.

Video one was of someone playing guitar and drums in a recording studio. Video two was two girls walking outside a building while getting into the car talking about something to do with poetry. Video three was by far my favorite… it was footage of Her singing. The heart melted away watching the video over and again.

Video four was taken at a rave. A lot of loud music making it nearly impossible to hear or make out anything else, but I knew what it was. It was of course the night we had met. The more I watched those videos, the more anticipation grew in my body that not even Master Madhi could calm for long.

Where there's a will there's a way they say. Waking up with computer keys imprinted to my face and drool on the keyboard, it is assumed a fair trade had taken place.

The video was paused. The frame showed them getting into the car. The eyes begin to play tricks as sharp forms of light turn to blurred colored pixels. In time my eyes focus back while coming to view the passenger's side mirror.

In this mirror was a reflection of the building's address. BINGO! "Objects in the mirror may seem closer than they appear." Ha, irony it seems is also a comic.

Borrowing Loki's Mustang makes going downtown easier done than said. Of course Loki had to come along. "There's no separating a dealer from his car for too long, unless the dealer has a brother with no ride of his own," Loki cracks a joke at me.

He also joked on how ridiculous I was being for doing all this James Bond shit just to find a girl. But she was no girl. She was thee girl, and only people who have fallen very hard for someone will understand what I'm talking about.

"But it's a little psycho, don't you think? I mean seriously, what are you going to say to this girl when you do find Her that won't make you sound like a creep? O funny bumping into you here, what's your number want to meet up? Ya right. O here's your Ipod back want to get some lunch? She probably doesn't even remember you. She probably has a boyfriend. You were just a shag man, get over this bird and let's go make some cash."

Loki rambles on. Brothers sure know how to bring out the side of things you choose not to see.

"I get the picture Loki but none of that is going to happen so chill out."

My fingers run through the air like fire on wax. Chills inhabit the body and all future concerns float away. Loki's voice slowly blends in with everything else as the music rises beyond the thoughts of many.

We find the studio with ease. Loki plays it cool with the female receptionist. He threw out a line and she bit just as fast.

"The people in studio seven have been recording for a few weeks, maybe they know who was there before them," the receptionist tells us, later adding how there was no phone number or name recorded from the previous artists.

"What kind of business is this anyhow?" Loki expels, making our way down the satin hallway. Pulsating red walls glistened multidimensional prism into my eyes. "I feel like I'm on Glow," saying with a big gasp.
"You are!"
"What?"

"Ya, I put a pill in my soda and you drank some... so I'm pretty sure you got some high," Loki says casually.
"What is your problem? Why didn't you tell me?"
"Cause it's funnier this way."

It's never fun having a drug creep up right when you're about to do something serious. I again pull out my backup plan... "Fuck it."

How that phrase can easily turn everything around. If spells were real, then "fuck it" would be the one that turned fools into kings, seekers into finders... I hoped.

In this case the foolish would indeed become royalty. Upon entering, the black-shirted man bumped his head to us, being busy with the recording in progress. His headphones looked fresh, the large old school Dr. Dre beats to be exact. To our left there was a younger guy alongside new PlayStation, controller in hand with Street Fighter to keep him company. The ego begins paying attention to the little details thanks to Mr. Glow.

"You hear to see Dru?" the video gamer asks while we sit on the leather couch next to him; the frostbite of air-conditioning was most comforting. Keeping focus was my concern while introducing myself, asking about the previous people in the studio. The video gamer laughs a bit at our reactions... he knew we were rolling.

The time spent losing at fantasy combat proved to sober me up a little. The lyrical rhythms turned out to be more than helpful in focusing on my musical goddess. An older gentleman in his mid-thirties emerged from the chamber of sound.

"Wait a minute," Loki stops a moment, "You're DJ Deep!"

"Yes sir… the name's Dru," he says while sitting next to us with his friend wheeling the chair over, forming a circle. Again explaining the situation and why we were there, Dru ended up being no help in the quest for my goddess.

"You'll find Her bro," Dru expresses while hopes are gracefully crushed. Subtly as possible, Loki pulls out a joint and sparks away. To my surprise everyone is ok with it so we blow rings and pass rounds.

"You like to party?" Loki asks Dru.

"Of course."

"Ok Dru Deep, would you guys like some Glow then?"

Loki throws the pills from backpack to coffee table. The pupils widen with curiosity biting ferociously. The video gamer knew exactly what it was, beginning to express his experience with it. His enthusiasm sparked the flame of the other two virgins in the room. And let's just say most men don't want to stay a virgin for long.

I go with my free samples to Dru; the positive approach yields them to buy ten pills between the three of them for later. Dru and his brother Dave, who still had his headphones on, pop a pill while Loki and the gamer start lining up slopes to hit with the help of Benjamin Franklin. "Drugs are always good for writing lyrics, right?"

Loki begins with casual conversation. Dru insisted on a mix of substance and sobriety in his approach to musical creation. The drugs came first then the clear mind to put the pieces together and perform the set on stage or recording booth.

Dru kept on rambling on and on about New Day, the music event of the century that was changing everything. Dru had been invited to participate in the next gathering. You see New Day was a surprise to all. Only a few people knew when and where the next major event would take place, there in adding suspense and anticipation to the general public.

It wasn't just a music event. This festival lasted anywhere from a few days to a few weeks. As far as the venue was concerned, it was located everywhere: nightclubs, restaurants, and mostly the streets. Parts of the city had to shut down with the public taking over, pitching tents in parks, buildings, even in the baseball fields, basketball courts and music venues. It was a migrating economy of music and art that moved from country to country at will.

I knew this because Dru knew this and wouldn't stop talking about how it was one big musical fusion for the masses. Influenced by the dub scene, enhanced with rock and roll and maintained with hip-hop, it was an event that changed lives.

"Let's hear a rap battle then Deep, I'm tired of all this talking about it… I need to hear this shit."

"Let's hear a beat," Dru insists. So Loki throws out a beat from lungs to lips, building the foundation. Dru laid it out for us to play it out. He would go first, his brother Dave, then me. The gamer would be the judge. So with nervous nerves I dive into the waters of calculated improve.

-Dru-

The story I type. The words I write.
Revealing struggle. Internal Fight.
Between the darkness and glowing light.
Just to be sure my son sleeps tight.

A man of virtue in a world of vice.
A woman's herbs is a lovely spice.
Stacking chips, rolling dice.
Crossing fingers, hoping like o Christ.

Win my luck. Page by page.
Gambling life just to make a wage.
This golden cage with filling rage.
Just a part living digital age.

Rap my lips around the bong.
Take away stress, what's right, what's wrong.
Smoke inhaled all night long,
Thinking what the hell is going on.

Mind is slipping, either way,
Time is still or fades away.
The things I say, day by day,
Is the only shit I know to obey.

Sitting here, digin the vibe.
Listening beats with the lyrical rhyme.
All inside, fueling the mind.
Creating self limits, personal crime.

-Dave-

Video game kicking it street fighter.
Spraying words as if he was a writer.
Forever trying to take himself higher.
Dropping guilt, gunna make him lighter.

We got the punches and we got the kicks.
Individual rhyme with the lyrical licks.
The chimes he says, the words he spits,
Evolving character, courageous wits.

I break words for you to relate,
Brothers out there you better concentrate,
Begin to meditate to elevate,
Our consciousness we call the mind state.

Could it be, what you see inside of me.
A little thing they like to call harmony?
Could it be, possibly, synchronicity?
All around me, feeling perfectly!

-Noah-

I be flowing and growing,
All the buds from AZ, I'm showing.
Trimming nuggets, sticky mowing.
Hanging dry until the next morning.

Let me see what we got here.
Popping pills with a bottle of beer.
Adventurous times are very near.
Enjoy the ride, focused we steer.

Aggression. Depression.
You better believe, let go.
Time to bounce to the cosmic flow.
You choose to forget, what you want to know.

Walking path of your inner glow.
Patience in action, take it slow.
You need time if you wish to grow.
Watching life as if a show.

The beat keeps rolling; the mind is in a most
receptive state. Eyes close. Ego surrenders in a blend of
fire and air, releasing the most poetic of talents…
spontaneous reaction.

Many things I will teach you son,
Today begins with more than one.
Many paths a man can take,
One of peace or one of hate.

Some are fake and can't relate,
That fate it seems is what we make.
We choose to live, choose to create,
From karma and destiny to incarnate.

Indeed father this must be true.
But what in life, what shall I do?
How do I choose the best of two?
List of virtues, I'm a bit confused.

Be mindful of your thoughts and feelings,
Lust, desires and everyday dealings.
Little acts of kindness everywhere you go,
Helps the world shine, lets your mind grow.

Life is spent, learning of the physical.
Time moves on, slips to the mystical.
Runs with typical, habitual that is ritual.
Days evolve into a spiritual miracle.

Follow the path that knowledge lies,
Coming as thoughts as wind in the skies.
The voice that cries love all lives.
The voice inside that fuels our tries.

Thank you father for opening my eyes,
The path of truth, the path of lies.
You have made me so very wise,
No doubt to my surprise…

Likewise.

The beat stops with the last word spoken. The wings of silence spread. We were left in retrospection, still as winter's morning. The frost melts with Dru and David lowering their heads in respect…

A smile is all that comes in moments like these. I lower my head to Loki for the rhythm while the gamer dubs me Sir Noah the winner. We crack jokes and spill more smoke from joint upon mouth.

We make our exits from the circle of rhythm with honor, exchanging phone numbers with a "Hit me up," and two fingers for peace. Loki made his rounds from local house parties to street rats. I kept to my clients as he kept to his, however there seemed to be an underlying theme to Loki's customers… they were all junkies.

"You got to stop selling this shit to junkies, it's killing them."

"They are just like everyone else, they want something and I am a provider. You do the same shit so don't go spraying that hypocritical bullshit."

What I'm doing is different. Im selling to people who don't want to decay, they want to grow.

"So because you sell to hippie people, that makes it ok?"

"It's not like that, my people can handle their substances. The people you sell to are zombies waiting for anything to feed on."

"Ok so just cause someone can handle a drug better, that makes them a better client and ok to deal with?"

"Umm, ya kinda!"

"You better rethink whom you are dealing with Noah. No smart-ass logic is going to get around the fact that you sell the same shit I do. You have some weird standards for reasons I can't find sensible. I deal to anyone and everyone. This is why I'm selling twice the merchandise than you are."

"That's not the point. You don't understand. There has to be a line that's drawn. A moral and ethical line where you stand on the side that's not causing pain, overdoses, or deaths."

"Ant nobody dying bro, why the hell you bringing up morals and ethics? If you want to get serious about morals then why you in this business anyways?"

"Because you asked me to help you!"

"I asked you to help me cause I needed help in helping you. And now you got some money right? Enough to get your own place and most likely save up for your own ride, am I right?"

"Don't kid yourself Loki, you did this for you, you needed help to get started and now that you are I think I'm going to stop all this while I'm ahead."

"Ah it's just an argument bro, you know you like living the life again. It beats getting a real job and slaving away in some corporate office or worse... living paycheck to paycheck," Loki rebuts.

"Is it worth it when you get caught and go back to jail for doing the same damn thing?"

Loki slams on the breaks while pulling over to the side of the street, almost getting us hit by traffic in the process. Brother looks me in the eyes saying,

"I ant ever going back to jail, don't you ever say that again. Don't you even think it! I ant like him, I'm better than him."

Loki continues to drive like nothing happened. Of course he was talking about our father. The very thought of going back to prison wasn't even in his universe.

It was far better thinking of my musical goddess than the bullshit that is a regular brothers feud. She consumes my mind once again. O how beauty is a cruel mistress. She eagerly tormented me with memories and desire, taking me away to another moment within self. However, a flame turned to embers is still highly ignitable with some paper and a few thoughts. My brother's anger and careless actions weighed heavy on the mind. The city's lights sneak prisms through the darkness of night. I am left in retrospection.

"Dig"
-Incubus-

There are a few things about Loki that should be known to fully understand his character and methods. Him and I share the same father, same upbringing and same background to a more or less degree; but everyone has a different story to sing, a different path to live out and Loki's story is far more aggressive than most.

We are sons of a drunken fool whose sex drive drove him to cheat, lie, steal and at times push away everything that he held dear. Cash, family, car, career, you name it he lost it to a certain degree.

When I was born our father Andrew was already fighting the war of addiction. In this case it was manifested in the form of booze and constant neglect for his own well-being. His intellect was genius in nature, however this was only the mind. The emotional body was far from developed.

Andrew was never married and when it came to my mother, Michelle, she was just another lover who bared child while providing a place of rest and comfort. Andrew's heart was in the right place, but his addiction to power calculated the odds and measures of life without a sense of respect for others. Driven from jealousy and greed, Andrew's actions wavered with the tides of our earth's milky satellite.

The ego overshadowed his soul's voice. As powerful of a tool the mind can be, it is a double-edged sword, leaving itself wounded and stuck in thought spheres deeper than the darkest tomb.

When I was three our father got another woman knocked up by the name of Heather, and so history repeated itself and my father lived with Loki and his mother. Loki's original name is Andrew, like our father... but as time would have it, Andrew became Loki after an upsetting series of events.

The November sun was setting in the suburban neighborhood of Mesa. Loki blew out the candles of his sixteenth birthday. Of course Andrew was drunk, naturally forgetting the birthday of his second born.

While we all dived into frosted covered cake, Andrew came home in a most unpleasant mood: screaming and yelling about unjustified wrongs done to him while searching the house for his bottle of Jameson. Unfortunately it was nowhere to be found. Loki and I drank it the night before with friends and females.

When this was realized and brought to Andrew's attention, he snapped. "Alcohol is no drink for a boy," he yelled. Loki, being like our father, snapped back.

"I'm not a boy and you're a drunk. All you care about is yourself. Do you even know what day it is?"

Andrew responded with a slap to the face, "Don't you talk back to me you ungrateful little shit." His voice grew deep and rough, raw impulses took over.

Heather could handle the outbursts that Andrew had. But when it came to her son, there was no bullshit to be taken. Heather slapped Andrew across the face. Loki stood back in shock; it had been the first time Andrew was struck by Heather.

Things escalated quickly when Andrew struck back with a closed fist, "Woman don't you ever touch me like that. You will learn your place you bitch."

Heather's nose started bleeding; drip-by-drip, tear-by-tear Heather sat in pain and horror. This was the tipping point when everything changed. Loki grabbed the baseball bat from his room and came at Andrew with rage, swinging towards the knees.

Painful as the strikes may have been, this was not enough to bring a grown man to the ground. Andrew repeatedly hit Loki; fist to face to floor, showing no concern or attention that this was his own son.

Immediately I jump on Andrew's back, beginning to choke our father in an attempt to apply the Vulcan death grip.

Six-three weighing two-twenty, our father was a beast when his heart pumped whisky blood. He threw me off his back with ease, crashing into the table and cake.

Loki lies on the ground with broken nose and a two chipped teeth, gasping for air. Heather grabbed the 9mm pistol hidden above the fridge, nervously pointing it Andrew's way.

"Get out! You touch my son again and I will kill you where you stand. Leave and never come back!" Andrew began to speak but was silent when Heather unloaded a round into the roof.

"I won't repeat myself," Heather says in a most serious tone.

And so it was done. Andrew left. We took Loki to the hospital. Heather filed a restraining order against Andrew for her and my brother. Our father was sentenced five years in prison for the degree of Loki's injuries. About a week later my brother told me to refer to him as Loki. "Why Loki?" I ask.

"Because all my life I have been at war with him. Every time I hear the name Andrew I think of how much I hate him. I never want to be called Andrew again. I hate that name and wish he was dead."

Loki's eyes filled with tears and a tightening fist. I said nothing and listened to his request. Ever since then, Loki has been different. He acts with a mild state of anger, selfishness and an unforgiving nature, unless it is towards his mother or myself.

It's said that a change in name is a change in consciousness. The vibration of a name and the changing of that name are reflections in what you are connecting to. The name Andrew had deep emotional scars; therefore introducing the opportunity to choose and embrace a new name that meant something more.

Although after looking back at it all, Loki might not have been the best choice of names to attract. Perhaps Loki's choice in new name was an effect of the things he was already being subjected to. Whichever one it may be, the result was the same. With the passing of years Loki's talent for getting himself into messy situations grew.

As for my father... five years in prison isn't a long time, it's a lifetime. At first I thought jail was going to be the end of him... however, fate it seems would have the last laugh.

The years pass while my visits to prison grew. The first time was a year after the incident, on Christmas day. Andrew gave me a chessboard and smiled. I felt terrible when the only thought coming afterwards was realizing I didn't have anything in return.

The second time was four months later on his birthday. Gift in hand Andrew rips the paper off, revealing a wooden chess set with a hug and enough time to play.

Just like that the games rolled on. I got better at chess. He got better with alcohol. Amazing what years of being sober will do to a man.

"It's just like chess, but a bit more complex," Father tells me when asking how he became connected and respected in the prison, inmates to security guards alike.

The foundation was respect and personal empowerment. Andrew understood that even though everyone in the prison was going to fight eventually, there was a way to curb that aggression. His aim was to unify instead of destroy. There were segregated areas like anywhere else. Most of everyone stayed in their own turf or in the neutral zones, being places of eating, sleeping, bathroom or showers. If you wanted to fight someone then you would tell him when and where like a real man.

"There is no honor in fighting or killing a man in the shower," he told everyone. These ideas quickly spread throughout the zoo of inmates, empowering their egos in a more refined way.

It was no longer an issue about fighting. If you wanted to fight then you had to and if you wanted to fight someone who didn't want to fight you, then it meant you already won anything you were trying to prove in the first place. And for the people who just straight wanted to kill, well they would be using nothing but their fists. There was no honor in using weapons when they had none.

This idea of refined aggression spread full circle. The fights grew to a point where the guards had to let them carry it out regardless of personal opinion or command. There were just too many fights happening. But in time the brawls grew less. The weak from the strong knew their place and with that strength came certain responsibility. Just like in chess. Different pieces make different moves and hold more importance than others at specific times.

Fights grew more into bragging rights or competition. The betting came later, guards and inmates alike. Andrew turned chaos into organized profit. Funny part was he had nothing to do with the betting... that came on its own accord. The very nature to compete was also to profit in more ways than one... preferably from someone else's expense it seems.

The dog eat dog nature was still in full effect. It fueled the flow of events in more ways than one. The guards allowed this to happen, most of the time being paid off to do so. Until the day came when someone wanted to fight Andrew.

Sometimes there's no reason for a man to fight another. Sometimes all logic is thrown out the door and pure rage is left to emerge. There is no honor or respect... no understanding or words, just intent to harm.

This was the case of Hector Hernandez, sentenced twenty-five to life for murdering Veronica Hernandez and Gabriel Gonzales. The two engaged couple were victim to a twisted love between brother and sister. Hector being confronted... realizing he could never have his sister, decided to drown his liver in vodka.

The record says there was a phone call reporting screaming and cries for help. When police entered the premises there stood Hector, cocaine on face, holding two butcher knives in a pool of blood. Hector threw one knife at the cop, missing by an inch, while the other officer threw a bullet to the upper chest. He was labeled "The Butcher" by the guards. Voices drop rumors towards the inmates, leaping from one ear to the other of a mad man wanting to die.

Hector took interest into these organized fights but didn't obey the rules. He started fights whenever in a large space with others. After the guards had their way with him, Hector came back from the holding cell more aggressive than ever.

You see Andrew was waiting for the moment to fight Hector. It was an outcome that most men couldn't escape being in that position. It was on a Tuesday in the month of falling leaves. The air smelled of rain since past with the birds drying in the blowing wind.

Hector came behind my father in an attempt to sucker punch his target. The Butcher was surprised with a fist to the throat. Gasping for air Hector was repeatedly punched in the throat and ribs. To be fair and honest Hector connected a handful of hits to the Andrew's face, but it didn't matter.

It was an all-out brawl ending with Hector's face being bashed into the concrete so badly, four men had to grab Andrew and end the massacre. Sometimes in chess, even the King needs to kill and get a little dirty.

The sad part was Andrew being charged for manslaughter. The jury took pity on him for it being in self-defense, but nonetheless he received eight more years. So while Andrew stayed in jail, my visits grew. Time and time again he kicked my ass at every game. I guess that's what happens when your dad has a chessboard and nothing but time.

"You're getting better I must admit. You don't make many mistakes other than miscalculating possible moves," Father tells son while moving his Bishop, taking my Knight.

Chess is mostly a quiet war. A bit of talking if you are amongst friends before quickly fixing eyes back on the field. I move, Queen taking Bishop.

"What's on your mind Noah?"

"Everything."

"Try me."

"Well the days are starting to roll together like a slide show. Telling dream from waking life is a bit of a mix at the moment and I can't stop thinking about a girl that is slowly evolving from habit to addiction. Everything I do to find Her is only crushed with disappointment and the harder I try, the farther away reality seems. I think that pretty much levels it out."

Andrew chuckles a bit moving his Queen, killing mine, with a "Check."

"Well aren't you going to give me some fatherly advice?"

"Well in chess most people are afraid to lose their Queen, they protect it at all costs unless pushed to the point where losing the Queen is the only way to win. They forget that the name of the game is Kill the King, not Save the Queen," he explains while my Rook slays his Queen. "So what are you saying?"

"I'm saying that even though it seems the Queen is important, she really isn't. And if she is that important then it's easy to get another one," he pushes Pawn to my end of the field, turning it into another Queen, "Check."

"So you're telling me just forget about it and wait for another one to come along? I don't think that's possible. This girl is special, she's different." My King moves out of check.

"Well then be sure not to give up because all it takes is one mistake on your part to lose the game," Andrew's Knight moves into place while his Queen and Pawns formed a barrier, uttering, "Checkmate."

"So you're saying don't give up on Her?"
"I'm saying let your opponent make the mistakes first."

"This isn't some chess game, what you say doesn't apply to anything, I'm not fighting anybody else."
"Exactly, you're not fighting anybody... just yourself."

"Closer"
-Kings Of Leon-

RING, RING, RING...

The phone buzzes with sleep-crusted eyelids making everything blurred.

"Got a solution to your dilemma," is the first thing heard. It was Chris. Still half awake in dream world, all that can be done was a simple moan of the throat, as to say, "Yes I'm listening."

Chris invites Mr. Glow and myself for a cosmic event of fun and games to celebrate his "forty-seventh" trip around the sun. How could I say no. Chris always had this way about him that was connected to the stars and the essence of nature.

It was more important to celebrate the heaven's events than any other holiday man had created. If his day of birth celebration was anything like the last party he threw, it was forming to be quite the anticipated event.

A few rounds of laughs were exchanged; Logan and I play baseball, hitting the bong back and forth. It's in a grower's nature to push the limits and adapt. It's just the American way.

The American dream was believable for those who were still asleep. A nation built on questionable foundations has molded us into units of consumerism and habitual ignorance. What ever happened to the days when sages humbly directed society to the inner fabrics of their souls?

Now it's being overrun by some ideal image of what happiness is. Somewhere down history's journey, presidents traded reason for madness… Kings mistook contentment for mere amusement.

The most ironic part must be the fact we know all this corruption and deceit is happening; yet all continue to do the same damn thing, day after day. This inevitably pushes us forward to a fantasy that has very little purpose in our lives other than keeping us at some normal level of consciousness.

The moment you want something different, whenever you think outside the cube, that's when you're labeled a nut, extremist or an airhead hippie searching for the utopian civilization.

This is how the world was viewed from Chris' eyes. Most people considered sex parties to be outside the normal, viewed upon as a cult or among free spirited fanatics. In a way this is correct… and on the other hand there was real progress being made with pealing the layers of conditioning.

Getting the Glow wasn't a problem. In fact David insisted on Loki and myself handling all the transactions. This was more responsibility than I wanted but it was good money and Loki handled most of the bullshit anyways, so it worked out in my favor.

David's habits turned recreational to troublesome. The track lines on his arms told a story all too familiar. Once you turned into a junkie, shooting up additive substances, it wouldn't be long before you started making hospital visits and ignoring phone calls. I try not to put too much attention into things of that nature; David was a grown man and could handle himself, or so I hoped.

It was hard not to look away. Shaking eyes, random mumblings, slurred words; his sister had to take care of him when Loki and Katie were out making rounds. It's never a good idea to shoot anything into your veins but shooting up Mind Glow? Now that was heroic by any means with consequences even the local drunk could foresee.

It was a sad sight indeed, David in a state of complete vulnerability. It was a sign not to trouble trouble until trouble troubles you. "Hummingbird," is the only word David is able to make out clearly. Turning over we find him smiling, pointing with his eyes closed. All that can be done is return the smile and let him be.
"I'll keep my eyes peeled David."

Omens… the language and voice of the creative force that is. Learn to read them and life shall be more directed, yet complex. What we see, we believe. What we feel, we come to know. So be sure you feel what you believe and know what you see.

Keeping this mental reminder, I walk into the white-pillared mansion of Mr. Adams. The tile reflects vocal tones at a distance with Chris' voice bouncing off floors and walls, eventually greeting my ears. Chris was more cheerful than usual, insisting we get straight to business. We gather in his chambers.

"Ok first thing is first, the things you do here stay here. The people you are selling this stuff to are not really them. Tonight you get to be transfigured and become your inner god, the inner Shiva or Krishna or maybe Pan, it is up to you. The females are playing the role of Shakti. We look at the goddess within each of them."

"What are you talking about man, we didn't play any role last time!"

"Well this isn't like last time, this is more tantric than just pure orgy fun. Now a woman may come up to you and make a gesture with her body. This is an offering and is answered with your full awareness and attention. You are holding space for these women... and of course sending them into a state of orgasmic bliss."

"Chris listen, I'm down for the freaky shit but all this is a bit fast don't you think? I mean I don't fully understand half of what you just said."
Chris laughs, shaking his head.

"Noah, all you got to do is go with the flow. These girls are playing a role, you can view them anyway you wish, or not at all. The choice is yours, but if you are going to swim with us, it's best to dive in head first and really taste the flavor that life is offering you."
"Well damn, now that you put it that way."

"Just don't forget to focus on your heart and breath while they take turns with you. And most importantly don't forget to see the Divine within them all."

"Ya sure man, whatever you say," I tell Chris while escaping the fact I had no idea what to expect.
"O ya, one more thing Noah."
"Yes..."

"Make sure to enjoy yourself. Release some of that tension. This will help with your music goddess. All in good time," Chris assures me.

Upon entering, the living room was covered with Indian attire. Silk cloth covered walls. Middle Eastern vibes pumped through the speaker. Sex-filled impulses thrived. People floated around the room in a form of speed dating for the spiritually opened.

There were no rules but rather simple guidelines. First was the respect issue. Nobody could do anything if the other wasn't ok with it. Fair enough, but it seemed to be non-existent as everyone was down for everything.

People humped on the couch, the floor and kitchen counter tops while stopping me, snag a pill or two, swallow then continue. No time to ask for cash now. A simple list of names with pill count was easy enough, and let me tell you, these fishes were biting hard. In a matter of half an hour I went through two hundred or so pills amongst eighty people until all that was left were two. I pop those like a virgin pops her cherry, hard and fast.

The second guideline was what Chris had mentioned earlier, and so I kept my mouth shut. I saw Nathan again, the man running for state senator. The sheriff of Maricopa County was there. The host from Entertainment Tonight and the actor from that vampire flick were surprising guests to say the least. A few porn stars with a list of other people who looked to be casual folk like myself.

All of this didn't matter though… it wasn't who they were, tonight they were someone else, Shiva, Shakti, Poseidon or Aphrodite herself, these people had completely left behind the masks of the digital age and dressed for a blast into the cosmic past.

To be honest the intentions were much more than meets the eye! Stare into her eyes and gaze. Feel the reflected spark within then focus on the heart and breath, focus on healing, focus on enlightenment, focus on making this orgasm last forever… focus on whatever you wanted to really. The intention behind it all was the key.

Most of the time I just focused on the girl's ass or face while tits bounced up and down like a rock show. The ladies tonight were so beautiful that most straight women turned lesbian for a night, but there was something with this focusing on heart that kept me interested. Viewing this foreplay speed dating, two bombshells come up with glossed lips and a seductive lure that made most men speechless. But in the end they all seem like that when you're horny and high, so who really knows what they sounded like without substance overload.

"You must be Shiva's friend?" one asks. I didn't know who Shiva was but I smile nonetheless.

"She means Chris," the brunette tells me.

"Ah yes Chris, he invited me to this shin dig."

"What's your name?" the blonde inquires.

"Noah, and yours?"

"What's your real name Noah?" The brunette asks me. She had a lot of makeup on but I knew who she really was. It was Amber. She noticed me and I noticed her but we say nothing and play our roles.

"Ah it's one of these parties, I see. The name's Maha, at your service," I answer, bowing my head ever so slightly.

"Kali," Amber answers, "Athena," the blonde responds.

The two girls step back, moving into position with a gesture or mudra in offering themselves. Athena had a personification of water, dressed in white while bent over, sticking her blossomed bum to the side with gaze to the sky.

Kali was undeniably the element of fire, with a hint of Aether. She was dressed, if you like to call it dressed, in red and black lingerie. Seductive legs open, forming a triangle while her hands touched magnetic eyes that fixed upon mine.

The goddesses posed for a few minutes, radiating their beauty into my body. Thoughts of passion quickly turned to feelings of rough sex and burning lust. And that's what happened.

They took turns with me after finding a seat in the theater room. Athena and I moved together like a school of fish in an ocean of pleasure. She had lovely lady lumps that rippled with the thrusting of my cock. Athena exploded like Niagara Falls with her juice spraying all over us. She screamed so loud it was a surprise someone didn't come in thinking she was being raped. If it was a rape, it was a willing one… she couldn't have me deeper inside of her.

Kali was more of a fighter than a lover. She hit me across the face and chest when orgasms were near or far. In a way this made me hate-fuck her harder. Not a real hate-fuck, just an unusual love of my pulsating member in for the jabbing with gasping air following every stabbing.

"Bite my neck," Kali orders.

So I do as told while she digs her nails into my back. With Kali, a little pain is closely connected to pleasure. From human to vampire, my teeth sink into neck, sucking away. When she did it to me it felt amazing, tingles of arousal in full form. But when it came to me sucking her away, blood was tasted, so I stopped.

"Why did you stop?" Kali asks to my surprise.

"Because you're bleeding girl," responding in a concerned, freaked-out way. I had lost myself in her energy and apparently sucked enough blood for it to start sliding down her neck.

"Fuck me like you would in grade school," she expels, continuing to ride me with intent to dominate.

Mr. Glow starts to hit hard when reality and fantasy collide. I put the headphones on… setting tunes to shuffle. Why did I do this? No idea! This is how the mind works in states of pure sexual turbulence. It just made sense. The air smelt of cum and cries. The music matched perfect with our tempo. The drug's signature move (sensory glitches in eyesight and memory) was in full effect.

The lights grew dim with everything around us becoming non-existent… except Kali. She glowed as bright as day… to the point where only outlines remained. Finally she radiated so bright, all that was known was light.

Then slowly whiteness turned grey, inviting dark blue and black to play. Her eyes beamed red, Kali became intimidating to look at, nonetheless I am glued.

Then things started to get weird. Inch by inch her face became different, literally transfigured into Her. Could it really be? The goddess I was searching for all along?

I apparently said this out loud while she took her finger, pushed against my lips with a, "Shhh, quiet now."

Whatever was happening, all that could be known was my music goddess had found me. Her touch felt the same, even Her smell. The moans and voice was all up to par. It was the closest I had come to being with Her again… and for now, it would have to do. With that being said, we humped like little rabbits in Wonderland.

That night… I had a most peculiar night terror. After the tender touch of transfiguration, I began being chased by the black menace; the movements came closer and faster than before. This force was playing with me from landscape to shifting landscape. The faster I ran, the slower everything got.

Typical it may seem yet extremely frustrating, I was being chased from one dream to another by this dark force. It was hard to tell if this creature was being playful or purposely trying to hurt me. This menace revealed the music goddess' voice with an evil underlining tone tormenting my soul… quickly escalating into rough sexual aggression.

I was lost within a dream, yet still had this addictive lucidity about it all. She came into my space, scratching the body then residing back into distance. She imposed her intentions on my will. Her ambiance only nurtured more auspicious investigation. Astral vampire perhaps, or maybe just a subconscious shadow? Whichever it might be, it is tricky business to say the least.

There was a faint voice in the background that kept calling my name. It was very dim but finally ignited with a slap across the face and a voice that screamed, "Maha!"

Eyes opened with guests greeting the sight of my naked self, condom still on with dried party juice flaking away. They stared at me like a freak show… and how could they not. I had bruises and cuts on my body, mostly on the back and chest.

Some were flesh wounds and others showed signs of going seriously deep. Only the red-stained chair could show the true bloodshed. It wasn't a massacre by any means, just some spots of dried blood. But in the eyes of many, a little blood was a little too much.

Amber was crying… trying to get out an apology. Her neck was almost as bad as my back. She had one bite mark that a left purple reminder. I had a few dried spots of blood around my mouth that was washed away soon after realizing.

Chris looked at me with a blank stare, expecting him to elaborate on what happened, all he said was "What happens here, stays here." And so it was.

Chris recommends taking it easy, allowing us to rest there for the day. Amber remains quiet, curling up close to me most of the afternoon. The only thoughts appearing to mind was how this happened and when could I see my goddess again.

"Razorblade Kiss"

-HIM-

"If our history can challenge the next wave of musicians to keep changing, to keep spiritually hungry and horny, that's what it's all about."
-Carlos Santana-

Static Radio

"Here is what we need to take into account. The human mind is made to move and manipulate matter. This is no magic trick. There are hazy lines between consciousness and dreaming. I mean it's all repeating itself everyday; wake up, sleep, live life. But are we exactly sure where we are? I knock on this piece of wood then believe it's real. So how many times have you had a dream and thought objects to be just as real. But ah it's just a dream so it must not be real. How the hell do you tell the difference then? What is dream and what is waking life? The very fact that you can dream is impressive enough. That you may create an image in the brain, which isn't really even there tangibly but is put into position and moves around like film on a screen. What is this?

To be honest we know a small fraction of what is really out there Alex. We are smart, no doubt, but in comparison to the fabric of the universe, we got a long way to go. Once you get to subatomic particles, the microcosm, everything gets thrown out the window. Scientists have observed a particle being in a super state. This is a state of movement and stillness at the same time. How do you explain that? The fact that you look at an object and the observer changes the behavior of that object… the viewer actually changing the atoms that are moving… this is extraordinary!"

"We know a lot for humans. I've had a lot of people come on this show and digest a lot of knowledge. But when we start diving into the mysteries of the universe, scientific or spiritual, we have to ask questions. Why does the universe stay together? Why is it not falling apart? Is this universe the only universe?

A new theory among scientists is that every galaxy has a massive black hole in the middle, and every black hole may contain an entire universe. Every black hole may contain countless galaxies. Life might just be a sliver of an infinite moving wheel that lasts forever. Imagination seems to be the real driving force behind the evolution of humanity."

"Exactly Alex! We imagine an idea, a concept, a product, or house. When we have this idea we build it up and kaboom, it's here. Real as can be. There seems to be no new thoughts of what this image was before you created it. Did it come from you? Was it sent to you?"

"What are the root signals then Sarah? Could imagination be information that is out there? Is it not full of endless possibilities? Is it not the remover of limitations?"

"The confines of our imagination are kind of based on what we go through in life. The experiences we have, even if it's photos or videos, they shift and mold us into our perspective. This enormous universe is just what we see. It is momentarily limited by our ability to go beyond what we have seen or felt. Every dimension has its own structure; its own laws that go into natural order… its own template reality. It might be so vast that we are unable to view it all simultaneously. This goes hand in hand with what is happening in the sciences of biology. It is turning out to be an information technology. The next generation of artists and scientists will be writing DNA at the rate of Shakespeare with the fluency of Mozart. We are beginning to play jazz with genomes; the canvas of life itself might be a new instrument for aesthetic design. Instead of praying for transcendence, let's engineer transcendence."

"A thing to remember is that when spirituality exceeds technology, species thrive. When technology surpasses spirituality, species are forced to survive. Humans are very good at blowing things up, if you catch my drift. The very idea of blowing stuff up becoming an option is a direct extent of who and what we are. We can use words to create poetry or we can use them to slander and spread hate. A change in consciousness is as important if not more important than the tools we use."

"Very true Alex. It is crucial to take these things in with the utmost importance. All life on Earth is born of Gaia. Each life has a spirit. Every new spirit is housed in a physical body, through their experiences on Earth each spirit matures and grows, returns to Gaia. Bringing with it the experiences, enabling Gaia to live and grow. Everyone knows about reincarnation, where the soul departs and returns to a new body, a new life. Rather like some spiritual revolving door where the transmigration of souls occurs.

When we view things from this perspective, it seems reality is this invisible thread that hardly seems to be tangible. But from this comes everything the imagination could possibly be. We put value on creativity but hardly give it the true merit that its status holds. It's information that the building blocks of reality are from... our ideas are simply neurons in the head, interpreted by the mind. Even though these ideas have very little physical substance, it has achieved more evolutionary change in our species than anything else. Thoughts that change reality isn't just philosophy; it is living actuality."

"This is like blowing my mind. To think that we are in the middle of all this right now. We can literally see reality unfolding itself. Life is showing us that our imagination has an effect on how things go on in the real world. When you believe in things, they come with great power. Who can say this isn't real?"

"I mean this is the human brain we are talking about; it links to everything and produces the world we inhabit. First we build the tools and in return they build us... we are a living universe. Customized utopias, or in some cases, ragged slums. Mostly how we perceive reality is handed to us by our stereotypes, altering the way we view things. Has anybody even given this any focus? Is it so imbedded in ourselves that we no longer give it second thought? Technology basically does what we do but on other levels. Smartphones, computers, text messaging is sending a message through space and time at the speed of light... and you use it on a daily basis. This is a reflection of our self and it's called telepathy. It's an extended phenotype, a part but separate. This will only speed up until the entire universe is at our fingertips, internally and externally."

"If I have learned anything from hosting talk shows Sarah, it's that we are pretty much antennas picking up signals from everywhere. Just like a radio can flip through stations 100.7 to 93.3, so can we. The life we are in right now is just a radio station. And on some other radio station there could be realities where humans are blue and green and breathe helium instead of oxygen. There might be endless channels out in space with infinite worlds around us every moment. Life might be just like radio!"

Musically Driven

"Parachutes & Sparks"
-Coldplay-

"I was listening to that... but I like this album so you're lucky." Amber crawls onto my stomach. We cuddle and play in bed.

"How can you listen to that hippie stuff?"

"You're telling me out of all that Eastern Hindu music you listen to, you find this talk show to be hippie?"

"Ya kind of," Amber expresses.

"You know you're just jealous cause you can't keep up with the science of it all."

"The science of it all? Please Noah. Just cause I'm not off in my head all day talking to myself trying to figure out the universe, doesn't mean I can't keep up."

I flip Amber over, biting her flesh hard enough for screams to leak out. It's a delicate balance of torture and sexual drive. We were in that middle state. When the friendship of two people get to be more than just friends, but no one has yet put a label on what's going on.

No worries though, this state doesn't last long. Up to a few months depending on the desire of the individuals. Every time we made love, we surged as one. And to be honest, I could transfigure Amber as Her. It was the only way I could see my music goddess. That and of course a nice cocktail of crunched up Glow and liquids to wash them down with. My weakness was the one that got away. She was into that transfiguration stuff anyways, so it seemed fitting enough to play with it a bit. At times the sex was so vivid that Amber really became the goddess herself. It was hard to get away from.

"Well my talk radio is far better than that show you watch about people on an island with AIDS. That shit's ridiculous."

"It's called ISLAND LOVE and it's a smart idea," Amber corrects me.

"The idea of people who have diseases going to an island just so they can fuck and not worry about giving someone else an STD is crazy."

"Well that's the catch, people are already having dirty sex, so why not have a place where people with diseases can have sex with other people with the same disease. This way no one gets in trouble for passing on an STD."

"The whole idea is fucked. The show has that weird host with the big creeper smile that just sits there trying to get a peak on the action. It's almost Idiocracy status. It's not even civilized."

"Well half of America likes it Noah."

"Half of America is retarded."

"Are you saying I'm retarded then?"

"No no. You are retarded beautiful. So fine you smell of wine in sunshine. So delicious I could eat honey from your bum hole if you wanted me to you. Now come over here so I can take you sideways," I say as she smiles, moving over willingly. But I'm still very serious about America and their education system… it is the worst.

Smacks across my face; Amber's hands point to her eyes as she begins to change. Hair twirled around so fast her face becomes a black tornado of electricity. And there she was, my goddess had returned. She was overwhelmingly powerful. Blood dripped down razor sharp teeth, biting into my neck with vigor. Screaming loudly… I woke up!

These night terrors became more frequent and unexpected the past weeks. It was worrisome. Waking up and sleeping had no definite line. It was four in the morning, Amber rested fast asleep. She hadn't even woken from my yell. Did I even yell? Can I even remember hearing my voice?

I walk to the balcony. The feel of Tempe Town Lake was quiet. Still. Distant ambiance of red-eye flights and early birds on the freeway made presence. Life glistened brighter than Mind Glow itself. Perhaps the residue of my party accessories was still in the system?

Every time the eyes set to view the city, flashing images of a rising bird was seen within the pixels of imagination.

These side effects had to stop. No longer was I ok with the aftermath of this red pill. But it was just too hard to stop longer than a day or two. If I didn't have Glow, then I wouldn't be able to see Her. No more fun transfigurations versus no more terrifying nightmares!

To be honest, going back to sleep seemed a bit frightening. When we go to sleep, what if that is really waking up? It seems so farfetched in your waking hours to think that it's all a dream anyways. Or maybe it was waking up that seemed to be filled with more fear than anything. What was I running from? What was I running towards?

While the phone vibrates, I care not. We have a choice with everything in life, even to answer the phone. Sometimes we go on living life forgetting things as simple as choice. The phone keeps pulsing its electric currents through the body,

First message was from Dru. He needed to pick up, with the message asking, "What's good… up-re?" Vice versa was re-up, you get it?

The second was from Chris, inviting me to his pool jam out. As always my party accessories were much appreciated. It was plus two guests this time, a little out of character by his standards. Chris usually played his whole tantric group thing on the low key. Maybe that was a hint it wouldn't be so cult-like this time.

The third was from Janelle; she needed help with crops and a little TLC. She followed the message with a heart sign. Ah digital hearts. They say so little but show so much. First thing was first. I needed to get some more pills!

Amber drops me off at Loki's. She sneaks in a kiss before making an exit. Butterflies start flapping around while an anticipation to leave overwhelmed the impulses.

Loki is already weighing out shipments like a Chinese sweatshop. Labeled, tagged and bagged for this weekend, everyone seemed to pick up from Loki now, even myself. He was slowly adapting himself to David's clients and most often dealing with David's complications as well. This is what happens when a dealer turns into a junkie. Things get flipped around with a twist at the end just to leave you dizzy and curious to the swaying tides.

We pack the pills in backpacks then head towards the Mustang. We flow Dru a hundred pills on the spot. He was good for it. It went against the rules I set for myself, never deal with credit, but what can I say, Dru was trustworthy.

Owing people or being owed money is by far one of the worst things to have hanging on your shoulders. It will drag you down sooner or later. This is how the Mafia does it. This is how the government does it; shit, the banks do it to us everyday, creating money out of thin air. But now is not the time to dive into economics and what is morally and ethically correct. So I digress.

We make rounds to the hood rats, street whores even some local bums hanging around QuikTrip for spare change. How the hell a bum gathers a hundred dollars for one pill is beyond me... as they say, where there's a will, there's a way.

We made some house calls; one in particular was Perkulator's house. Never trusted the kid even though I never met him until Loki and I walked in his place, smoked a bowl and started shooting the shit. It was small talk to make things go over nicely, more of a formality nowadays than anything else.

The reason why I didn't trust him was threefold. For one his name was ridiculous. I mean some could say that about Loki and a lot do. But if you said anything to Loki about his name, he would snap like a loose cannon fighting the British in some civil war. Number two was he always gave excuses rather than reasons. Perkulator always had some story and never the full truth. Reason three being he had been a junkie for far too long.

To make things short, Perkulator didn't have the full amount owed. He made up some story about a guy dressed in black beating him up, leaving him with lost cash and pills. This sounded like bullshit but I had a similar experience so I empathized with him a bit. But to Loki it didn't matter.

"I guess I'll just have to take your Xbox and anything else I want until you get my money." The scared candy kid didn't like this but had no option. I watched Loki rip apart his house in search for anything worth value, bong, DVDs, watches, even his new pair of shoes. "For fuck sake his shoes, really?"

The funny/sad part was his girlfriend was with him. Her name wasn't important enough to remember, some Asian name that was harder to pronounce than to spell. How humiliating it must have been for them both. Loki put everything next to the door in a pillowcase then walked towards the kid, forcing him to empty his pockets. The kid refused, but when you find yourself hanging upside down by Loki's fists, things seem to change a bit.

"Look mate, you find yourself in an unfortunate situation here and it's up to you how it ends!"

"Fuck you," Perkulator expresses while hanging like a pig.
"Wrong answer."

Loki begins kicking his head like a soccer ball, dropping him on cold tile floor. The girl screams and runs after Loki. I stop her gently as possible. The kid got his face kicked in no doubt. Loki takes the nine hundred twenty-seven dollars from his wallet and adds,
"I'll be back for the rest soon."

The kid had the nerve to spit blood on Loki's pants with another F-bomb.

This spelled out the end for Perkulator. Loki repeatedly went off on the kid's face. The girlfriend just sat and cried while the golden retriever barked loudly towards the kid. Amazing, this junkie's dog didn't even like him.

I sat frozen in debate, watching the massacre of flesh to bone. Blood and a bent nose proved most noticeable, other than the obvious broken ego. Loki continued to punch skull like a sandbag. I rushed over to stop his rage-infested state, pulling him back. I take Loki by the throat and chest yet still he drives his anger into the kid.

"Loki stop... he's done...stop... ANDREW STOP!"

Finally he lets off. Head remains down, adrenaline pumps vigorously.

"I told you to never use that name. That's the last time you will call me that." His voice was dark. Evil. Far beyond any state I've seen him in lately.

"I just don't want you going back to jail bro, that's all."

"I can handle myself," Loki snaps, walking towards the door.

Perkulator yells out in tears, "Please don't take the bong, it's not mine."

"The hell your bong," Loki yells, smashing it on the floor then walking out the door with a whistle to the dog. The golden retriever follows along outside.

"Bro did you have to steal the dog, I mean come on, it's his dog."

"Fuck him bro, he'll get his dog back when I get my money."

"You just kidnapped an animal, if he calls the police..."

"He ant calling no 5-0, he ant that stupid."

"You got to relax man, this is what gets people caught. Be smart, just cut your losses. Stop dealing with junkies and this won't happen."

Loki reacts fast, not giving one word a chance to digest.

"Sorry I don't have such high class customers like yourself who pay upfront."

Sometimes it's just best to let people win an argument. With Loki you never win arguments. It always turns into a fight. Actions sometimes speak louder than words. And with that we drive away... all three of us.

The body leaves tracer marks. Perspective glides into elapsing motion. The magic of instrumentals sound the same in every language... Today's message: move without thinking. Just let the feet guide you and bump to the beat of your heart.

"Love Music"
-Jay Scarlett-

Chris called asking twenty questions. To sum it all up, he needed our help. We were to pick up his astrologer at the airport.

"An astrologer? You have your own astrologer?" asking Chris with a hint of interest.

"Yes I have a friend who is an astrologer, he is an old Indian man having long dirty white dreads that go past his waist. You can't miss him, he will be looking for you."

If that's what Chris needed help with, then I was much obliged to help him. At first Loki was a bit sketched out, rolling up to an airport with enough pills to throw you away for a lifetime wasn't first on his list of adventures for the day.

"Na man, let's just get him a cab," Loki tells me.

"Just relax, everything is fine."

Chris was right. You couldn't miss him. The man wore clothes that seemed to be once bright yet turned grey with age. Wrinkles of the skin told stories beyond the simple laugh or joke.

"Name's Veena, you must be Noah," introducing himself, "And you must be his brother."

He nods his head while taking Veena's bag, introducing himself with a handshake.

"Call me Loki."

"Veena, that's an interesting name," Loki starts conversation sharing the back seat with his new dog while I drove.

"Same could be said about your name. But something tells me that isn't your real name now is it?"

"Why would you say that?"

"Because Veena wasn't my first given name either. It's just another mask. But what is a real name anyways?"

"What's your real name then?"

Veena pauses, looks up, going through the files of memory.

"My mother called me Ananda, but in the end it's just a name. Another ego."

Veena made a good point. Loki didn't have a thing to say, which was most surprising because he usually had a list of topics to talk about.

"So what brings you to Arizona?" I ask.

"New Day!"

"What?" We both say in synchronization.

"I'm here to play for New Day," Veena says with his Indian accent most elegantly. Loki and I both look at each other in a shocked state, still trying to comprehend what Veena just said.

"Did you say New Day? Here?" The retriever barks in excitement.

"That's how it starts my friends. First it's rumors, then out of thin air it happens."

The first thing that came to mind was the music goddess, strangely enough. My high instantly wore off, being replaced with another highly additive substance. Love. The first thing Loki thought of was money and business opportunities. I could feel Loki's thoughts while he quickly scrolled through his phone list. New day was just another opportunity for Loki to make another big score. After looking back on it all, I should have paid more attention to Loki and his plans for wealth.

"So what do you play then?"

"The Rudra Vinya," Veena answers.

I had no idea what that was. Veena explained it was a seven stringed instrument that was the father of the Sitar and the grand father of the modern day guitar. Seven strings for the seven chakras of the body, the neck of the instrument was as long as the player's energetical spine. Sushumna Nadi. Only a musician who's made his or her own Vinya would be able to play with such perfection to be recognized as a master. Loki had partially tuned out, already talking business on the phone.

"So you just travel with the event? You get paid? How does it work?"

"Something like this. I get compensation enough to live. I play music for the simple feeling of playing music. Everything else is a bonus."

Veena seemed to be a bit of a purest in the truest sense. He connected the dots, took the simple path. His virtue was the natural way, among other favorable qualities. Veena also had a knack for guessing people's birthdays. No joke, he perfectly guessed Loki's birthday, being a Scorpio, and myself, being a Pisces. He knew our age and could tell we shared the same father but not mother. He was that good.

"It's all the symphony of life. Astrology is just a means to view the story of the cosmos," Veena explains, looking at Loki through the back mirror.

"You brought us a mole? Who are you," Loki exaggerates, cracking jokes.

"I am no mole. I am a musician who understands the planets and stars."

Veena had this way about him, sort of like old man strength, but in the mind. His presence was one of great confidence and humble warmth. I understood he wanted to help us, and help he did. Arriving to the mansion, we are welcomed with open arms.

"Loki this is Chris, brother this is friend," words fall. Hands shake.

"Ah Loki, I didn't give you a proper greeting," Chris says.

"What's a proper greeting?"

"It's somewhat of a hug tackle that puts you in a laughing wrestling state," I explain.

"Well I'm glad we cut that part out of the introduction," Loki adds.

Chris shrugs his shoulders, holds his mug up high yelling out, "Non shall pass these gateways without the love hug." Chris' Roman attire made it safe to assume that a toga pool party was in full effect, a simple Saturday afternoon in the life of Mr. Adams undoubtedly.

The picture I am about to paint you is the version I saw. I'm sure most of the people there shared the same vision, but we all see what we want to see, not to forget Glow was fully in my system again. By now popping pills seemed like chewing on Tic Tac mints. Highly expensive mints that make your brain go whack attack. My tolerance was at an all-time high.

Most of the girls lay flat by the pool, bottoms up tanning on the sun deck. It was a must when summer heat shined in Arizona. The females had names like Jasmine, Eternity, and Aubrey, most of them models or in the porn industry. In fact I wouldn't be the least bit surprised to find out that all of them had eventually slipped a tit or clit on camera before.

The male-dominated poker tournaments and beer pong games held strong inside. The stoner's lounge was at the bar where hookah clouds kissed ganja rings. "I think I have a solution to your dilemma Noah!"

"That's what you said last time Chris... and I ended up with incisions on my chest and back. But it kinda worked, so what might be my dilemma this time?"
"Same dilemma... the music goddess!"

"What about Her, she's lost, vanished into my imagination."

"Noah I'm telling you, imagining Her every time you have sex with someone else won't solve everything. It's somewhat healing no doubt but it's an illusion. You're suppose to be transfiguring the woman as her true self, not picturing another every time."

Chris had good points that mostly got overlooked. I thought about Her everyday, where she was, if she had remembered me, what song was she listening to. Perhaps it was the same song Her Ipod shined into my heart.
"So what's your solution?"

"Well it's not so much a solution than it is a signpost pointing you in the direction of clarity."
"Well then show me this signpost you speak of!"

I am led to the last door on the left of Chris' infinitely long hallway. The room was well lit, but not overly bright. It had a relaxing nature when sitting down on the cushioned floor, Asian style. Chris poured me a glass of chai tea from the Himalayas of Nepal. He was big on the little details, and it showed.

"You are here to relax. Veena will be with you in a few moments," Chris tells me, excusing himself from the room adding a "make yourself at home" courtesy gesture of the hand.

Not long after, Veena appears with a bright ambiance holding a few papers and pen.

"Noah Savage."

"Yes?"

"I am here to give you an astrology reading."

"You're here to tell me about my planets?"

"You could say that. I am here to bring understanding into your life with hopes of your solutions being realized." Veena had a strange way of viewing the gravity of any situation. We sit facing each other, cross-legged with teapot and all. He says nothing at first, focusing on his papers.

"You were born at seven-forty-seven a.m. in the Land of Enchantment on March 4th, in the first year of the new millennium. Would I be correct?"

"Um I think so." I mean honestly who really knows their time of birth. Let alone refer to New Mexico by its proper name and the year 2000 by new millennium. His mystical side surely took over when in the element of stars.

Veena started asking questions about my youth. When I was this age did I go through something like this, or around this time you must have done that. A lot of the questions I had no memory to link to, although to be fair he was spot on about a lot of things to do with my father, brother, and relationships.

"So you can just look at my planets and know everything in my life?"

"It doesn't quite work like that, there is an internal process that goes on as well. I can tell the type of energy you will be in thus having a number of effects that can happen. This is looking at fate and things that cannot be avoided. Your free will is always a factor."

"What do you mean things can't be avoided, isn't that the whole point of free will?"

"Yes it's a bit of a loophole. Your fate is your free will. Your free will chooses your fate. You chose to be born here and now, not hundreds of years ago. I mean you could have been born long ago and really you're living that life simultaneously but that's besides the point."

"So what does it say my fate is?"

"You haven't chosen yet, you are between crossroads."

Veena was beginning to throw me around loopholes that never really answered my questions, however I did understand a bit more than before talking with him. He finally broke it down in words I could relate.

All the planets were in some place in space and time when I was born. All the constellations were in a portion of the sky and even the earth had portions of the sky that are divided up into twelve houses in reflection to the constellations.

Your Sun sign, Moon sign and Ascendant are the three strongest influences in your chart or structure. Why is this so? Well think it like this... the Sun influences us on the most tangible of levels. Without a Sun we would have no life or very little of it. The Moon controls the tidal waves, swaying our emotions, as we are made of water, just like the ocean. The farther away the planet, the more subtle the effect is. The outer planets start going deeper into our subconscious and universal mind.

"And your Ascendant governs your physical body as it's determined by the portion of the sky rising at our birth?"

"You catch on quick Noah," Veena is caught in a surprised manner; which was needless to say very enjoyable. Veena turned into a curious kid asking more questions to determine what planets held greater impact in my life. He thought it was funny my Venus was in Aquarius, this made sense with all my relationships moving very fast, having friendship at its core.

Ya I had some ex girlfriends that I still talked to but for the most part it was in and out of my life like that. Gain the philosophy behind the matter and move along.

Not by any rude conscious choice, just the way I was programmed it seemed.

Veena begins to point out the position of Saturn, in the all-accumulative Taurus. I had no real idea what all of this meant. I took from it that Saturn was the same as karma. It had to do with cycles of time. Apparently it connected with my Pluto (the planet of transformation) in Sagittarius, which was all about knowledge, spirituality and the long journey of it all.

With the current transits of Saturn in Pisces and Uranus in Taurus, it made out for one high octave of karmic debts that pushed limitations. And how could I forget my Mars in Aries being transited by Chiron. This was a whole other story in itself. Every aspect held so much depth.

"Trouble with girls, trouble with substances? Let me guess... having trouble sleeping and keeping track of time? Do you even know what day it is Noah?"

Ok so he had me there. I was no more than clear glass in his eyes. Veena could read me like a book. But for your information it was Saturday, or better yet, Saturn day.

"So what's all this saying, you're telling me things I already know. What's the future say?"

"It doesn't say anything in concrete. It points out the probability of events that might occur based on the energy that is there."

"So what might happen then?"

"Hard to tell. It will be a bumpy ride though. Saturn is never much fun in the long run. She is a wicked goddess that one."

"What do you mean she? Goddess?"

"I mean it is feminine in nature. Well from the Hindu point of view. Most of our galaxy is feminine. The Milky Way, milk comes from the mother, you getting the picture! Of course this is all Prakriti, another goddess, another concept. Now our closest neighboring galaxy, Andromeda, is masculine in nature. The polarity of life continues on a grand scale."

"But why goddesses?"

133

"Noah my friend, it is just a point of view. In India we use symbols that are influenced by our imagination. The Hindu religion uses the concept of deities to be symbols of life energy. Shiva is consciousness, awareness, male or yang! Shakti is energy, movement, female or yin! Saturn is just a small aspect of Shakti called Kali. Just like the pictures of Ganesh, the elephant man, being an aspect of Vishnu; the preserver of life."

"Kali. Tell me about her? She sounds interesting."

"Well she is mostly about destruction. Death. She holds a sword cutting off heads at will. She wears skulls around her neck. This is one form of her, the other is seductive, lucrative, the bait that wheels you in. Her chocolate skin and near-tantalizing eyes stare deep within. Razor sharp teeth wait to kill. Let's just hope she doesn't kill the physical part of you hehe," Veena chuckles like it was some joke. I was terrorized by everything he described because oddly enough all of this reminded me of my dreams and transfigurations during sex."

"So you're saying you can physically feel these things?"

"Most of the time it has to do with our mind, the concepts and barriers are what need to be destroyed. She is a goddess and doing you a service, it can just seem a bit harsh sometimes when you get a goddess like Kali."

"But let's say if physical things did start happening, what might those things be like?"

"Well you or those around you could get sick. People can experience a close encounter with death. Certain plans could end up falling apart, losing a job or changing a location in living space. Anything that promotes change instantly through hardship."

"What about physical wounds?"

"Noah, is there something you're not telling me?"

Like I said, Veena could see straight through me. I told him everything. The girl, the vivid dreams, the hallucinations during sex, the bite marks and scratches afterwards. Even the experience of Amber not being in control or remembering what happened that one night, and of course Mind Glow. Veena looks at me with intensity,

followed by a careful relook of my chart. He makes tiny noises like old men do when thinking things through.
"You only see the girl while making love?"
"Yes. She's more vivid with Mind Glow."

Veena pauses for another few minutes while silence begins to consume the ears. High-pitched noises ring loud enough to break willpower.
"You ok?" Veena asks.

"Ya I'm fine, I just get these high-pitched noises in my ears from time to time, kinda like after you go to a concert or something."
Everything said Veena took in with the deepest concern.

"Noah, do you want to go through a relaxation with me? It will help you understand these events and help with future occurrences."

Well of course I did. Anything that could help was much appreciated at this point. I lie down in comfort. Veena takes me through some deep breathing, and the body rests. Deeper and deeper, arms and legs fall like iron rods. The other body parts catch up without haste. The mind floods with shape and form. Veena guides me in a trance.

I was walking in a forest… perhaps a jungle. It was all fused together with bird songs greeting the senses. A little bit of Glow was still in the system, giving the experience full lucidity. Stone steps covered with moss traveled downward. Tall trees watched from above. Walking farther I came to a very large tree at the end of the stairs. There was a fuzzy outline of someone sitting down meditating. The closer I got to him, the clearer everything became. His face crystallized into an older gentleman. By now the words Veena spoke became faint sounds off in the distance, blending into the ambiance of deprivation.

Taking a seat in front of this man, he says nothing. I wanted to ask questions about what was going on in my life, but it felt so out of place. It was like any question I wanted to ask was either answered right away with a feeling of yes or no. Some of the more complex questions were meant for a later time. This was a peaceful place that had its grip around me full throttle. The tree behind him was a grand tree by any means.

"His name is Mulu. He has been our friend for many years," the man finally spoke.

"Who are you?" having to ask.

"I am only a reflection. An oversoul."

His words were soft, yet held much value. His voice was direct yet most soothing. We sat together saying nothing much, yet everything at the same time. It's something that words try to explain yet fall short nonetheless. In this state I dwelled for countless amounts of time. He held up two fingers saying, "Love all," then placed his hand back down and continued to sit in stillness.

If you've never heard a Rudra Vinya before, I suggest you do so. If you ever get a chance to hear a Vinya played live, this is a must. Veena's talent greeted the return to physicality.

"It is the song of protection," Veena explains to me.

The sound was multi-dimensional; it even had the ringing noises in the background, yet more complex than the average high pitch ambiance.

"You will always hear this ringing sound, for it is with you now."

"With me? What?"

"Some things we can't know all at once. You have experienced a lot dear friend, soon everything will start clicking and all this mystical talk will be grounded in your experience. Metaphysics is a good place to continue your investigation."

Veena gets up packing away the Vinya.

"What was that trance you put me in?"

"It was a hypnosis."

"So everything I saw was myself, even the man and the tree?"

"Precisely."

"You know I have had that vision before. I have dreamt that dream."

Veena smiles handing me a little book titled, "The Six Sided Self."

"It is something my friend wrote, its right up your alley," he tells me.
"Thank you Veena."

Finding my way back to the party, the music rises with everyone jumping around, dancing to the beat of rails on mirrors. Loki of course has lines cut up for mass consumption. It was in that moment I realized, heart to heart, one of my biggest addictions was not just the goddess or Mind Glow... but love in revelry itself.

"Animal"
-Miike Snow-

Synapses surged with emotional intelligence coming forward. Day turned to night; drugs, infatuation, addiction passed. Now what greets the eyes is a mixture of bright lights and sweet smelling buds.
"I know this place, it's the cave."

"You ok man?" Logan asks in a concerned manner. It took me a few moments to gather composure. Realizing you just lost all recollection like some bad Xanax episode is a hell of a thing. I don't bother much in explaining what was experienced.

"Yes I'm fine, just high!" Tensions relax, continuing to slice a few plants from our personal stash.

Logan had cutting the clones on lockdown. His master craft was growing plants... and smoking them. No matter how many times the bong was hit, a small feeling of fear was still left inside the body. Never before had something like this happened where having that vulnerability was so overwhelming.

We had orders to fill. People wanted a lot of pills out of nowhere. So many in fact that it was time to start thinking outside the box. We cheers White Russians as Logan, Loki and myself sit back after a long cloning session.

"Thanks for helping out brotha."

"It was my pleasure."

"You sound like an English man with that voice," Logan points to Loki.

"You been hanging around David too much, letting that accent rot your brain."

"Ya ya ya," Loki nods his head, getting on with more concerning matters.

"Speaking of David's black ass, we all need to talk."

And then it was so. Leisure turned straight back into business. Loki begins to lay it out for us to play it out... The Big Score!

"We all pitch in for as much as we can get. The orders are already overflowing compared to our rate of import and export; it won't be hard to get rid of it all. Coming up with money won't be a problem, for the most part."

"So what's the problem Loki?"

"The problem is when you deal in high amounts, you need to go to the source or else it's not worth it. And I don't know any source yet. Not to mention the risk factor of caring that much weight anyhow... we would need security no doubt."

"Is it really worth it if you get caught?" Logan butts in.

"I'm out. Don't want anything to do with it; I'm getting bad vibes. It's just too much weight and too much of a risk," I express to Loki after Logan's valid input.

"Now why would you go and say that?"

"Because it's the truth."

"What about you Logan, you want to make some cash?"

"No, I just like taking the stuff."

"That's why we love you and we hate you," I crack a joke to lighten the mood.

"Well there are more ways than one to skin a cat," Loki continues.

"What do you mean," Logan inquires.

"The Big Score. You could just pull off a heist, of course you need a distraction, a crew, and a mark," Loki pauses.

"I'm listening."

"You need a crew who is trustworthy and has a common goal bonding them together. After pinpointing what or whom you want to take from, you then create distractions that force the best conditions for your Big Score. Then you sit back and enjoy the fruits of your actions. The more people you have, the bigger the game is. The bigger the distractions, the more time you have."

"I think you're forgetting something though."

"And what's that?"

"Karma is a bitch. Stealing from people, using people as a means for gain."

"Ah come on Logan, don't tell me you believe in that shit."

"It's not a matter of believing, it's a matter of cause and effect. It's science."

"Well is it stealing if you're taking money that's already stolen? Is it using people if that's what they are asking for?"

"What you're asking is a matter of morals and ethics and can't be correctly measured without a sense of subjectivity. What I am talking about is the objective lenses of action and reaction. What comes around goes around."

"Yes what comes around goes around, now hit this," I tell Logan while passing the bong.

Loki says nothing more on the matter but says nothing much at all. This was a tall tale sign that he was working out the kinks and leaks that was his Big Score. It was much harder to get his mind off money and success than it was drugs and girls. Scary thing was his plan included them all.

Loki eventually left. Logan eventually passed out. And Janelle eventually got home. She came on hard in full character (church school girl) the entire time. So much so, it was hard to tell if it was her real side or just an act. Janelle over dramatized words making sexual comments with food.

"I think I'll toss a salad for dinner. Should I take a thick cucumber or go for the long carrot?" she asks with a winking eye, putting the carrot up to her mouth.

Laughter consumed the senses with a quick nod of the head in agreement. She made the salad as well. We ate it right up with balsamic vinegar, olive oil, croutons and a splash of crunched walnuts and cheese. A vegetarian's aphrodisiac. It tasted amazing… as did her lips.

"My dad doesn't come home for another hour. I better get clean. I sure hope no one comes in and controls me!"

Janelle stands up, slowly taking her skimpy walk to the shower. Undressing along the way, leaving a bra on the door handle. And so I popped a pill and did what was expected of me. After all, I was a guest in her house.

Again I transfigured Janelle as Her. Stillness with sexual bliss rocked the heavens. And then like an asteroid from space it hit me... the letter K on the back of the Ipod, Kali. Holy shit!

Had I thought this before? Had I been so caught up in the day-to-day thoughts that perhaps, unconsciously, I chose not to realize this until now? Perhaps this explains the chill up my spine.

This was the most realized trip experienced to date. Not to forget the fact this went on while having sex was indeed the cherry on top of the cake. I was starting to understand why Chris had chosen sex as a path of enlightenment.

I wake to the sounds of throw-up echoed by tiled floors within the bathroom. It was not a sight for the faint of heart. Janelle threw up blood, splattering everywhere. Tying her hair back from puke, I rub the back in spinning motions then begin to clean her arms and face. Don't know why it took me so long to see this, perhaps it was the blood that was distracting, but right next to the bathtub, was a needle, spoon, torch and all.
"My God, why are you doing this shit. Stop!" I tell her.

Janelle doesn't speak, or chooses not to care. It was serious and had to be stopped. I take the equipment and throw it away in the neighbor's trash down the street, get her cleaned and fresh with a nice meal. Then she went back to sleep, so I went to go take care of other pressing matters.

What the hell is going on in society today? It seems we are lost in our search for knowledge and clarity, never being given the whole truth without a sense of doubt. Not to mention the lack of giving back to the world at large. Now please don't get me wrong, there is more good going on out there than bad. This is a fact. But it is not what is shown on the televisions of the world. For some reason something is so addictive in watching destruction and chaos, and then we do it ourselves... to ourselves.

You see it out on the streets, at your job... on the weekends... in the bars... people acting off pure impulse even primordial frustration at times.

Come to think about it and all, is this train of thought not negative in itself? Or is the intention behind the matter the real message of the situation? Are both not equal in their own right? Perhaps thinking is the one to blame! Perhaps thought is a blessing and a curse! Then should we even be thinking?

"Jesus," I say out loud while eyes focused to an almost fatal accident on the freeway. Gripping the wheel I check myself.

"What the hell Noah, you retarded or something. Do you know how much loot we got in the back?"
"I'm sorry man, I drifted off."

"Well don't let it happen again, pay attention. Stop narrating bro," Loki expels.

Chris' Black Moon party was tonight, meaning work hard now so we could party hard later. What does this mean exactly... well it means once again I helped my brother move weight and collect cash. I wasn't comfortable with the methods of collection as Loki was to say the least. "Don't worry Noah, we got Zeus with us."

Loki already named his new K9 companion. We hit drop after drop, popping trunks from the Tukee all the way to Apache Junction. The suburbs of Gilbert proved to be simple with young teens and foolish college students biting the hardest. Mexican Mafia overran Mesa so when it came to dealing in that turf, we dealt straight to Victor and let him take care of the rest. It was easier this way, not to mention safest.

Tempe was another microcosm to take into account, too many people walking around in a haze of consumption. What was needed were people on the inside: the clubs, the bars, the street rats, and the event planners. This is where Loki came into play with his lucrative skills and of course… girls.

Girls can make their way to anyone in any industry, for sex always sells. Loki's connections stretched out towards central Phoenix, with my connections being mostly in Ahwatukee or Scottsdale. The fast cash and high expectations made it easy for wealthy folks to invest once again in Mr. Glow. Katie became Loki's right-hand woman. It was business and pleasure for them both as they used each other for position and power. They loved it.

The sun rapidly approached the horizon in an attempt to kiss the earth goodnight. As light turned to dusk… dusk into twilight… and twilight into translight, the music rises with guests making their way into the mansion like Black Friday.

There were at least four hundred people all dressed in basically nothing. This wasn't just a party for the moon, it wasn't just a party that embraced the elements… this was a party of pure expression. Pure emotion. Pure feeling that dragged the night along with it, beat by beat. Deep inhalation by deep exhalation, I allow the music to take charge once again with rhythm and ecstasy. The New Age hippies had alluring taste with acceptance reigning over all.

"Shiva Moon"
[Moon Nectar Remix]
-Prem Joshua-

Substance abuse was at a maximum. No longer was I dealing with orders of pills and such. Loki had this under control while the vortex of impulse slipped ever deeper.

"This technology! It's hijacked the brain, electronically. We plug into reality… so-called consciously, that our blind perception is thrown down vigorously. In the time that is given stay grateful and glade. Focus on purpose and what you already have."

To be all fair and honest this is a messed up thing to see when you're tripping. It can be some heavy shit… and it was. The unknown quote carved into the brick wall leads me to a more surreal standpoint. At times it was information overload. Focusing on my breath helped ground the spinning waves a little as I stumble through the people zoo.

Dizziness rounds up like a tornado in Kansas. Finally I make it to the bathroom in order to gain composer. That's when I broke the golden rule in my book of keeping cool. Never ever, ever look at your face… let alone your eyes when you are tripping. It is an abyss of self-reflection and mind masturbation that unravels the ego at an undetermined rate.

There was this sense in the actuality of emptiness, where the natural perfection of reality lies. Continuing to ponder at the uncontrived sameness of every experience, my conditioning and ambition resolved with a sliver of finality. Giving myself to the art of listening, my views on life were abandoned.

I had a discussion with self, casting away all the childish games that fetter and exhaust the bodymind. We talked about the various abstractions in life without any foundation. It was only with this constant inquiring that truth was found. If we have to believe and become attached to any doctrine, that belief would be based more or less on a self-centered idea. This is when I discovered that it was absolutely necessary to believe in nothing. Approach everything with the beginner's mind.

Neon blue lights made the bathroom seem like a Smurf dream. Amber walked in with a smile, "There you are!" My gaze fixed on the mirror. She walked up, looked me straight in the soul and laughed ridiculously until focus was broken.

"My God Noah, snap out of it. WAKE UP," Amber screams with a love slap to the head... indeed I was now awake.

Walking back into a crowd of lost souls, the party was silenced when police officers walked in, cutting off the DJ. Everyone stands still. Two people jump over the fence quicker than the eye could see. The cops say nothing at first, giving a hard look to each individual. The cop picks up blunt roaches and smells them with a look of disgust. Standing on the beer pong table, he speaks,

"Gentlemen, I'm going to need you to stand on the right of me and take out your wallets. Ladies, I'm going to need all of you on the left of me and get ready to shake it... pump the music back up!"

The DJ begins right where he left off and the party continues. It was a joke. A prank. O thank God. The heart skips a bit. O he was a real cop, but in the world of Chris, there were no bad guys... they were all friends, "For are we not destroying our enemies when we make friends of them?"

Amber skips down the hallway with her long dress flowing ever so lightly in the air. The everlasting image burns tracer marks into my retina. I moved slowly. No way I was keeping up with that bunny.

The mansion seemed bigger when under the influence. I went into every door looking for Amber. Chris had three bathrooms just on the top floor; all being occupied by the local druggie who liked to get high on their own supply. Gritty little buggers they are.

I am beginning to train myself to see truth in all things. It may not be your truth; it may not be my truth, even if we can agree to disagree. But it is still truth nonetheless.

With thoughts like these zipping through the brain at speeds impossible to record, I turn on the light to find the strangest of sights.

There stood Veena, paintbrush in hand, crafting a landscape of detailed pictorials, highlighting a city in flames and ash. Wait a minute…

"Were you just painting in the dark?"

"One might think so," Veena chuckles.

"That's impossible, it's so vivid… so detailed. How do you do this?"

"Once focus is cultivated, we can determine our own vision. With this comes clairvoyance. I am peeling the light spectrums, revealing what's already there in another so-called dimension or thought space. Most of your New Age books will teach you this."

"Ok… practically explain to me how you see in the dark then."

"Most inquisitive. Very good." Veena utters with a delightful tone in his Indian accent. Bobbing his head side to side, Veena appreciated the opportunity in sharing such knowledge to a listening heart.

"With practice, patience, and persistence, you will go far. Trust in yourself, and see fear turned into courage, faith into knowing, believing into seeing.

The power that is held within the physical is but a mirror of our true potential. Understand your limitations by not being bound by them, you see.

Do or do not. Accept or deny. It's the middle area that leaves so much mess of the mind. Now with that being said and to answer the question that's on your mind… everything seen in this illusion is energy. Before something happens there is an energy outburst, I simply see what is in the astral and manifest it in the physical. Everyone can do this and a lot actually do on an unconscious level. It's all a matter of awareness and a little purity of intention."

I'd take my hat off to Veena if I had one. He was a most excellent painter. The sun was abstractly done to symbolize a phoenix. The buildings silhouetted behind a classic AZ sunset. The sky was so tastefully done that multiple images appeared then disappeared, just like fading clouds. Fists, feathers, burning ash, it was a somewhat tragic painting yet empowering in some odd way.

"Do you have any hobbies?" Veena asks.

"I'm not sure. I like chess if that counts. Any suggestions?"

"Well the only thing that comes to mind is making sure it's something you love, cause if you don't have love in your life, what's the point?"

The first thought was listening to music oddly enough, and then Kali. Even stranger was the music thought of was on Her Ipod. It was Her music. Then a little stress set in and all I could think about was having Kali. The anxiety outweighed more problems than a serial killer on trial. I mean it was nonsense that was placed upon myself. Thinking of what could be... then getting sad that it wasn't happening. How ridiculous.

Taking a second glance at fresh paint, there seemed to be a storm in the background. The storm had glowing eyes with lightning and dust spreading like wildfire.

"Why did you paint a storm?"

"She represents the dying, the suffering, the sickness of the city... and the rebirth of the people at large."

The number of homeless wonderers was growing, being pushed out onto the streets. The number of new fixes and quick rushes was large at hand. Hell, I should know; I was the one who helped sell some of the worst stuff that's out there. Was I one of them now? Taking a hand full of narcotics of uppers and downers can really mess with the head.

If we are to speak more directly about Mind Glow... well then there is little to talk about. Don't know what's in it, how it works, why it works the way it does, or even where it came from. But one thing was for sure; it did things to your body that seemed irreversible.

Something in our DNA was changing. Evolution was granted a leap forward... but at what cost? Maybe finding a more direct source was a good idea, if it could lead in knowing what was in this stuff. It's funny how you choose to over look some things, then out of the blue, decide to start worrying about other tedious details. I suddenly realized I had no control over myself. Whoever I might be.

"Wow man, you are in it right now!"

"What?"

"Your face, you are in it. I can tell, too much thinking, too serious all the time. Stop psychoanalyzing everything."

"You know Veena... I think you're right."

"Of course I'm right. Just do what I do."

"And what's that exactly."

Veena took a quick look at me then began to laugh. He laughed and laughed until he couldn't hold his sides anymore. At first Veena was forcing the laughter. Minutes later he was battling them away. He became possessed with giggles and tears. Veena was laughing at the way I thought. The way I held myself. He was laughing at everything about me. Like yawns laughs are, so contagious. And with that, we laughed together, fueling each other downward into a giggle fest for the ages.

In those moments of laughter everything is lost and forgotten yet all happening at once. You don't think, you don't worry, you don't mind anything but the moment at hand. It is a blessing that humans can experience something such as the laugh. It can be used in the most obvious of situations or the most uncomfortable of times. After it's all said and done, the laugh is what brings unity, giving spark to compassion, forgiveness, humility and joy.

We now found ourselves outside. Laughing at anything anybody said. It was contagious. When guests came up to me talking whatever whatever, all I could do was laugh. I laughed at their reactions. Laughed at their remarks. I laughed harder when Chris and his friends asked for Glow. And I laughed the hardest at the fact Loki was nowhere to be found.

"Wait, what do you mean you can't find him?"

"That's what I've been trying to tell you and Veena this entire time," Chris explains.

"Is his car here?"

"Ya."

Attention shifts to detective mode. Information is searched for like Sherlock Holmes playing Clue. The Mustang was parked where we left it. The pills were still safely hidden amongst the dog food in the back trunk. Loki wasn't answering his cell phone and Katie was nowhere to be found. Conclusion? They must have found a perfect spot.

This was the most obvious of scenarios, but it wasn't the most believed. Something just didn't feel right. So I help the guests get some Glow and with a collection of three-grand in an hour, it was safe to say that tonight was a good night. Well, for some of us anyways.

Loki's disappearance was still in a shard of mystery but nothing could draw my attention from fireworks blasting over the valley. The night sky was now lit with a rainbow of colors and noises. Everyone screamed in a roar of excitement while the sky blossomed vivid sparks... fading into the night. All the way from Gilbert to North Phoenix the fireworks presented themselves in a haze of infatuation.

"Butterfly"
(Bass Flo Remix)
-Talvin Singh-

We all sat in presence of it happening. The music was a foreign technology. Forever I am bounded by it. A puppet? A puppeteer? A willing one at that!

Music says what words cannot. It is heard, felt, and recognized almost instantly. This was the first language we experienced when nurtured in our mother's womb. The grace of birth upon this root we call Earth is the beginning of our recognition in self. If this doesn't make sense to you... read again.

It is the moment you split from one into two. No longer do you hear the beat of your mother's heart. Life was made for pain, made for separation... and the juice is always worth the squeeze.

What is meant by this second part? Well take a look at myself for instance. I smoke weed that hurts the lungs. Take pills that fry the brain. And drown myself in mind masturbations of girls and details of debate. All which are not healthy, yet somehow molding me in a way that pushes to fight the system. No longer will this tyranny be permitted! No longer will we be a product of manipulation, sucking at the tit of the greedy and ruthless.

"Fuck the government and the world order. When did these politicians forget that we gave them their power, that we pay their salary!"

"What the hell Noah!"

"Say what?"

Must have been talking out loud. The look on Nathan's face was one of anger and sadness, a strange combination to say the least. Before I could begin to say sorry for talking down on his career path, Nathan just nods his head and agrees.

"You're kinda right actually. That's the sad truth of it all. I try and make a difference but to be honest…"

"To be honest what?"

"It's not even a choice anymore. Voting for this guy or that guy! In actuality it's already known who gets in. It's a joke. I've already won the seat for senate and no one has even voted yet."

"What are you saying, you rigged your election?"

"No. But I know my investors will make sure I win in order to protect their own interest."

"Please don't tell me you're going to go on about corporations and the Illuminati. Truth or no truth, this flood of information leads one to soak in the good and the bad. I've done my research and all it leads to is more theories and a negative manipulated mind," I tell Nathan whole-heartedly.

"But in the end it remains some type of truth. We prioritize money and economy over basics like air, water, food, community and environment. We use an economic trading system that adds death to millions a year. We divide land into sections, then fight over who owns those sections. We call people soldiers and assume it's ok for them to kill people. We send our kids to schools for their entire childhood to memorize facts and skills that they will rarely use in life. Love and compassion, which promotes life, are mocked as facile. Whereas war, which harms life, is seen as honorable... I joined politics because I wanted to make a difference, because I think we can do better. But, as I find my role in all of this... there's this fear that I might not have what it takes!"

"Don't ever say this Nathan. Make them accept the truth of compassion and act upon that. Only the weak are cruel. Gentleness can only be expected from the strong. Don't give up man. Investors or no investors... you got my vote."

Nathan nods, remaining silent. It was a good silence. The kind where you're comfortable with the silence and don't need to think of topics to talk about with the other person. It just came to my realization that Nathan had been there all along. Who knows how long I was talking for? Who knows how much he heard? Now that I knew he was next to me, some of his soberishness was drifting my way. It felt like fresh snowflakes on a winter's breeze.

Being able to stand again provided good time to search for Loki. I hadn't forgotten about him, he was just on the back burner. Problem being he was nowhere to be seen. I found Katie, but her story of my MIA brother was the same as mine. The party rolled on. The crowd thinned out. The rooms became occupied. The kegs tapped. The bottles dry. The pot heads asleep. The rollers still rolling, in the grass that is.

Amber lies between my arms upon chest. We were one in the same, watching the sun's eyelashes streak the yawning sky. Twilight became dawn and all was at peace. I slowly leave Amber's embrace for a fresh wake and bake.

Now we all have those times where things seem a bit absurd, a bit intense and a bit confusing. Sometimes, if we are lucky enough, we have a state of pure enjoyment and curiosity. Today was without any exception. For today was NEW DAY. It had come early, as most traveling groupies could have guessed.

Now when I mean it was a "NEW DAY," I mean just that. Everything was different… people became affected, leaving no one behind.

Let me try and paint it out for you readers in cyber space who are having technical difficulties seeing the big picture. First it started with the fireworks. But it evolved into the televisions, the radio, the stores, and most importantly… the mind-bending souls who lived on the streets.

All the networks simply cut out commercials and replaced them with YouTube videos. MTV actually played music videos again. The radio played sound bits of pop culture films, never having a break for the sponsors. Movie theaters were five dollars all day, every day. The light rail was free while the streets of Phoenix and Tempe merged into a giant festival of pure stimulus… eventually leading towards sensory overload.

It was Halloween everywhere. The inner hero or villain emerged as the city grew into a World of Warcraft replica. Artists took towards the streets beginning three-dimensional landscapes on buildings and sidewalks; by the time it was twelve o'clock, nothing was what it appeared.

I hardly slept, the pills were to thank for that. I was tired yet full of energy. The city and people were fueling my every step and thought.

A quick shower and coffee to restart the body never fails. "Ah, there we go!"

The day begins with a few major setbacks. First I needed to find Loki. His car was here. Zeus was with Katie, yet Loki's phone went straight to voicemail. Chris and Dru both wanted orders far beyond my capacity of export.

"I'll see what I can do and as always, it's been a trip," I tell Chris. Phone rings. (Aka the theme song from the old X-Men cartoons.)

"Who is this?"

"It's me motha fucka!"

"Loki… where are you man, what happened to you last night?"

"You wouldn't believe me if I told you."

"Is that why you're calling me from another phone?"

"Ya."

"Well spill it out!"

"First I kinda need your help with a ride situation. I'm far too messed up to drive right now!"

"Bro, I could barely drive your car to drop off Amber this morning."

"Noah, listen, its NEW DAY! OK. Now do your brother a favor and bring me my ride… please. It's the least you can do, after all you are driving that car more than me these days."

"Well since you asked so politely I guess there's no choice now is there? Where are you?"

"Scottsdale."

"Text me the address!"

The situation was far worse than imagined. Loki slouches in a careless manner, greeting me with a smile and a glass of Bourbon, even some bumps of Glow if I liked.

Apparently Loki had left the party with David.

"We jumped that fence like a couple of niggas man," Loki exhales with a laugh. He remembered getting a ride from a friend that David knew.

"That's all you remember?" My curiosity was transforming into agitation.

"Like I said, we got out of there when the cops came and partied hard once the fireworks started."

"So you remember the fireworks then? What about David, where is he?"

Loki stops and thinks, as if dusting off old memories, and then resumes in explaining the day's mission… import and export. Pay and get paid. His mind was on one thing, as it always was. A hiccup in the plan being Loki was too hung over to do any serious transaction. Of course this wasn't stopping him in the least.

He had a knack for getting himself into trouble when under the influence of drugs and power.

"Yo bro… bro you're vibrating," Loki gestures with a pointing hand.

The text reads as so…

-GOT LOKI'S PHONE. DROP BY THIS AFTERNOON AND WE WILL MEET UP WITH STELLA AND GLOW-

"Well David has your phone and it looks like you're meeting someone to get a bunch of pills."

"Correction… we are going to get some pills."

I knew what Loki was trying to do. He pulled the same routine every time. Different strokes for different folks but in the end it always came down to living like a gangsta.

"Even though I need more for Chris and Dru, I told you I didn't want any more of this mentality. I'll drive you and help out, but I'm getting bad vibes about this shit. You keep acting like you want to go back to jail!"

Loki goes on the offensive changing the subject back to me.

"Who wants to go back to jail? Are you serious? When are you going to show a little ambition and do something with your life? All you do is sit back and wait for shit to happen. Only reason why you are where you are is because of me!"

"You need to close your mouth before it says something you can't take back!"

"And who's going to make me hu? You? I doubt that, you wouldn't hurt a fly."

"I'm telling you Loki, take your tone down."

"Or what?"

"Let's find out!"

We stare off at each other while the phone rings again. I pick it up as we both make our way out to the car. It was Janelle. And if you didn't guess already, she was booty calling me. I play it off cool, promising her a rain check on the matter.

The air was a bit tense after our argument, but as the day rolled on, it was kind of hard to stay mad. I mean, the city… it was in such a uproar. So much that at times it was a trip in itself. Life became chaotic in an intuitive way.

There were people who dressed up like zombies, monopolizing the streets in a battlefield of the blind, deaf and dumb. Then there were the real zombies who resembled more of a vampire feel than anything. They were the ones who could snap at any moment, go crazy over any wrong look or comment… drunken fools they are.

The math was simple. Getting the pills was easy enough. Except the pills weren't pills, only powder. This sucked because anytime you play with powder, you always lose weight in the handling and exchange from one bag to the other.

The money was a bit hard to come by but not impossible. I mean twenty thousand dollars is a lot, but in the world of drugs and high rollers, it was just the tip of the iceberg. By now I'm sure Loki was as hard as a rock. His pants tighten when eyes met glorious desires, Glow of course.

There was something up with Stella, David's connection. Her accent was a mix American and something else the mind franticly tried to keep up with. She wore an arm patch that resembled a phoenix with rising fist inside of it. She didn't say much unless spoken to, but her attitude was fully present. Stella was somewhere in her forties being extremely magnetic. In some small way she reminded me of Kali.

I had been pushing Kali away lately. Too painful to think about the one who got away. Better to focus on less hurtful thoughts. I have my self-preservation to think of. I mean my God I'm only in my twenties and still going through high school attachment drama.

Stella begins talking about Mind Glow with a flare. All though she never called it Glow. She simply referred to it as "The Mother."

"Why do you call it The Mother?"

"Why do you call it Glow?"

"Because that's how it makes me feel," I tell Stella.

"Same here," She simply says.

"So you're saying this stuff is connected to a Mother?"

"Not a Mother, thee Mother."

"How do you know?"

"Well I hope I would know, I helped make this stuff."

At first I didn't believe her. So I began asking more questions as anyone would. Just the way she began to express this drug made me believe her. She used words and terms way out of my awareness on the matter, talking about DMT extract, combinations in brewing, factors to take in when drying, how to cut it... why to cut it and when to cut it.

Scopolamine was a leading cutting agent among other ingredients. It wasn't comfortable knowing you were playing around with the Devil's breath mixed with an arsenal of mad chemistry. And I thought all along the stuff we got from Stella was pure. Everything was carefully cut and balanced. This was power and where there is power, there is always darkness lurking around the corner.

"To be all fair and honest, it's a love-hate relationship... It's an amazing drug, but there are too many unseen factors that come with it. I mean everyone trips differently on this stuff. That's something new in the arena of drugs. Not to mention that it mixes well with anything. But it's all terribly bad for you in the long run. Why the hell are we even doing this if it kills us in the end?"

"Because life is suffering. And we must learn to be ok with that. Not to run from it like a child. This is the whole point of it all. This is the aim of the stuff, to destroy you down to your very last breath... and from the ashes shall rise a more evolved being."

"Damn Stella. I got to hand it to you, that is some dark twisted shit right there. But it's a bit unnecessary don't you think?"

"Unnecessary you say?"

"I mean who says it's got to be all sad like that. Why should we do keep hurting ourselves all the time? A little pain here and there to show us what is real is one thing, but when did this habitual downfall become the normal without question or thought? ”

"It's a path. That's all."

"Well it sounds like an unfortunate path to me. That's why I'm letting Loki take care of all this stuff."

Loki butts in, "What do you mean me… I'm going to need your help bro. I can't push all this alone. You see how crazy it is out on the streets?"

I say nothing. I am used to Loki trying to use me like some parasite.

"Looks like you can't get away. She has you now," Stella remarks.

"Who has me?" I say with great interest.

"The goddess."

Stella made sense. Like most of the people in my life, which left me only more lost and confused overall. There was something lingering over my shoulders that had been put off for some time. It was far too soon to put any words on such an overwhelming feeling, although the emotions grew like weeds.

"Loki I'm not doing your work. I'll drop off the Glow to Dru and Chris, but you need to take care of the street rats. And that's that."

"You don't need to refer to them as street rats. Harsh."

"Are you serious Loki? You're the one who is saying niggers. You're the raciest one."

"Hey. I take offense to that. I just think everyone should own their own nigger! That's all."

"How is that not racist?"

"It's not racist because I have black people in my family tree."

"NO YOU DON'T!"

"Sure I do bro, they're still hanging out front!"

"Shut up Andrew and be real once in your life!"

And with a slip of his name, a brother swung at his own. Hitting me down to the ground with a sledgehammer slam, I make way, charging at him, bringing us both into the wall.

Fist into ribs… elbows into face… knees into chest… blood and anger of repressed aggression finally released. We crashed into the flat screen… finally making way towards the ground. It was high school wrestling all over again. I laugh a little. Attention is taken off of stressful matters, trickling towards Loki, laughing himself.

"You see, now that's what I needed. That's the Noah I miss. Bring that guy back."

Loki begins his new angle of persuasion. The master manipulator was hard at work indeed if he resorted to fighting as a way of twisting intentions. Although I must say, letting the rage out every now and then is a most peculiar rush.

"You're an idiot getting involved with these people."

"You wanna go another round speaking like that?" Loki feeds off my aggression.

Stella's wickedness sets upon us! In a lot of ways I felt Stella playing with my mind. Searching for something. It must sound weird, but if you have ever just stared at someone for longer than thirty seconds, you will begin to understand the language beneath the words of magic.

"What the hell. Who is going to pay for my T.V. now?" David comes out from the bathroom.

"Sorry David, we'll find you a new one," I tell him with little concern.

I grabbed my share of Glow and thanked David for his hospitality, as short-lived as it was. I make no gestures or goodbyes to Stella. And as for Loki and myself… it was to be continued.

"As The Rush Comes"
(Gabriel & Dresden Chillout Mix)
-Motorcycle-

New Day was getting wilder than foreseen. Electric Daisy Carnival, Burning Man, Lightning in a Bottle, Coachella… they all had their spot on the podium, right below New Day. It was no longer a city. It was a

157

migrating evolving organism. In some ways it was a plague, turning inward fears into outward actions.

Vanity was everyone's best friend. Attitudes polarized. People's shadow ruled. Protests turned into riots. Riots turned into occupying public space, eventually leading to far worse things. Considering most of the protesters were whacked out of their minds, few in the streets still remained within their own light.

As for me, the battle for balance was always present. The chess pieces pour into position as the cold metal atmosphere echoed throughout the jail's visitor center. I say nothing much while my father moved white Pawn to begin the game. The eerie background tone was in reflection to the stillness before battle.

I was five moves ahead in four different scenarios. We exchange Queen for Queen early in the game. He comes on strong. My defense holds up in keeping an even balance of Pawns and Rooks, leaving my Knights and Bishops without their brothers.

It was a battle for the ages. My father's poker face was a brick wall. The only tells I got off of him was the little sighs he unconsciously made when his attack was naturalized. As for me, I was sitting tight, letting him come with the offensive. His advantage in going first was a lead in position. My advantage in going second was seeing his form, then act accordingly.

His defense was near perfect but when thinned out, became weak; more room to move created greater possibilities in checkmating him. As much as I wanted to win, in the end I didn't. But either did he. We each had our Kings with one Rook each. Chasing each other around the board. Just like every other cycle out there.

"Good job, you didn't lose."

"Ya but I didn't win so what's the point?"

"The point is you didn't lose. You're getting better… seriously."

"Ya well a tie isn't worth much now is it," I tell him with disappointment.

"Noah, why do you think I started playing chess?"

"Enlighten me!"

"It wasn't because I wanted to win or be good at something," Father pauses, giving a moments time to figure it out for myself.

"Why play then?"

"I play for the simple fact of just playing. It was fun, win or lose."

"So then what's all the bullshit about linking chess to situations in your life? Saying it's all just one big game."

"Yes. A game that I hope one day no longer governs us."

"It's our choice to join the game then right?"

"Is it much of a choice to live without eating? Sometimes we can bend the rules. But breaking them… that takes much more courage than I've come to know."

It wasn't hard to understand him. It was just hard thinking that it was all a joke… a joke of our own making and our own undoing.

"… Can I ask you something?"

With a nod of his head, I began to unravel threads that haven't been pulled in many years.

"How did you know mom was the right one for you?"

"She wasn't the right one for me. We were young and foolish," he replied with a sarcastic laugh.

"Is that why you left her and went for another?"

"Listen, I don't need your investigation ok. If you have something to say just say it!"

"I'm just trying to figure out what is me and what is you. Cause frankly I am tired of being pulled apart." Father's eyes widened while listening ears flapped with interest.

"It's just this whole love thing. It's a real mother bitch you know."

"I assume you're still trying to get with that girl?"

"Her name is Kali. Well I don't know really… it's a long story. Every time I think of Her it brings me joy with the deepest sorrow. I mean the only way I see Her is in my dreams or when I picture Her while with another."

"Do you know why I named you Noah and your brother Andrew?"

"No not really."

"When you were born I saw a strong soul, much wiser than mine. When I saw your brother, all I saw was myself. I'm no saint… you know this. I am sad how things turned out between Andrew and I, your mother and his. But if I could do it all over again, I wouldn't change a thing… well maybe a few things here and there."

I chuckle a bit while the mood is lightened, yet still grasping some insight, and dare I say, contentment?

"To be honest Noah, I hope you don't come back here. I hope you never visit these walls again. And when I'm up for parole, I hope you aren't waiting for me outside these gates."

"Why are you saying this?"

"Because then I'll know you have found your way. Walking your own path. Creating your own game with your own rules. Not playing by someone else's. Then you'll know what I know and hopefully do much more with it."

"With what?"

"Your life!"

The guard comes in yelling, "Let's go Mr. Savage, times up," while pounding keys upon door. My father's eyes close. "I'm not done yet," he says in a most serious tone.

"Well you are now."

"It's ok, this was a good talk. I love you dad, "my father is shocked as much as I am… it had been years sense the last time I said that, and it felt good.

The hour and a half drive home proved therapeutic. 89.5 KBAQ. 100.7 KSLX. To close it off, a little peace and quiet while the city sprays neon graffiti. The 101 freeway was transformed with artists tagging geometrical spirals running along vibrant walls… resembling Tron with a modern twist.

The most excellent psychedelic trip by far was the sky. Creative minds, scientists and artisans alike developed a way to paint the night sky. Never fully understood the complexities of such a magic show. I vaguely remember hearing about the process. Just like printing logos on shirts. So they printed the sky with stories.

Most pictures lasted about twenty minutes before fading away, making room for another. Like falling leaves upon autumn soil, the landscapes alone left most people drifting off in fantasy.

In the heart of Phoenix, everything was gridlocked. Raves migrated into the streets, the malls, and even the grocery stores. Why the grocery stores? I have a feeling it had to do with bright white lights and munchies. It wasn't much of a guess why the police stayed away from the inner city. It was just too out of hand.

The light rail transformed into a paintball battleground. There were events like zombie walk, vampire hunt and robot dance off. People who dressed as zombies were stoned and wasted beyond reason; they aimlessly walked Mill Ave in a flash flood of impulse and emotion.

The robots gathered mostly in Scottsdale, as electro and dub moved people like hands on a clock, ticking and grinding with Molly and Mr. Glow. The last was the vampire hunts. I never fully understood these events, but it consisted of absolute rage, aggression, anger, and release.

Mosh pits seemed elementary. With coke-filled veins, monsters endlessly fought each other. It was called a hunt because once someone found another to rage with it wasn't over until the last one was standing. The ones who fell were the hunted; the ones who stood tall were the hunters. In the end they were all predators.

The ego flourished. The dark side revealed itself in many forms. For some reason everyone wanted to destroy everything from relationships, friendships, to cars, buildings, even hospitals.

The news blasted reports of rape, murder, even kidnapping. Amber alerts began to play on constant loop, with a different name every time. The police could manage the suburban and rural areas. But as far as Phoenix was concerned... it had become its own identity. Those who went in rarely came out.

CNN, CNBC, BBC, FOX News, you name it they were covering it. New Day had grown into a black hole in just over a week. It was the first time New Day had hit America... and by the way things were looking, it seemed this would be the last.

The eyes weigh heavy and rest is taken. Amber, the sweet goddess gave the best back rubs, coconut oil with eucalyptus aromatherapy. She had a most addictive quality.

In our state of union, I transfigure Amber... I just had to see Her. Kali was always on the back of my mind. It was a little hidden pleasure. As time was fractured, hazel eyes quickly became red and yellow. The skin turns black, the teeth into razors. Two arms become four. I now reside in a state of terror. I was mummified, paralytic, and unable to move in the slightest degree. That part came fast!

Her hand grasps the neck, holding a sword in the other. Kali was vivid yet blurry at the same time. Hot on the outside with flames surrounding us, yet coldness on the inside. That part came slow!

Unable to breath, she opens her mouth wide, detaching her jaw in the process. She unleashes the most horrifying screeches. The jaw clenched so bad, teeth crack like brittle glass.

It was the first time I felt completely helpless, vulnerable to everything. It is a pain I wouldn't wish upon my worst enemy. Death crept slowly. Kali and her sword drew back for the kill strike.

With the power of sound, I was able to breath. It was the Rudra Vinya. It came fast and spontaneous. No soft smooth transitions like before. It was a progressing scale that added bending notes with forceful picking. This force threw its will upon me so greatly; I stood still in awe of it all. It was like viewing myself from afar with a sense of curiosity and urgency.

Kali stops screaming, the Vinya overpowers all. With each wave of sound her flesh was ripped. Flaking away like burning ash. Bones release steam. Her heart was as black as the hole it came from. With a last strum of the Vinya, Kali was washed away with a gust of dissipating smoke.

The eyes awake, the mind resets. I find Amber on the phone looking towards me.

"You ok?"

"Ya."

"Ok never mind, he snapped out of it. Thank you." Amber hangs up the phone.

"Snapped out of what?"

"You were having a seizure or something. You started twitching and not breathing. Then blood started coming out of your ears and I didn't know what to do. What happened?"

This was going to be hard to explain. Dots were still connecting.

"I think I was saved."

"What?"

"This might seem weird, but I think I heard Veena's Rudra playing when I saw Kali."

"Kali... You transfigured me as Kali?"

"I transfigured you as a goddess."

"That only works when I know about it you idiot."

I must have flipped a switch. She got angry... fast.

"How long have you been doing this?"

"Babe it's nothing, calm down."

"You tell me you think of another girl when we have sex and you expect me to be calm. How long Noah? How long have you been thinking about Her hu? HOW LONG!"

Now I was scared. She wasn't the same. She reminded me of Kali just a few minutes ago. Chris was right; this was blowing up in my face. I had this wavering guideline... it was never tell a girl the complete truth. Always leave a little mystery or buffer space for yourself. Girls want the truth but can hardly handle the truth when given it. This ended up building relationships on total lies I later realized.

At first it seemed like a good idea because whenever I was truthful about my feelings, it always ended up with the girl bitching at me. They always had to try and change my viewpoint. This is why I came up with guidelines. So after what just happened with Amber, it was time to tell her the truth.

"I've been thinking of Her since we first hooked up, I can see Her so vividly with you. She looks like the one who gave me this Ipod. I'm sorry, I thought you were cool with it because that night at Chris' and everything."

"That night at Chris' completely freaked me out. You felt me crying in your arms. That's me being scared. That's me not liking it you idiot."

"Amber I'm sorry... Please forgive me. I don't know what else to say."

"That's it Noah. There is nothing else to say."

Amber gets up, putting on her clothes.

"I think it's time for you to leave now."

"But it's like two o'clock at night."

"Maybe you can call Kali and see if she has a bed for you... o wait you can't, cause she's not real."

Amber's eyes begin to tear. Nose clogs up with snuffles and tissue. I walk over to comfort her but she pushes me away. She grabs my shirt and denim, throwing them at me.

"Get out. I can't see you right now."

"Amber please let me –"

"No," she interrupts my words, "I like you Noah... a lot. But now I see you for who you really are!"

"What's that?"

"You're a fool who is in love with love. You don't care about anything other than your next fuck or living a life of revelry. All you care about is the feeling you get out of others."

"That's not true at all."

"Well it's true from where I'm standing. Just because you're sweet and nice doesn't mean what you're doing isn't mean. You're just like your brother."

"I am nothing like my brother," I tell her in a defensive tone. None of us like to be put on stage and crucified with words of slander, however true they might be from perspective to perspective.

"Actually Noah, you're right. I'm wrong for once. You are worse than Loki. At least he is straightforward with what he wants and does. At least he has the balls to tell a girl he doesn't like her."
"But I do like you."

"Then you have a twisted way of showing it. Now please, put on your shit, and get the fuck out."

Amber wasn't playing around. So I left without a word. I stand out front of her house, leaning on the Mustang. The sky paint was fading; the stars barely peeked through the light pollution. An incredible feeling of guilt set in. Have I been that blind all along to those around me?

It's amazing seeing to what extents people go through in dealing with their problems. Some hit the bottle. Some hit the bottle hard. Some drown themselves in food and expensive toys. Others find their comfort behind narcotics. For me, I find contentment with a good old fashion fuck. Ironically this was the problem at hand. So putting the pedal to the metal, the tires spin and all concerns burn away. The night takes me. O glory to spontaneous reaction.

"When The Levees Break & No Quarter"
-Led Zeppelin-

"Seriously, to think about art as a crime is beyond reason, it's pure insanity. To think that fast food companies can post ads on billboards to eat shit food, but putting a painting of a rose, or a woman, or even a name is considered a crime punishable by law! Punishable! They are actually going to slap you with a fine for expressing yourself. They have gone too far. When did they forget that We The People pay for these streets, We The People grind it out everyday to pay for that building, that bus stop, that sidewalk. The hell with politicians and their words of fancy... the hell with the system and their golden chains, We The People will no longer put up with this suppression. We The People speak loud and clear. We are your bank clerks. We are your high school teachers, your neighbors. We are the all Seeing Eye of society. From darkness we are born... from ashes we shall rise!"

The city pulsed with street activists and poets alike. Oil, spray, or just plain chalk, the buildings blasted expression from head to toe. Dripping with eager impulse from pleasure to survival, kindness to sorrow, people vomited their sickness into the gutters, cleansing their demons and virtues. The scales of life wavered in the new wind of revolution.

The Europeans made their mark on Mill Avenue down past University, spraying beer on the mouths of many, throwing bottles at will. Circus folk and hippies gathered towards Tempe Town Lake. All who wondered that far remained adrift. The lake and its residents blended together like a rainbow, in reflection of the color festival of India.

Sweat lodge camps sprung up, meditation circles, healing wheel centers, channelings for messages both astral and extraterrestrials alike. The eco culture posted in the parks yet somehow reached towards the cement jungle, terraforming it into a forest of bushes, flowers, palm trees, and cacti.

The city was at your fingertips. Holographic images filled in the negative spaces. There were virtual interactive guides and tours with news on anything from sports, politics, even where to find the nearest drug sector. What is a drug sector? Leave it up to the scientists and nerds to refer getting fixed as a drug sector.

I was no longer on Glow yet the world popped out at the speed of thought. No longer a mouse click away, it was here and now. Intake, digest and repeat. Intake, digest and repeat. In this rhythm Tempe took over. The flow of life began bouncing to a more surreal tempo.

Watching a man tag the side of a Walgreens store turned into a very subjective space to say the least. And with this space, the intensity of life revealed its flavors.

There was "We The People," a faction that had spawned from the middle and lower cast systems. They were the pirates who fought against the system of control; most of them wore Vendetta or Dead Presidents masks while they spoke about freedom, tagging the remaining blank spots of the city. You could tell it was them by their Gonzo looking fist stencil within a phoenix rising.

To say the least, they made good points and had excellent artwork. To say the most, they incited fear and chaos. They enjoyed adrenaline rushes, feeling they were doing what was best. So with no room left to judge, I observe more.

There was the "Feathers Of Freedom," aka the armed forces. It was a joke yet scary to see them recruit anyone they could get their hands on. Kids seventeen and above, criminals, bums…even the elderly. I mean what in the hell is a seventy-year-old man going to do with a nightstick and handcuffs. "Protect and serve" my ass. The old man would have a heart attack before he knew a riot went off.

The feathers of the eagle resembled unity and brotherhood in the vision of the U.S. Marines. The only time I saw anything to do with them was at banks, fast food chains, and supermarkets, or on people's clothing. A patch on the arm was a label upon the soul.

The more I found myself walking the streets, the more I realized: you truly don't know until you experience things for yourself. That was New Day in a nutshell. Robots, vampires, zombies, and…

"Fucking clowns man."

"What?"

"I hate clowns man, they creep me out. I rather draw the president's dumb ass than look at these carnies."

I didn't know his name, didn't understand why he started talking to me, but every one has their story to tell.

And so I listened to an old man covered in painted overalls with spray can in hand.

"What's wrong with circus folk?"

"They're gypsies man. Can't be trusted. Always scamming you of your wits and energy. Not to mention your wallet."

"You really think they are all like that?"

"I don't think. I know. I used to be one. And trust me, ant no one want the karma that gypsies bring you. It is a most unfortunate one."

"What the hell are you talking about man?"

"I'm talking about the little thieves. Robbers they are. All of them."

"You guys are tripping me out man," I express while shaking my head.

"What do you mean by you guys," the man asks, blowing cigarette smoke between a few rotting teeth.

"The fist within the phoenix," I point to his tagging on the wall, telling him with a curious mind.

"This is a sign of revolution. We The People shall rise."

"What does that even mean, we shall rise, We The People? Why would you want everything turned into a revolution?"

"When you come to be my age and have seen the shit I've seen, both in and outside the United States, you will come to know this nation's greatness and its malevolence. This is the only country that expresses its freedom in individual rights yet makes laws that hinder any rights given to us by birth. They are rights and therefore should not be subject to the law. That's the whole point of it being a God-given right. These rights can't be taken away and should not be suppressed. This is a nation of monkeys who watch stories be played on T.V. about school shootings and suicides like it is just another television show, and they flip the channel to watch a commercial that supports war and death as a video game or action movie that's deemed cool. How dysfunctional is this? This is literally what's tearing us apart."

"So you're going to use that as an excuse to do what you do with anger? I mean why can't we all get along, you know what I mean?"

"Because the world isn't nice. It's a horror story wrapped around a fairytale. The sooner you wake up, the sooner you will face your choice."

"What choice is that, between you guys or The Feathers?"

"Between what is fair or what is unjust."

"If you say this phoenix means revolution, then you're talking about civil war. Now I'm no clairvoyant but war solves nothing."

"Are you sure about that kid?"

The streets ascend in rage. Vulgar language was common tongue. People spilled venom from mouth like ink on skin, after awhile it was hard to understand what they were fighting about. It was anarchy.

No reason. No care. People did what they wanted, when they wanted. If they were not fighting, they were yelling, if they weren't yelling they were shady. If they weren't shady then they were con artists that eventually tried to sell you something or join their cause, putting you in some future hope or dream.

Again, who am I to judge this much? It was just a thought. I have grown accustomed to having emotional reactions make up thoughts in the head leading towards thoughts making up emotional reactions. The war within was as deadly as the war without. A vicious cycle that left no mind unscarred.

When fighting became ordinary, people found ways to unleash their stress, their fear, and in some ways even joy. Problem being the streets became a hostile environment. Mischief ruled. Planets shifted. In the midst of the anarchy came a distinctive voice that spoke around me...

"How many times must we watch our governments become ruled by corporations? How long will we sit by and watch the world bend over for the greed of others?

I come before you today with truth, with reason, and with purpose. It is time for us to take back that which we have become a slave to. The enemy has come as your Shepherd. Break free! We The People are here.

Let this be a declaration of God-given right. That everyone here is equal and shall conform no longer. You may leave in peace, or disintegrate in war. We give this country back to natural law... We The People have spoken."

This voice came from all directions. Car radios, televisions, phones, pubs and clubs all broadcasted the same channel. It was a hijacking and I knew that voice. It was Stella. And where there was Stella, there was Loki.

The raid sirens roared alongside the smoke of cars burning. A thick cloud of dust slowly crept in between the lungs. Rays of light shine through thickening dirt. I knew just what this was. This was no ordinary dust storm. It came slow yet constant. This was a Haboob, at night no less. Blackness took the streets, death creped on us all.

There was nowhere to run. Every escape was quickly analyzed then realized as failure! I watched a city tear itself apart, turning all into a void of helpless cries. The darkness latched onto everything. Hard to breath... Hard to see! An overwhelming presence forced its will against mine. It was fear that crept up inside. The ground shook again and again. I felt this presence rise above the public's cries. The ground rumbled in a symphony of destruction as gas stations leveled entire city blocks in an explosion of terror. In that timelessness of catastrophic events, a minute felt like an hour.

This force blasts me onto oiled concrete; the grimy smell of tar and gas consumes the senses. The flames revealed Kali. Frightening yet fascinating still. Her laugh unveils gruesome razor teeth I had not yet forgotten. Her tongue hangs down as she devours all manifestation.

Kali stands upon body with feet of flames... burning flesh and muscle while dancing on my decaying corpse. Her necklace of skulls twirls around like a tornado in zero gravity... trophies of her most beloved victims. Kali easily broke the courage of men. Her all-mighty powerful sword guarantees gruesome rest. This goddess' intensity is but sharp thorn on rose stem. Her naked body glistens in the fiery aftermath of embers and flame. She is a universal embodiment upheld by the eternal power of time.

The city transformed into a graveyard within moment's notice. All began to perish. Kali pulls the hair, lifting me up off the ground. The body begins to ring. The closer her sword comes, the louder everything gets. Her laugh heightens with an atomic blast.

What does a man do when the universe is thrown onto him? I released my fear and remained calm. Settling in pure stillness, I accept her sword. Slicing my head off, blood sprays red then black. Awareness knows only piercing darkness and…

"Coma"
-Buckethead-

Bardo

How can we precisely navigate this density and discover the thematic statement of our life? In order to do this, we must question everything. Leave no stone unturned. When we find an answer, take it in, and then throw it away. We must learn to accept failure while never getting discouraged. We must embrace a sense of gratitude. We must diligently strive.

It is mans urge to investigate, and in so doing there will always be this sense of overcoming something far greater then ourselves. The goal? To gain full confidence without a reference point... total confidence in all skill and form... like a tiger in the jungle.

In today's society we take information in as false, then look for facts and reason to prove it is true... generally speaking. This serves purpose, but we need balance. We need to take in experiences as truth, and then look for evidence that suggest otherwise... innocent until proven guilty, as they say.

To move like this is to see with a discerning eye. This process helps us understand the difference between information and knowledge. To explain and speak is to understand. To know is to breath in direct experience... to be the very moment itself. You see, knowledge is truth and truth is lived out, not taught in a class.

It is no wonder why pilgrims, sages, and prophets travel far and long. They are where they need to be, when they need to be there... just like awareness itself.

This being said, opportunity for individual investigation is essential. The rituals we perform come into greater light, as it represents the godhead of our life. Within our own space, all truth is recognized. No longer is it about her facts matching up with his reason in order to believe. These ideas versus this theology no longer have to contradict one another. You and me become we... interdependently. This is the true reality.

-AUM-

Long before the rise of iron and intellect, plastic and capitalism, there was an entire reservoir of intuition flooding the gates of humanity. The physical body was seen and used as a vehicle for migration from one level of expression to the next.

The pure witness then jumps from one dream to another with absolute fluidity. Omni-consciousness is the aim. To do this, the temple is kept clean with diet. Moral integrity sets the foundation... ethical behavior the pillars.

The adept of spiritual liberation seeks in a detached manner. Like a butterfly towards a flower... it moves only because it needs to move. So asana and pranayama practice is developed in all its grandeur and guidance. Patience, persistence, and perseverance are to be embraced then nurtured. The state of contentment abides.

A student of the occult sciences will know this to be the tip of the iceberg, the external aids to union. Clairvoyance, clairaudience, and clairsentience are to be expected, depending on the individual's karma. By no means are these degrees of perception the main goal. By no means are they to be used in an egotistical manner. By no means are they attained with arrogance or neglect.

With such a ritual, time weaves a web of exploration, concentration, and meditation. It is here where we enter the inner fabric, completely surrendering to the undisturbed flow. Distinct and separate, that space of thought draws true meaning in knowing thyself. To find eternal truth is the greatest drama of them all, with only one end... Samadhi.

The grand masters of all ages found refuge in their own forms of Samyama. And so life pushes forward, sprouting new seeds of application and approach. Countless villages and communities bloom between the eons of peace and war, all sharing and adapting these investigations on the human experience.

Who is the pilot? What steers? Why am I here? Where am I going? When am I going? These are general questions when crossing the fabric of immensity. From this point of view few observations will serve better then more. We can speculate that the observed is not the observer; therefore the driver of the Higher Mind would be the essence of what we call the soul.

The digital age breeds' Digital Yogis'. The power of balance is always in play. The individual story is one of hardship. The gradual decrease of the unessential is a constant obstacle.

The theme is integration. Adapting the higher vibrations into the lower ones. The sense of surrendering synthesized into the controlling will of mankind. The 4th density mixed into the 3rd, through the chemistry that is the 7th ray.

Graduates of the great harvest know your truth to be true. Stand within your light and let others stand in theirs. The inner way in an outwardly material world… a path most fitting for the Digital Yogi, such a journey is riddled with awareness, triggering emotional responses too deep for words.

"Hayling"
-FC Kahuna-

It is decision making without foundation that leads humanity astray. Realize the time wasted in trying to decide between this and that, wondering and worrying. Knowledge does not deliberate; it simply waits for the time to act and then does so.

You are becoming a student of knowledge, to learn how to receive and give. Practice is giving and being present to serve the world. The world calls desperately for this greatness to be revealed; yet you must learn how to reveal greatness in the world.

Come with great reverence for what you are attempting to do. Remind yourself of the importance in these times of stillness. Remind yourself that these are times of worship, times of true dedication to give yourself to that which gives itself to you.

Everything you have ever said or done has been an attempt to express self. Learn how to express yourself, how your true expression will affect others. Allow yourself to be instructed in how to reveal greatness in the world... you must let knowledge give of itself and not try to give from your own ambition or a sense of inadequacy.

I am committed to learn to learn. To give what I am meant to give. I am committed because I am part of life, because I am one with knowledge. What is commitment but the natural expression of your true desire?

It frees you. Does not bind you. It engages you, does not limit you. Honor all who have served you in life. Consider all that is given to you. Let this day be a day of accomplishment and gratitude.

Know that knowledge is real in you and that you are real with knowledge! The next step is waiting... to engage with all!

-AUM-

Wake up Mother Kundalini, thou whose nature is bliss eternal, the bliss of Brahman. Thou dwelling like a serpent asleep at the lotus of Muladhara. Sore, affected and distressed am I in body and mind, Do thou bless me and leave thy place at the basic lotus. Consort of Siva the Self-caused Lord of Universe, Do thou take thy upward course through the central canal. Leaving behind Svadhishthana, Manipuraka, Anahata, Vishuddha, and Ajna. Be thou united with Siva, thy Lord the God. At Sahasrara; the thousand petaled-lotus in the brain, sport there freely, O Mother, Giver of Bliss Supreme. Mother, who is existence, knowledge, bliss, absolute... Wake up, Mother Kundalini! Wake up!

    I viewed my entire life up to this moment... the pain, the joy, the suffering, the organic orgasms, all the crazy facets that was event after event. Just like a movie, perspective spirals outwards. The spark within was viewing a steady projection away from the known universe.

    This awareness revealed my existence lived from within the eye of an organism far larger than comprehension. The godhead of life stared back into my soul. Words appear with a tender voice saying, "Thank you for playing as Noah Savage."
Below reads,

Continue... Yes/No?

"Spark"
-Nitin Sawhney-

" When the power of love overcomes the love of power, the world will know peace."
—Bob Marley—

Static Radio

"Reality check… You are alive; a breathing, caring creature that finds themself on a journey of awareness throughout space and time. As you listen to these words we are traveling on spaceship Earth at 140 miles per second, circling around a giant ball of burning metal we call our sun. The universe is 99.9% empty space, just like our atoms within the body, all originating from the belly of a star being in polarization with another star, our solar system in conjunction with another solar system, our Milky Way congruent to the Andromeda galaxy and so on until you find yourself on the edge of an ever-expanding reality. Reside in this space… for you are now listening to Static Radio, an investigation into the known existence… and beyond. I'm your host Alex Summers accompanied by our guest Dru Deep aka DJ Deep."

"Hello."

"Our discussion tonight is New Day! It has become the hot topic on everyone's tongue. What it is, why is it, and will it ever stop growing are some questions that get brought up."

"Well that's easy Alex. It's a creative induced bubble that separates itself from one illusion and creates another. It's here because we have willed it to be here, even on some unconscious level. What happens in the world is only a reflection of our internal expression. And to answer that last part... there is no stopping what must happen, it will only continue to evolve."

"Understandable yes. But these words have major effects that take time to reveal themselves. From drug use, rising crime, extortion, rioting, public unrest, social mental breakdown, not to mention the most recent attacks brought on by rising factions that deem themselves radical realists. An entire block destroyed by gas station bombings just a half hour ago. The police are gathering to enforce Martial Law. You say this must happen?"

"I actually have a lot of friends who are there as we speak. Unfortunately there are those who resort to manipulation and fear when presented with opportunity. We The People... Feathers Of Freedom... this is only the beginning. We changed things in Phoenix, and with this change will always come power. There are those who are fighting desperately to guide this world in the right direction... and there are those who would try and oppose this."

"Now you came from Phoenix before you got to our studios here in California?"

"Yes, I was recording a new album and did a few shows."

"Let me ask you, throwing away all the political talk that we'll get to later... from firsthand experience... what is it like to be involved in one of the largest gatherings America has seen since Woodstock?"

"Yes the rising count of people is a constant. But to be honest with you... it's something that's incredibly hard to put into words; it goes beyond our speech into the language of dreams. Being out of the vortex is proving to be more intense than any other festival I've been to. All things will eventually end but it doesn't matter because I have taken part of that time and place with me, spreading it across my life. Across the radio stations and into my music… It's a way of living! A message of freedom… of choice and purpose!"

"New Day has indeed arrived and continues to grow. With his various methods of music, slam poetry and truth! I hand over the microphone and present to you… DJ DEEP!"

I'll be your host for the rest of this show.
Spitting words into rhythmic flow.
I'm turning it down, very, very slow.
Allow me to say what you need to know.

These people here, you see on T.V.
There just like you, there just like me.
They live in a world of hypocrisy.
Turned upside down, no longer are we free.

This digital age… technology.
It's hijacked the brain, electronically.
We interface with so-called reality,
Through squared illusions of our fantasy.

There is hope; there is faith, there is harmony.
There is sadness; there is hate, even misery.
This sphere we inhabit seems obscurity.
Three questions, two answers, one shot, your destiny.

Releasing emotions, the dice of chance.
This life you gamble is no longer your dance.
A change is coming, inside we enhance.
To feel life's trance as addictive romance.

Let politicians throw words, reasonable to the whack.
From logical to the absurd, both white and both black.
Unity is what we seek, let's try and stay on track.
In the end it's all the same, republican to democrat.

179

What must be known, is unfolding as we speak.
Intuitively living, the knowledge it will leak.
From classrooms to arenas, out on the street.
Word of mouth travels fast within a week.

Together we are one, standing firm on the ground.
Let the governments of humanity hear our sound.
We embrace you as family, lost and now found.
There is room for compassion, for it circles around.

Civilizations will become civilized.
Individuals will become realized.
Virtues become baptized.
Ways of life, decriminalized.

There was once a vision, whispered among the many.
Weightless as a feather, yet held value among plenty.
Its magical charm left you full, yet still empty.
Crystallizing effects living pure and simply.

We are the barriers of courage, strength and noble deeds.
We overcome fierce battles of desires and selfish needs.
From power to money to the root of our greed,
We begin anew, planting respect as our seed.

Let this message be a symbol that burns bright in the night.
Through darkness' veil we bring light into sight.
Enemies, egos, whatever your fight,
Just be sure to do what feels right.

Musically Driven

"Building Stream With A Grain Of Salt"
-DJ Shadow-

The ego was dissolving. No more creating concepts that limit self. The words 'my' and 'I' were only used because the English language had no better way of explaining what resided in this flesh vehicle. The Internet, radio, television… all connected to the lotus petals of Ajna, the universal mind.

I had the collective unconscious at my entire disposal. Bits of information leaked from skull onto intuitive canvas. The body lies still, covered in ash and dust. The soul had gone through much more than your average victim of violence is prepared for.
Rebooting… Rebooting…Ding
Interface upgrade. Density shift. Consciousness attained!

The eyes open to smoke covered air. Riot sirens blared in the distance; cars burned through the retina. The body was an antenna for global communication… intergalactic planetary awareness. I sit motionless, still digesting the residue from a glimpse into the Bardo.

Living in the now is the purest essence in life. Everything just is. The solar now dissipates past karmic repetitions, growing closer to the only reality of the living "Now!"

The lunar now has no light of its own; it only reflects the light of the solar present. It is up to the individual through awareness of their alter ego, themself, that expression of their being can reflect that of the "Now!"

The present is ever changing. The acceptance of the relationship with self is symbolized as a mercurial energy of thought arising in the conscious mind of the "Now!"

Change stays constant. The presence of love and harmony is viewed upon all things. While this presence is cultivated, gratitude and contentment permeate the entire being. The effects of Venus are very real within the everlasting "Now!"

Movement is constantly stimulating the present, creating vivid sharpness, continually re-awakening one's software. This Martian energy impresses our own very small yet unique identity into the significantly powerful universe. The role we play unfolds our soul's desire in the "Now!"

From this come ideas and experiences being more than personal. Co-consciousness is attained as a cooperative, collective understanding from the Divine intelligence. Self-suffering is released when one learns to enjoy experiencing clearly what life has offered. This energy of Jupiter is achieved when one learns how to see the light instead of classifying the darkness of the ever present "Now!"

With all this weight in knowledge and experience, responsibility is imposed. Saturn can burden individuals in understanding the importance of our needs. This establishes the central theme of one's life and guides us to know our own strength. Realizations and goals may be well into the future but it is what we do in the present that creates this reality. We become the taskmaster of life; eventually evolving to mastering the task when living in the "Now!"

In all that has been, comes awareness. The heightening of intelligence opens an individual to new insights far beyond ordinary thought. A useful breaker in illusions, Uranus (the forerunner of our Aquarian Age) enlightens all with true freedom of thought in the "Now!"

With illusions broken, the mystical sleep we entered upon birth is revealed. Neptune is the unspoken present connecting to an eternal flow of time. Physical words hinder the nature of its reality. This continuity is found within the "Now!"

O Pluto, our unconscious horny friend… how you help us with lingering thoughts and attachments we put to end. Automatically creating changes within our structure, these experiences bring realizations of identity being a product of what one does. Then the hardships and trials of life can be appreciated for all the amazing wonders that the "Now Brings!"

Be here, be now, be one with the you-niverse!

Kali… what is there to be said? A part of the imagination? Energy perceived as another to be idolized and conceptualized to fit a mold… the so-called normal human? Does it make it all any less real? Perhaps with time we shall truly never know… like fading snowflakes upon fresh snow. All is dissolved within the life stream flow.

I loved her, passionately. She tore my innocent ignorance right underneath me. She destroyed the ego in every way, until all that was left… a child within cosmic play.

The all-revealer? The accidental healer? It is yet to be fully seen. All that is known is that a quickening has happened. Kali Yuga shines its grace in the most distasteful of ways… all a part of growth through hardship that frays. Bits of data kept spilling and spilling. There was no stopping it.

The body rises. Thinning dust vaporizes. Hue and glow reflect the remaining smoke particles. Everything is ambient. People are screaming… crying… even laughing. Chaos was the condition of the streets. Had to escape. Had to leave. With this thought a hummingbird flew by with a flare.

Of course I followed this bird through the city of burned-out humans. Running through the camp of Area 51 was a most delicious adventure for the eyes. The theme was sacred geometry and psychedelics. The bird races past the party-planning tent and on to the troll village.

Merchants from Asia with cheap goods… "Yes you buy now, you like!"

Forget this feeding frenzy, the little brown guide speeds with haste. Past the Hare Krishna Bhajans, deeper into the robotics of electro drum and bass… digital junkies navigated the city with their Google glasses. I ran for what felt like an hour.

Finally a clear view of the city; its skyscrapers magnetically pulled my curiosity. Buildings were covered with graffiti around neon fiber optics... transforming everything into red.

Epic was the view from ground towards towering heights. This is where the journey ended... and began. There was unfinished business. O brother turned God of mischief, how we have words to share. The sickening past stares upon judgmental eyes no more. It was time to clear the air.

All I had to do was think of Loki and I knew where he was. This is due to the volume in which the senses were turned up. Images flood the mind of dear brother upon his throne, overlooking the city.

It couldn't be so easy, could it? Just walk right in this pulsating city, find brother and make peace? Every move in every scenario surfs around the hemispheres.

Like moves upon battle... so I calculated the odds of peace. Sixty-two percent in favor of going bad, factors depending on drug substance, myself and of course Stella. That little manipulating bitch... she was twisting Loki's ambition and there was nothing I could do about it. How could I have been so blind?

The only hope now was hope itself. The feet did the walking, the mouth in verbal talking. Thoughts fired neurons from one sliver to the next within fractions of a second. The eyes continued to follow this lovely hummingbird.

The cities various sounds sowed a multidimensional museum of ambiance in awareness. Bits of conversations weave their way in the mind state, and not just from those around me. I could hear Dru on the radio, Logan smoking with Janelle, David talking with Chris, Stella and Loki.

It was hard keeping a solar presence while receptivity flushed sporadic insights and mumblings. But there was one useful thing that got highlighted within the rambles, and that's Loki's position.

Chase tower… many possibilities attached to Stella being at top. Why be here right now? What was so special about this location? Why were the doors unlocked and security cameras off? Why had a bird so playfully guided me to these glass reflections of rising anticipation? Perhaps somewhere there is a spark that screams justice in every way possible!

Doors open upon the thirty-sixth floor. Legs make way towards voices within and without the head.
There stood four guards with semi-automatic assault rifles.

"It would be a good idea for you to leave now," the brute mercenary forcibly tells me.
"I am here for my brother, I am expected."
The guard remains silent and still.
"You're not moving?" I ask in a playful yet forceful tone.
"My orders are not to let anyone in."

"Since when did you take orders from anyone other than yourself?"

"Since I joined the revolution. I have my place and yours is outside on the streets you maggot!"

This is when I felt like punching him in the throat. Have an epic battle that most likely would send us all to the hospital or worse… six-feet deep. But I was no fighter of such physical anger, especially to a military jarhead. I was a warrior of balance, thus approach needed creativity and the elegance of intelligence.

There was no leaving without talking to Loki. Outnumbered and most definitely out-gunned, there only remained one course of action. Use the force.
 "You wish to go home and rethink your life," I tell him.

The guard stood still, pondering what was said. With force and unshakeable deniability I spoke again. However this time I emanated violet light from my forehead onto his third eye. The battleground of the astral was far beyond his reach or comprehension. I mean he wasn't even in the same league.
"You wish to go home and rethink your life!"

The brute stood still. Silent.

"Mind games don't work on me kid," the mercenary says with a fist to the stomach. Ok maybe his battleground was in the same league. Stella walks in from the double doors gesturing the guard to let me pass.

"Stella will be seeing you know," the jarhead says with a smile.

I am led to an office near tall glass windows.

"Brother."

"Noah... how in the hell did you find me here?"

"I'm sorry for not listening, for pushing thoughts and not accepting who you are. Forgive me for this violence in projecting fear and tragedy. I see you brother... I have love for you!"

"Jesus Christ Noah, you've become a hippie!"

"I'm serious Andrew, I love you and I'm not afraid to say it. I accept you brother."

Stella walks around the table next to Loki.

"Thoughtful Noah, yet changes nothing," she speaks.

The city's lights crept in through tinted glass. Stella need say nothing more, her presence told it all. As the Queen stood still, placing her move, I came closer to Loki. Emotions leaked like water from breaking dam.

"I'm not going to try and convince you to leave Loki, so Stella you can calm down now. Just know what chaos you are contributing to!"

I walk to the window and open the blinds to show what lay beyond towering heights. Looting, scattered fights with riot control. Burning cars with fields of smoke rising in the distance. Square blocks became pits of rape, murder and rage. Martial Law was beginning to take effect as our view showed tanks and drone predators upon the horizon.

"You act like I did this. As if the entire city's in flames because of me. I didn't summon the sky to throw a dust storm over everyone or for the army to retaliate to freedom."

"No you didn't, but Stella is manipulating you. Deceptive, selfish she is… and We The People, what the hell is this all about?"

"Pick a side Noah… We The People are free by birthright."

"Listen to yourself you sound like a robot. Who are you, you barely know Stella."

"And you do Noah?"

Silence stills as we catch our breath.

"What did I tell you, he doesn't understand," Stella begins to influence Loki.

"I understand very well, Stella Stone, much more than you think. I am truly sorry what happened to you… I hope you find your peace and are able to forgive yourself when the time comes."

I fully didn't understand what was just said; however trust was placed in what I felt needed to be heard.

"Is this a threat Noah?"

Stella's eyes widen with a hint of tears from tensing impulses. She was looking for a fight. Must have plucked a string she forgot about. The mind wanted to rip her head off, most likely fighting Loki in the process. But another part of me felt sad for her with emotional intelligence granting insight into sympathetic action.

"Not at all Stella, I only mean to help you from certain demise."

"You're either with us or not!" Loki cuts in.

"You're searching for revolution?"

"It is upon us Noah."

"A real rebel is one who doesn't act against a society, it becomes irrelevant because they understand the real game of it all. This is the beauty of real rebellion; this is the door to true freedom you are seeking.
Revolutionaries are not free; they are constantly fighting with something. You are reacting against something… how is reaction freedom? All of this is preventing growth. If this is your path, then this is your path… I must walk my own."

"And what path is that exactly… you just going to forgive and forget without wanting to destroy the people that drove this world into slavery? You think it will all just disappear because you hold no attachment to that shit? You think just by leaving this world you don't belong to it anymore? You'll become an outsider, a fucking bum. You will be nothing, a deserter, a traitor to his own people."

"You're right brother... I don't have all the answers... do you? Do you even know why you are doing this... do you have clear objectives? Because if you don't then anarchy will set in and soon after the old regime falls, a new tyrant will rise to bring order. The systems that follow revolutions are often just as totalitarian as those they replaced. Don't you see, they want you to fight like this, it's a chess game."

"Join us Noah and together we shall shape the world as we see fit. We fight for peace... for freedom."

"Fighting for peace? That's like holding onto hot coal and expecting not to get burned. There is nothing more dangerous than armed men and women with utopian dreams... I cannot follow you."

Trying to save someone from what they choose not to see had come and passed, so I left it at that. Holding my hands together, I bowed to them with full eye contact... then walked away.

It is their undoing. His faults his own, none of my own choosing. Their future clear as day, yet ignorance clouds the way. Her own rise and her own fall... to each is own... their fate... their call.

Sensing Andrew's response was deep to say the least. Mixed feelings with idealistic reason clashed. What was left... a brother stunned with the unordinary turned actuality?

No drama, no fighting with a huge climax of battle for survival, it's time to spin a new web. This is awareness in action. All past attachments released... cares, worries, even the inner beast. These are the crossroads of humanity!

"Faultered Ego"
-On! Air! Library!-

Everything is in slow motion. Walking away from the madness that is a city stripped of its chains, people react with full impulse. Wheels and rubber spin towards Chris' pad. Cheers and beers greet the eyes with a nice big hug to my surprise. Words from mouth spill out whatever whatever. Fancy talks from drama to fighting out emotional weather. The gang is there: Chris, David, Amber, Katie, and some new cutie whose name is Mercedes. Logan was missing, trimming nuggets with Janelle no doubt. Blunts with laughter trickles towards ideas worth going after.

"Noah o brother, how I have a proposition for you!" Chris makes his presence known with a hand over my shoulder.

"I don't know if this is good or bad."

"Well, how would you like to look after this place for me?"

"What? Where you going?"

"Back to India. The mother land!"

"Why?"

"Visit the family. Detox from the grid of consumerism and false dreams. I need someone I can depend on, someone who is honest and trustworthy. I could think of no other man in town!"

"I am humbled for sure, but I don't know. Sounds kind of surreal."

"No pressure just throwing it out there."

"To be honest India sounds more exciting than staying here!"

"That's what I'm talking about man."

David joins in while we catch up on lost time. He was just like a kid again. Mind Glow made David like Logan used to be, and changed Logan back into his old self like David was; an awkward observation yet most interesting. These thoughts led more awareness onto my own very unique transformation.

David had a few good stories to tell about Loki and his newly acquired underground drug ring. He made deals with Stella; who was connected with the Mafia supposedly.

Mafia from where remains a mystery, although the gut says she's a part of something far more sinister than Mafia.

All that's known are chess pieces moving into history, a story that I neither wish to tell or dispel... only caring thoughts for all to remain well.

Amber walks onto the second floor terrace. Chris knows body language, he signals David, leaving us alone. We say nothing to each other; just holding one another was enough. For countless moments we remained in our love. So many downloads. Like dripping rain they are, images of a fragile heart torn apart... to be sowed together by Cupid's dart?

"I'm sorry Amber."

"Me too. I should have let you be you... I just thought maybe you liked me... liked us."

"I did... I do... it's just complicated. I was looking for something different... something more... an escape. While being blinded to what was in front of me all along." Silence with tender embrace holds us close at hand.

"So you do love me."

"I do."

"Then let's forget the past and build the future."

"I can't."

"What! Why not!"

Amber pulls away in distaste.

"Because you deserve better. I'm not ready for this, I mean how am I going to give half of myself to another in a relationship when I don't even fully understand who I am?"

Amber says nothing. I am fully present to her pain... anger... and sadness. These were the times of deep thought, the letting go of attachments and expectations.

"I'm sorry Noah," she says with a kiss on the forehead, and then she walked away.

The tragic truth shines bright today. Sundials dance with music dripping conscious trance. Clarity in action had found union with satisfaction. Hermes flies in with a flash! Beginning to laugh with realizations of astral friends is beyond a blast.

"O messenger of the heavens it is good to see you. Idolized God turned brother, who would have known."

"Maha old friend, you are aware! News I bring, news I share! Veena wishes you good day and farewell, his journeys have taken him off to sail. Sooner than later, again your paths will meet. A listening ear helps you follow your feet. The thread that's presented, untangles… unravels. Speaking of great length, one of mystic travels."

"Good news beyond most, I will reflect on it and toast to the endless coast stretching beyond the eyes of most. It has been awhile since we last spoke Hermes."

"Retrogrades I'm afraid, dragging some karmic weight of self reflection along."
"You wouldn't be getting old on me now would you?"

Hermes smiles with a spark in his eyes. We sat outside overlooking fading skies. The city fell in power. The grids descended into the rising night with electrical hijacking falling short of sight. All that was lit, the heart of Phoenix at her grip. A faction was happening, unchained from their trapping.

And with this, I sat. Meditated in the silence of the void, which had been completely morphed by the perspective of light and dark thanks to some passive aggressive extremists. In this space all was at peace until dawn greeted the eyes of those who realize…

"All These Things That I've Done"
-The Killers-

"So you're saying the Phantom Menace you dick-punched at Sound Wave was your shadow self?"

"Yes… and a bit of Kali it seems. And a bit of something else perhaps, I don't know."

"You totally fucked up and let Amber go because… you have found some type of respect for her?" Logan inhales smoke, holding it in, awaiting answer. "Respect for myself as well!"

"And you didn't get in a fight with your bro because you were tired of the drama?" Logan says with an exhalation and a cough.

"Because I was tired of seeing life repeat itself… and yes, if he must repeat his own cycles, better me not being a part of it! Although I still can't figure out why Chase tower."

"What?" Logan inquisitively asks.

"I found Loki at top of the Chase building with Stella."

"Holy shit!"

"Why do you say this?"

"Have you been living under a rock the past three days or something?"

"I don't understand."

"It's all over the news. Someone hacked into the database of JP Morgan and deleted all the security feeds, most likely adding a bunch of phantom accounts, and robbed most of the banks in the metropolitan area. Millions of dollars for the taking, it's being called the greatest heist of the 21st century."

"Are you kidding me?"

"I'm serious. That's why Martial Law is taking so long. They are looking for answers. I think the power outage had something to do with it no doubt. Do you not watch the news or something?"

"I try not to actually."

"You think your brother was a part of it?"

"To be honest, all of that doesn't even faze me right now. Being off Mind Glow these past few days has left me so systematically numb to other people's drama. I told Loki to leave me out of his Big Score and by the looks of it he did. The less I know the better."

"Well you're probably right about the less you know the better. So what about the girl."

"Kali!"

"Ya."

"She was just a fabrication of universal energy… such a beautifully vicious goddess."

"…Wait, if she isn't real, and Mr. Glow helped you see her… then what about the Ipod?" Logan rightfully asks.

"What about it?"

"You still have it… that's real… so isn't she real?"

"You know Logan… I have no idea. Perhaps some things are meant to stay a mystery!"

"Ok, now I'm really seeing something different… you don't even care about Her anymore. You're not chasing after Her?"

"Nope, nothing to chase. I care a lot about whomever I got this Ipod from. It's changed me. It's what kept me going through this roller-coaster ride… but you know, sometimes we just got to change. If not what we do at least how we do it."

"That's some deep shit Noah. Kinda cheesy though."

"There are enough dicks in the world Logan, don't be another."

The harvest was just about over. I helped trim the last quarter pound. Fingers hurt like hell but having a ceiling full of hanging nuggets wasn't such a bad sight.

They pass around the Master Madhi blunt. I decline on the notion. I was still high from my slight overdose into the Bardo. Janelle helped trim, as did her two brothers, The Turks. Pretty nice guys after you get past the three hundred pound deep scratchy voice.

You know after looking back at it all… life is somewhat foretold in the language of dreams. Nothing is ever what it seems. Memory jumps from one event to the next with everlasting recollection.

This life we live is the truest dream. It is the most psychedelic trip ever! The densest most effectible governing system we know. We are but stardust emerging in a world within a world. Live it. Breathe it. Be it for you are it.

Adrenaline fueled the body non-stop. Freedom was the anthem of New Day. The flame had evolved… spreading like wildfire upon summer's eve. To express freedom is a delicate task. To truly express our self is limited by our bodies and our minds. This was the fatal flaw with New Day… eventually it all had to end. The struggle for it to continue was ending up in chaos.

How could we be so blind, of course it would end up in chaos. What did we expect would happen when everyone did whatever they wanted? Somewhere along the line, freedom becomes restricted in place of stability and security. How far down the line and to what degree is of our own choosing, our own undoing.

It's a huge universe out there, let alone our galaxy, our solar system, our Earth, our personalities and realities. This idea of freedom… it echoes throughout the Milky Way.

We are so fortunate to have individual freedom with creative expression. We are fortunate to look upon the stars and know we can be self-sufficient. If we can work together in selfless acts towards a foundation for the future, a foundation for the now… we got it made.

Free will and fate, freedom or not… this is the paradox of paradoxes. This was the driving urge to run. To scream and call out to the Isness that Is "Show me a sign!" This is the part of self that reverberates a respectful challenge to the universe.

"What do you mean you're leaving?" Logan gets excited, most likely feeding off my excitement subconsciously.

"I mean I'm getting the hell out of here!"

"Why?"

"Because I've done this before. Lived this life day after day. I know what to expect for the most part. Only until New Day hit have I really been feeling the urge to live in the moment and experience the unexpected… I got to go!"

"What are you running from man?"

"I see it as what I'm running towards! This is much more encouraging. This is what I need."

"And what exactly are you running towards?"

"The unknown!"

A gradual pause overcomes us. We both retreat to the imagination. Reflecting. Digesting.

"I feel you're looking for an answer."

"You know Logan, you might be onto something."

No more thinking. Only doing. I grabbed my backpack, jamming four T-shirts, two shorts, a few underwear, toothbrush, soap, journal pad, pencil, The Six Sided Self book, Ipod, wallet, shades, bandanas, passport, twelve thousand forty-seven dollars, a whole lot of ambition and a willing heart... then off I went.

"Forget the phone and the digital age. I'm escaping the grid for awhile."

"Wow... you got that spark in your eye!" Janelle says, leaning back with a sense of appreciation.

"And what spark is that exactly?" having to ask.

"It's that twinkle, that glare that lets you know you're in for an adventure."

The Turks say nothing much, other than singing along to their headphones blasting hip-hop. Heads down, trimming away, they manage to show a little care when passing the wax pen my way, however I respectfully decline.

"What shall I do with these keys then?"

"I'm sure Loki will be looking for his car once he realizes I'm gone... actually on second thought, is the airport still open?"

"...Ya."

"Can I get a ride?"

And with that, I was gone. Being so full of rushing energy it was only right to cast a sail and see where the wind blows. My ocean reflects the many uncharted locations Earth has to offer. The vortexes... the lay lines... the Earth chakras await my arrival with anticipating joy.

New Day in the year of the wooden snake was a very special time to be a part of. All explanations fall short. No mix of words, music, or memories can touch that sense of being right here, right now.

There was madness in every direction; the city was alive! Free! Chaotic order of the masses rained supreme.

People's intentions shine like grace upon the blind. Our vision is now clear.

This push in awareness molds our inevitable victory over the dogmas of fear and evil. These wicked ways are outdated, brittle and faded. We need this no longer. Our energy will prevail because the revolution is within our minds, within our soul.

We are carrying all the momentum; we are riding a high and gorgeous wave of consciousness. With mystical eyes and a little inspiration, we can finally peal into the unknown… where drops of unity finally dissolve into the ocean of eternity.

I had to add one more song to this new playlist, the perfect tune to put a closure and opening on what a musical goddess revealed "all-destroyer" could do.

I labeled the playlist Edible Jazz, finally adding a bit of my spark within a spark… a little individual character among multiple playlists of stories that found its way through many hands. Many lives. I am but grateful steward of this Ipod. O Kali, you magical creation… how you work in mysterious ways of tantalizing curiosity.

Waiting standby for the cheapest jet across the sea proved useful time for such reflections. There is no such thing as wasting time to a traveler now is there!

Just off the corner of my eye rests an intriguing musician whose name I came to know as Zoe. We found common ground fast.

Her backpack had the rising phoenix fist woven in the middle. From being robbed of her guitar and wits to finding opportunity in playing at New Day, her karma was one of balance yet everlasting rotation.

"Your brother's a part of We The People?"

"Unfortunately yes."

"Why is that unfortunate?" Zoe asks.

"I just don't want him to get hurt. He gets extreme when left unchecked."

"Not all of us speak back in such harsh ways Noah. There are parts of We The People that are peaceful in a lot of aspect. There will always be non-violent solutions to any crisis… at least on the physical level."

"I'm listening."

"It's a simple fact of looking at the situation objectively. What if a million people didn't pay their taxes. What if ten million stopped paying? Now paying your state taxes that help with your local county is one thing. But to the government that uses it against the people. No thank you."

"The government would most likely catch you. I'm assuming of course."

"Well stop assuming. They can't lock up ten million people. Sure they can lock away part of the main core. We The People would suffer. But the actual people, the ones who aren't a part of this fighting. They too have power."

"I must admit Zoe, that would be one badass scenario if we all stood up like that. You should go on the talk show Static Radio. He has musicians and conscious artists come in, sit down and just reason."

"Yes I've done this as well. Just reason… I like this Noah."

Within the two hours of knowing one another we had expressed and released so much to each other. It was more of a continuation in friendship than a new acquaintance. She had been traveling for some time and had many flavorful tales. Zoe and I spilled story from lips that eventually inspired future encounters.

"Wait, so you're telling me you're just now starting your travels? That any flight you pick will send you to another clue in the endless search for yourself?"

"Well, now that you put it that way ya."

"And you don't have an instrument?" Zoe adds.

"Nope. Fresh out of instruments… just an Ipod"

"Shit Noah, I don't even carry an Ipod but I always carry instruments with me."

Zoe rumbles through her backpack. "I present you the Sansula. Better known as the thumb piano. May it keep you company on your travels!

"Wow… I don't know what to say Zoe."

197

"Don't have to say anything. Just play it." Announcements rang for Alaskan airlines flight 247 non-stop to San Francisco. Pre-boarding. "This is my flight, I got to go."

"It's been good getting to know you Zoe. Hope to run into you again!"

"Ya keep in touch," she writes down name and email with a, "Find me on facebook."

We hug with a kiss on the cheek. And off she went. In and out of my life just like that. I wonder when she will notice the Ipod I slipped in her backpack side while hugging? It was all I could do to return her kindness. An equal exchange I presume.

With this action comes some understanding in how I might have acquired such gift myself. It is still not fully understood how I got the Ipod… why I shifted my addiction from the love of women to the love of music! But it felt more liberating than anything else before. Placing hand upon heart, I pay respect to all souls within the great dream.

In an existence where the source of life is experiencing itself subjectively, it is surely a high form of intelligence not to grasp onto judgment to tightly. By all means speak your truth; it's all-serving purpose.

All we have to decide is what to do with the time that is given to us. And it's about time we start playing the game by our rules. Trust in the universe and the universe shall place trust onto you.

And as far as time and patience are concerned… humble companions hitchhiking along the glorious journey.

"Outro"
-M83-

-Mystical Junkie-

Vengeance

White flakes fall patiently upon stone and blade. The bitter coldness of Japan's Kokoku-ji Temple echoed nothingness into the unshaken night. Like an owl, Soka sits in perfect lotus, perfect coherence. She was waiting for someone… something.

The presence of evil was laced with a sense of urgency along the now-howling wind, carrying with it an arsenal of rapid thoughts and emotions. Soka remains still, holding total composure.

The eye before the storm… the crowd before battle… the cold sweat before war, our Sage knows all too well the faint taste of death lurking around doubt and panic. The fight begins in the mind, thus engagement of the physical was soon to follow.

A subtle crunch of snow eventually crept from the foreground. One man appears out of the darkness, pushing his way through the winter chill. The stranger's stride blends with the eerie ambiance shrouding his arrival.

Black leather stretched across a frame whose shadow now reached the vision of our Elder. Words were spoken across an ever-expanding breeze swaying with power and speed.

"Soka."

"Krill."

"Where is he?"

"Whom do you speak of?"

"Tell me or die."

Soka levitates just above the incubus remaining in full lotus. Krill takes a defensive stance, extending joints in the fingers and wrist, morphing his structure at will. Our Sage reveals Japanese Steel.

"There is only life. You are but a cataclysm."

"So you have accepted death then."

"Krill you mean nothing to me, you are but shadow of your formal self."

"My soul will soon taste your pathetic existence."

Krill jumps towards Soka with a slice of his sharpened claws. Our Sage deflects, jumping off the menace's face in a kick of yelling fury. Higher she floats into the trees holding puffy glistening powder. Cloud to cloud they jump as the moon shines silhouetted poses of cat chasing mouse. *"What are you running from? Scared you might like the thrill of a fight?"*

Soka responds with a thrust of her sword and a whirling tornado of snow and metal. Krill deflects, taking damage to his arms. Blood drops three red islands into the White Sea. Skin begins to heal quickly; our Sage takes notice to the grave danger this presents.

"Like I said, I will devour your existence, now tell me where he is and I'll promise you a quick death, a clean sacrifice."

"You just don't get it, no matter how many times you kill us, no matter how many ways you hate us, we will always prevail, enduring parasites like you."

"Save me your petty opinion. All your worth is in your memory. If you will not tell me, I will rob you of it."

Krill's speed was unmatched when given the element of surprise. Cold pale hands now grasp our Sage's neck. The menace pealed into the images of her life with great precision. Krill was abruptly stopped with an equal amount of resistance.

"Awe… where did you learn this power?" his condescending voice slips between her pride.

"I'm not about to tell you," Soka responds with another combo by her blade.

Krill weakens; trying to evade the onslaught of jabs and strikes. The play of light and dark was ever persistent, finally resulting with Japanese Steel going straight through Krill's chest.

There stood Soka in disbelief of fatal wound. The beast takes a gasp of air, trying to absorb what energy he could. With a slight smile and a forceful push, Soka is flown into the distance. Slowly the blade is pulled from heart. Inch by inch the smooth surface glides outward. Second by second the wound is healed. ***"Your sword, greatly accepted dear Soka. It's a bit old fashioned for my taste, but I shall need it… in the times ahead."***

The storm blasts with rising fear. Krill screams, running towards Soka… however she was not without a few aces up her sleeve. Soka lifts all the rocks around her with telekinesis, throwing the stones towards the oncoming beast.

Strike, block, and a miss… block, strike, block. Stones fly alongside wind and ice. The menace dodges what he can before getting smacked in the face. ***"It's good to see an Elder still keeping up with their talents. Finally… a worthy opponent."***

Krill taunts with sickening laugh, momentarily looking upward to find a two-ton bolder flying his way, driving anger and arrogance into the frozen ground. Our Sage takes rest, now mentally exhausted.

In that time of rest, of charging the batteries… tragic glimpses find the mind's eye of Soka… sights of the infinitely abused decay away. Past victims only find refuge in memories of oblivion in our now-healed puppet. Our Sage's link was still close to Krill, feeling the karma of a thousand souls scattered throughout time.

An explosion of rage burst minutes later. Krill was still alive and rushing past the stone shards that fell like meteors. Moving in between the zipping rocks, Soka rams Krill into a nearby wooden house. With swiftness and cunning skill our Sage throws the rubble towards Krill who becomes overwhelmed by an ignited fire.

Moments later a blast consumes our villain with Soka throwing everything she could find his way. House full of flames… Sky full of smoke… Screams and smells of burning flesh slid across the nearby witnesses. Neighbors curiously wander to see the aftermath of battle.

From red flames emerges Krill, still sizzling from the inferno.

"What are you?" Soka asks.

"I am Earth's fallen angel."

"You're a monster."

"...I know."

And like this, the final round began. Metal swung, just missing the elegant movement of wind and agility our Elder creates. Surrounding bystanders draw closer in search to end such gruesome hatred.

Jab, block, strike... slice, twirl, block... kick, strike, block. The combos grew longer with our Sage receiving help from brave citizens acting in defense. A few men got caught between the wrath of Japanese Steel as blood sprays like mist behind the hue of fire. Soka reacted with emotional drive, sending her into the magnetism of Krill, just as planned.

And with this, our villain saw opportunity and took it, slicing the left arm straight off our Sage. Down she goes in agonizing pain. *"Look what you have chosen, and to think, you could have made things so much easier on yourself."*

"I will never tell you."

"I'm counting on it," Krill responds raising sword in air, slicing her other arm clean off. A pool of blood and tears flooded the blizzard's path. Again sword raises high, ready for the kill.

Suddenly Krill felt a rock hit his head. Turning around pupils fix on a small girl barely eight years old. The child stands tough and confident. The tyrant looks back at our Elder's mangled corpse still fighting for life.

"Would you like me to send her with you?"

"...Don't."

The girls fear rises after seeing our Sage's body. She runs off into the storm screaming and yelling. Without a second's hesitation Krill throws sword, striking the little one's chest. Down goes the young life.

"NO!" Soka yells as the beast drags her by the feet towards burning building.

"Now I promised you a clean death… but you didn't listen. Once I have my revenge then I will have power… when will you learn."

"Power?"

"Now I do believe I owe you a gruesome decay."

Krill grabs her throat with one hand while he tore her heart out with another. He then threw Soka into the flames, watching her slowly burn away. Focus stretched outwards on a puddle's reflection alongside dying winds.

The incubus collects his newly acquired sword, licking the red syrup from frigid blade. The flavor of victory is sprinkled with the absence of life. The beast found short-lived glory… eagerly awaiting his grand prize.

White flakes fall patiently upon stone and blade. The bitter coldness is much embraced by the silent tyrant. It matched his hollow heart now resting between frozen ribs. The wicked own this night by tribute of blood and fire.

Red Road

"You wish to learn the ways of life do you! Well young one, you must first recognize the great presence… only then will nature be able to reflect what lays deep within."

The Elder Shaman smiles while Inti sits still, waiting further instruction. Most boys had questions and couldn't keep their mouth shut or legs still. Not this child. Inti was of another tribe. Another time. The kid was twelve and already showed signs of taking on of the first test every Shaman takes… to enter the jungle as one of its own.

The Elder and Inti ate a grand meal (mostly rice and meat with mixed veggies) overlooking the hills of Peru, just outside Iquitos to be precise.

"Your mother has left you in my care for the time being." Inti said nothing yet had a twinkle in his eye of the mysterious kind.

"Bring enough food and water with you to last two days, the rest we will gather along the way."

They walked north into the thickness of jungle, guided by the Elder who knew the land as well as he knew his heart.

The boy stopped many times to catch his breath and rehydrate. It was so hot, sweat dripped off Inti's face onto the ground. He never complained and kept pace behind the Elder.

"This is one of many entrances to the jungle, remember it well."

The Shaman walked in first while the boy took notes, memorizing the type of wood the trees were made of. He made a reminder of the birds nesting nearby from the pitch of their voice, continuing into the thickness of trees and plants.

When Inti entered the jungle, life began to sing. Birds chirped, crickets rubbed their legs together; butterflies made their way around the young boy, studying him like a science experiment. Monkeys peeked their wide eyes from behind the branches above. An overwhelming feeling rushed Inti's body. The jungle was alive and watching him.

"Try and keep up now," the Elder says, popping his head out of the brush.

Hours went by trekking. The sunlight beamed its way through the leaves, lighting up small patches along the path. Slowly but surely they arrived.

"This is Mulu," the Elder pointed to a thick tree whose heights gave the neck a stretch.

"Mulu views all, hears all and knows all in these parts. Make friends with him you will in good time. Mulu this is Inti; this young man wishes to hear what you hear, see what you see and perhaps know what you know. He needs to remember what he has chosen to forget. He listens well, yet still has much to learn."

The Elder then grabbed a thick stick, making a circle on the ground big enough for the boy to sleep in. He handed Inti the stick saying,

"Now look at this circle, look at nothing but this circle until I arrive back."

Inti's eyes widen.

"Where are you going?"

"I have a gathering to go to, don't worry, you will be safe with Mulu, he is much older than any of us and the jungle listens to him. It is half past midday now, I will arrive this time tomorrow... and don't forget to keep looking at the circle," The Elder points his fingers to Inti's eyes then the ground.

Off the Shaman went, deeper into the thickness of trees. And so Inti sat against Mulu, watching the circle. At first nothing happened. Inti kept looking at the same old rocks, leaves and bits of sunrays passing carelessly. This act tested Inti's patience greatly.

A group of giant ants marched along carrying bits of food for the queen. Single-filed, soldiers they were. A dung beetle casually made its way into the path of the troops. Within seconds they attacked. The beetle fought heroically, killing at least five ants before it became overwhelmed by the waves of onslaught. Power in numbers served the red fighters victorious.

Inti watched carefully as they broke up the beetle. There were ants to tear away the hard shell of the carcass. Others would take smaller bits and make way back to the colony. Some were messengers, directing others where to go while others didn't even bother. Flies made their way like vultures, picking up any remains left behind. Nothing goes to waste in the universe and this was a perfect example.

Sporadically, drop-by-drop, the clouds became lighter. The rain begins with a drizzle. Inti watches mosquitoes lay their larva within the circle. In the same spot there was death, hours later, began motions of life. The rainfall picks up a bit and what was once dirt, now was mud.

Frogs perform a symphony of sound. The water was emotionally cleansing. Inti fell in love with the smell in the air. The taste of freshness widens, soaking in every drop.

This paradise was soon interrupted. The feared emerald tree boa made its way near the boy. Strange that this snake was on the ground in weather like this, the boa must have wanted his presence known to the young boy, but why?

Inti stared at the snake that entered the circle. His gaze fixed upon the boa persistently. They remained like this for some time. The clouds ran. The rain ceased. The sun made its way to kiss the horizon. The night shows its sprinkled starlit face once again. The snake found a piece of bark to burrow in and rest. Peculiar this boa was indeed… its actions were peaceful and temperament calm.

Inti stayed up for hours. The moon's smile appears through the puzzle-piece tree leaves. Inti fell victim to the physical body, leaving him in the dream world.

Sleeping in the jungle has its advantages and drawbacks. Some drawbacks are you're always getting eaten alive by insects. There's never really a comfortable place to rest for long and if it's summer, it's like sleeping in a sauna. You have to rest with one ear open, always on alert for predators. Any sleep you do get is a light sleep.

Advantages are quite nice. Peace and quiet from the outside busy village or town. Stars scatter like sea salt across the pitch-blackness of eternity.

The night passes, carrying the humidity with it. Dawn transforms the night sky into a variety of navy blues, purples and magentas. Mr. Boa made his way out. Inti nods his head in friendship.

Perhaps the boa felt safe around the boy like Inti felt safe around Mulu. Perhaps it was Mulu all along. The circle being washed away had only slight glimpses of its structure remaining. Highlighting where to draw a new one, so Inti did just that.

Mulu watched Inti like Inti watched the ants, and so Inti sat still, waiting for the Shaman to return. By the time noon arrived, the Elder was nowhere to be seen. Very uncharacteristic, when a Shaman said something it was seen as already done.

Something must have happened, he must have gotten sidetracked or injured. Inti's worrying scenarios flood the mind like a tsunami. Of course there was the sneaking suspicion that the Shaman had left Inti there on purpose. It was a strange thing, having a few days' worth of food for only one day. Inti believed the Elder was playing games with him, testing his patience and commitment. Perhaps the Shaman was watching Inti all along!

Boa made good friends with the boy, finally making his way around Inti's neck. Monkeys continue to play in the trees above. Sounds of laughter from restless mammals echo throughout the jungle. Inti remains fixed on the circle, but today was another day and nothing more than falling leaves and a few insects feasting upon smaller ones made their story known.

With the sunset in motion, along comes a Black Panther cub. Surprising as its playful charm was more than comforting, making its way inside the circle. Inti's gaze fixed on the darkening eyes.

Boa and cub made their way to greet, both being amazed by one another. In the act of playing the cub hurt our boa with its sharp tiny claws. The snake bit back instinctively. The cub screeched out a yell of despair.

Once, twice, louder and louder the cub continued to scream its baby roar. The snake was not amused, switching into defense mode. With lightning speed came the mother panther to defend its youngling. The mother rushes closer to Inti and the boa, now perched up against Mulu.

The monkeys saw this. Swinging from branch to branch they became the audience: rioting, hooting and cheering. Without a second's hesitation boa struck at the feline's right eye, stopping her in mid-striking distance. The panther quickly backed away, covering her cub in the process.

The snake came between Inti and the now-furious mother. The circle became a coliseum, with front row seats given to Mulu and Inti. The mother paced around the snake waiting for the perfect chance to kill, and she did just that.

The boa was heavily outnumbered by the weight of an angry mother with the taste of revenge on her tongue. She caught the snake in her mouth, using her paw to stomp its tail on the ground… beginning to pull it apart, viciously.

The panther had its fun with killing then turned towards Inti. For a glimpse of an instant the boy thought to run, but this would have ended up fatal. The darkness of her coat began to blend with the ever-setting sun.

Her white teeth shine like planets appearing in the east. No choice for a child but to stare back and let fear set in, semi-paralyzing his muscles and mind. Inti grabbed Mulu behind him while the cub came forward between the mother's legs.

In between the breath of death, life flashed before Inti's eyes. Inti saw himself become adult then Elder… crossing the bridge of life into the realm of spirit. This moment was not his death. Inti heard the Elder's voice from the day before, a clip from his memory.
"You will be safe with Mulu!"

The monkeys became louder, eagerly watching from above. Branches begin to break then snap. Down fell the monkeys with the large tree-branch landing straight on the panther's back. The mother's spine was now broken. The monkeys ran around franticly while the baby cub becomes startled and confused. The mother lay helpless, unable to get up.

Inti was in a strange state of empathy. Fear soon diminished. Feeling the sadness and pain of the panthers, they three sat in a state of mourning. The mother's eyes began to cry. The cub snuggled close by her mother's side. Emotions spin inside the circle of life and death.

The Shaman finally comes back with a soft enchanting song of his flute. It was not a song that one can understand with words of intellect, but with intuition. The boy was more than glad to see his new mentor. As soon as the Elder saw what happened, he stopped the song, closed his eyes and sat next to Inti and Mulu in respect to the panther. Much time went by before the Elder opened his eyes.

"Thank you Mulu, the boy will soon understand if he has not already."

It was the way the Shaman spoke that helped Inti realize what happened. Perhaps Mulu had in some way saved Inti's life by taking another, giving a piece of itself in the process. This was a bit out of the boy's belief but still within grasp.

The Shaman took a blade from his handbag, hinting towards the boy to come closer. They stood within the circle in full presence.

"We now help this soul return to source."

The boy's eyes widened with the Elder making a quick jab into the jugular of the dying panther.

The daughter cub gave a long howling scream. Inti hugged the baby, placing her in his lap. The Shaman begins chanting a mantra. His hands guide her soul into the afterlife. The jungle screamed; every living creature becomes louder during the process. The last ray of sunlight reflected off the clouds towards the dead panther... showing the way back from whence she came. Silence overcame the jungle now. The crossing had passed.

"What has been learned here these past two days?"
"Life and death," the boy replied with a slight hesitation.
"So you realized the level of consciousness of the ground?"
"Yes, I guess," Inti pauses... "Why did you come late?"

The Shaman remains quiet for a moment then utters, "A friend, a fellow Elder has died, I was helping in the process of her transition."

The Elder then picked up a stick perched up against Mulu. Carving a big circle that went around Inti's smaller circle, the Shaman speaks.

"Now everything in this jungle represents the unknown, the questions and mysteries of the universe. Now the circle you have been gazing upon represents everything you know... everything experienced in this lifetime is within this circle. Now the circle I drew around yours represents my knowledge and everything I know. At first it might seem that I know more than you, and somewhat this is true, as it appears bigger than yours. But you can see my circle is connected to a larger part of the unknown, therefore I have more questions than you. I may have more experiences in this form, but im learning how much I don't know as well. It requires constant attention."

"So that's why you came later than you assumed, you were overwhelmed with emotions and questions?"

"Your insides serve you well Inti," the Shaman bows his head in humility.

"Come, let us shed this animal of its fur and take in its meat. One way or another energy will be transformed into something else, so best have a part in the process and do it correctly."

The boy's reaction showed he wanted nothing to do with that, but nothing shall go to waste in this world. First thing's first, the Elder begins to cut off the neck while Inti digs a hole next to Mulu. The fur was left to hang and dry. The cracking of ribs gave the boy chills.

The heart was placed next to the head; Inti quickly grabbed the snake, throwing it in with the dirt, covering them both like quicksand.

"Why did you bury only the head and heart?" Inti asks wiping dirt from hands.

"When we cross the bridge of life from one density to the next, it is a much safer passage if head and heart are together. Your heart is the way; your mind is the key. They need each other for they are a part of each other, balancing one another."

"Mind in the heart, heart in the mind," Inti adds.

The now-orphan cub sat nearby as they peeled flesh from bone, now cooked over an open fire. The Elder ripped the middle claw from the right paw. Then he took a thin piece of drying skin and wrapped it around the sharp bone making a necklace.

"A present for passing your first test," the Shaman said, putting it around Inti's neck.

"I don't understand... all I did was what you told me to do."

"Precisely. That's all you had to do and have to do. Listen to your ancestors, listen to the jungle, and most importantly... listen to yourself."

Inti felt overwhelmed. It had been the first time he received a gift from someone other than his parents. The Elder lifts the meat up high and spoke,

"We offer this food to the ancestors of the past, present, and future. May it go into the earth and trees as it goes into us! We become instruments of Father Sky and Mother Earth, to paint the world with joy and laughter.

They ate silent and cautiously. Only the songs of crickets and frogs remain. These lovely lullabies sung about a young boy who stared fear in the face, gaining courage and insight.

"You see this is what nature does, it speaks with one another, holding a space of love for all beings to grow in harmony. It sends out the perfect vibration to learn and create. This is more than just a fable or story for the lighthearted and truth seekers alike. It is real, raw, and measurable in the biological make up of the environment and its inhabitants. This understanding is being lost in today's age. They are telling people what to learn instead of how to learn. The oldest and wisest are the true teachers and this jungle is much older than either of us. It holds nothing back for we are their children... we are their legacy!"

Inti's eyes reflected the glow of knowledge, mirrored by embers of a now burnt-out fire. Still the boy had questions, "Why would trees and plants view us as their legacy, we are humans, not trees, right?"
The Shaman's hands lay upon Inti's shoulders.

"We are spiritual beings within a physical body. We are not searching for spiritual essence but trying to cope with being human. Knowing this, living this, being aware of this will put things into perspective as you evolve."

The moon was big and o so bright, filling up the darkness we all call night. Its crescent smile fell from sight with twinkling stars coming to light. The Shaman sat still, the Shaman sat tight; he let out a riddle, falling asleep just right.

Teacher of teachers.
Wisdom's best friend.
Molds all creatures.
Thoughts it will bend.

Silent among preachers.
A voiceless trend.
Garden of features,
This virtue will send.

Vengeance

Pointed towers echo footsteps. Lovely whispers float inside a Catholic church just off the coast of Spain's midday laughter. Children play. Grass grows. Trees sway. Birds chirp. Mass begins with Priest Nala Adaeze standing upon altar.

Heads lower, prayer is taken, words spoken, faiths realign. The Priest gathers hope, shining insight and wisdom. She was a messenger for some and a guide for most. Her hair was thin and light, complimenting her green eyes brilliantly.

Nala carried her presence with mystery, always leaving residue of curiosity. She carried the spark of awe… that charisma that slips straight through our delicate fingers, leaving us franticly searching for more. Finding any reason behind such emotional reactions words convey is as short-lived as lust itself.

Language was the masterpiece gods adored most, speaking being the authority itself. However… a sickness grew inside Nala. The gut draws weary. A sharp pitch punctures the ears, leaving most sounds in ruin.

The church doors swing open. Men and women stand to meet white skin and dark leather. The hands of our villain clap steadily… calmly…waiting for Nala to gain composure of her senses.

"Forgive me Father for I have sinned. It has been many years since my last confession, and I have killed many to come this far."

Krill reveals Japanese Steel, cracking his neck with a quick twist left then right. People scatter in a panic of terror. Nala stands ground, throwing her cloak off. Nala's true form is revealed. Sharp eyes on dark skin, thin blades on dark dreads, Nala held white plated armor on her left arm, gathering energy in a pose of defense.

"Tell me dear Elder, how does a woman become a priest. Is it her uncanny ability to hide from those she fears?"

"What do you want Krill?"

"You know who I want."

"If who you seek is there but you are here then his here is your there. Apparently you two are somewhere yet nowhere for certain."

"Enough. I will find him and destroy him!"

"What peace will this bring?"

"There is no peace, only power"

"Then you are blind."

"If you will not tell me, I will rob you of your life."

"You will try…"

Krill jumps high in an attempt to gain position but is thrown across the navel of the church by lightning and thunder. Nala's armor glowed blue with white electricity pulsing in waves. Krill smacks into brick wall, hitting wooden floor below.

"You didn't think I would be unprepared… did you?"

Volts surged in a seemingly endless sting. The aftertaste of shock only fueled the beast… wiping blood from mouth he utters *"Fancy equipment for an Elder,"* before bolting towards Nala.

Sparks flew with a few misses and a few hits. Blade comes closer strike after strike, only to be blocked by a field of energy. The shield of lightning curved with the unison of Nala and her words.

Krill stands back, observes. *"Old magic and new toys… where is your honor?"*

"Your honor has overshadowed the common value of life. You are broken. You are nothing but darkness."

"Well… you are right about one thing!"

Krill's eyes close, blade floats above rising arms. Our Elder went on the offensive, striking a thousand volts of electricity his way. Just like that, Krill takes the hit, soaking energy from the white armor. Like a black hole our villain remains.

Shadows crept through stained windows… down fell car after car into the church, crushing everything in its path. Nala blocked most of the debris with her shield but was taken by Japanese Steel swinging violently, slicing her armor. Catching her off guard, Krill went in with a death grip around neck, piercing into the images of Nala's soul.

"Yes… yes, just a little more. I must find him. I must have revenge."

With seconds to react, our priest straps her armor of electricity around Krill's chest, sending him with a kicking push out the doors. The armor explodes and with it the menace.

"Let that be an end to your destruction," Nala says, limping away from rubble and car alarms.

Moments later the police come with no lack of force. Nala puts hands on head, lowering to her knees, looking behind only to find the tyrant levitating in mid-air. "Correr rápido," Nala yells while taking cover.

Rubble, stone, metal and glass circled the incubus in a firefight, leaving only the savage to survive. Men ran from blasts of colliding cars. Bullets zip by stranded soldiers caught in the ambush of hellfire. Krill was an abyss, devouring his prey at will.

Nala ran fast and bold. So the chase began. She had the brush of trees and sharp sunlight on her side. As Nala ran, so the beast flew. The faster she ran, Krill easily followed.

The Priest's only ally was the now-approaching coast. The sea raised a mighty wave towards the demon, drowning him in a ball of water and magic. The words spoken remain quiet yet forceful. The mantra is repeated without breaking stride.

Our Elder's tricks worked. She now had the beast within liquid cage. The police and local bystanders watch as Nala holds the sphere. Agile and without warning, Japanese Steel flies towards the emanating mantras. Down falls the cage. Krill lands on the ground, coughing up lungs of water.

"Your soul… is mine."

"It is neither yours to take nor mine to give."

"I will drain your power then watch suffer… just as I did to your sister."

"All this talk about power. Revenge. You're a puppet. A slave. I pity you.

"I will never be a slave."

Krill reveals broken armor from the explosion, soaking in the last of its electricity. A lightning show of energy blasted its dominating sting, citizen's burn from the heat blast. The grim carnage drops darkened bodies upon asphalt.

A ball of lightning consumed Krill as he gained mass, expanding with every pulse. Our Elder stands back ponder options before action. There was little she could do, but the safety of the people was her utmost concern.

"You want my memories… you want my power… come and get it!"

Nala jumps into the sea in a daring escape and lure of the now-following menace. Off they disappear into the Mediterranean horizon, bouncing off one another in a deadly dance of flesh and bone. Wind blows, water moves, sharks hunt, fish die.

Slight echoes bounce from fishermen's ears to curious mind. The old timer looks overboard into the rippled reflections of grey hair and a tough tan. Nala zips underneath watery surface, carrying with her a streaming ball of light.

Krill slams into the sea with intensity… throwing the boat and its captain into the blue desert. Nala is dragged deeper towards chilling depths. Farther she endeavors. Down they hit… leaving Nala's throat at tightening grip. *"Into your past I take. Your knowledge, your power… you lost."*

Krill absorbs all that our Elder had seen; however… what our villain was seeking did not exist. Hidden the memory was. This trickery was upsetting to say the least as anger overwhelmed Krill, sending fists of fury into ribs and face. Heroically Nala fought, struggling to escape this dark tragedy. Glowing light shows a forceful punch into the chest of Krill... sending him to the atmosphere above.

Our Elder quickly follows going on the offensive. Japanese Steel blocks the attacks, cutting open flesh and white bone. The chase continues with quickening speed.

"I could use your help about now," Nala whispers to the connected Elder's. With speed Nala dodged the blade, finally landing herself onto glistening shores of Ibiza's west coast.

Slowly Krill floats onto the shore of shells. Waves kiss Japanese Steel, now approaching our exhausted Elder. *"Any last words?"* Krill raises blade.

Nala looks above to see fellow Elder teleport twenty feet above, gliding down with a helping hand. Our Priest looks in the Devil's eyes saying, "Veena..."

Rolling out of the way, Nala is caught by our Elemental, instantly being teleported on contact... leaving the beast with a roaring scream and a tightening fist. Krill returns to the scene of crumbling towers slipping media whispers of a massacre resulting in thirty-nine deaths and eleven casualties.

Our villain finds broken armor amongst wreckage of the ill and blind. His presence went without notice, as did his loss when collecting his unsuspecting prize. There served some purpose to Nala and her intellect of imagination. A blue and white glow faintly returned to the armor, giving with it a spark of clarity for the cruel to sink their teeth into.

Krill blends into the aftermath of vigor and rubble... taking with him the memory and smell of the rotting corpses still lingering in the afternoon sun. The wicked own this day of death and sin.

Red Road

A Shaman is one of healing and guidance. Known as medicine men or women, the village holds them in high regards, like most people today hold a Priest or Guru. Every Shaman has their own approach in making people realize the inner nature of self. Most of the times they watch while people make their own assumptions. The Elder never worries, sits comfortably and continues to offer presence and support. They know the land, live off the land and respect the land because they are a part of the land.

In regards to the Elder of this story, his heart was warm and eager. He was one to unite the surrounding villages and circles, embracing every idea that was beneficial. He helped the sick and confused in their most desperate of hours. He communed with the trees and birds, flowers and clouds, men and beast in this physicality and the next.

The Shaman answers to many names that hold such meanings as light barer, humble one, and truth seeker. When asked for his true name, he always chuckled with a grin saying, "Does a name really matter when given so many?"

One of the founding members of the Elemental council, the Elder Shaman's communion was highest when in meditation. His ambiance was one of a holistic nature, his philosophy... kindness.

Our Elder was given the grace and opportunity in being able to teach his former Master... which is not an easy thing to do. The day came when Elder received approval in being the successor of Baba Hanuman, the White Magician from the west.

"Here lays twelve generations of writings from one master to another, may their guidance follow and embrace your journey."

The young Shaman did not understand, "I don't need this, all we need is in here," he answers while pointing to Hanuman's heart.

"Then take this as a token of your accomplishments at such a young age," Hanuman replies.

Now our young Shaman was no fool, although from the outside it may have looked like that. When this was happening it wasn't just in some room or house; it was in front of the entire community so the people would know directly who the successor was.

They had food, music and a grand fire in reflection of burning ignorance from within. So when our young Elder received this book of generations, he paused for a moment, soaked in the essence of the writings, and then casually tossed the book in the fire.
"What are you doing?" Baba yells.
"What are you saying," our young Elder replies.
Hanuman was displeased, looking upon event as burden.

"Layers of conditioning, attachment to teachings our mind can't let go are the real burdens. My master, let us forget about silly words and enjoy each other's presence," the young Shaman told the Baba, being embraced with a hug.

The community saw this two different ways. First was that the young Shaman had indeed surpassed the Baba, the second being one of confusion and uncertainty.

"Let people think what they want and gossip as they will. The lesson in the matter is one of gratitude, being our attitude."

The changing of seasons passed with the ageing of Hanuman. The final test was one of a conscious passing, to greet death as a friend, not foe. The Baba said very little to few people, but of course he had some last words for his successor. Hanuman's voice was old and frail; two years of seclusion will do that to a man with little aspiration... his time was fading in this density.

"You were right...that day with the book...you were right," Baba gently spoke into the Shaman's ear as pale wrinkled hands fell from face to chest. Baba's brother cleared space in preparations for the crossing. Our Shaman stood outside the bamboo hut while the Vinya player orchestrated one last song for the crossing. Om Nama Shivaya!

In the communities of Peru there was a general rule. If the youngsters didn't like school, didn't attend school, then they spent time with the Shamans in the jungle. Their teaching would be different, but they would learn nonetheless. How this came to happen in Inti's case is quite coincidental. Every now and then the Elder migrated through different villages where time was spent with the younglings. Mostly they asked silly questions and made laughs of the Shaman's grey hair that reached beyond the shoulders.

This time however was one of argument. A group of kids were fighting over the money that Inti stole. Inti explained the same story every time, "I didn't steal anything, you're lying."

Each time Inti said this, he grew in anger. Spraying words of reason quickly turned into unbalanced reactions.

The Elder said nothing much at first, but finally broke words. The young kids stood still and listened.

"The matter that this boy stole money or that you boys are lying about it is not the point. This will come in time. Now who will help these young gentlemen come to an understanding?"

The kids remained still, staring at the ground like they were just yelled at by a parent. You could say our Elder's voice was quite strong and forceful when perceived through the eyes of children. No answer surfaces, so finally the Elder speaks, "Then I shall help those who ask of it." Inti stood up, walked over to the Shaman and spoke.

"Those boys bully me every day, they make fun of my dad running out on my family. They are jealous because they have no love in their lives. Please help them so they stop hurting people!"

This surprised the Elder. The group of boys stood up and laughed, they didn't want any help. The bullies walk off with their Oakley shades and bent baseball caps. The Nineties American culture rolled in swiftly for our younglings to say the least.

With permission from his mother, the Elder took the boy under his wing and explained to Inti the ways of the ancient world that was still thriving. The story of Mulu and the Panther was just another omen. Inti learned the ways of nature, of language and communication in all living things.

"It's a never-ending cycle, forever learning more about life's greatest mysteries," the Elder rambles on. He was full of stories and riddles, some just words of poetry; others were finely tuned pieces of art, turning most people into novice word mechanics.

So it began. Inti found passion for a life somewhat in solitude. It was a need to connect to things of his nature that guided the boy. Inti's fascination with the natural world turned out to be the soul's calling in remembering past lives. In the span of nearly eight years, the boy learned from the Elder. The list of stories and spiritual accomplishments grew taller with the shedding of seasons.

It was a hot and sunny day in the thickness that radiated insects and sweat. The jungle could eat you alive if it wanted to.

"Stare into the bushes," the Elder tells Inti.

"What am I looking for?"

"You are looking for nothing!"

"Then why am I looking master?"

"So you can listen with your eyes of course," our Shaman says with a smile.

So Inti looked. And looked some more. An hour went by with very little talking. The Elder began to lightly laugh. Inti had written a curious look upon face.

"You're too much in your mind my friend. You must look and listen without thinking...like a movie."

"But I don't understand, how can we listen with our eyes?"

The Elder says nothing more, staring back at the bush. So Inti did the same. After gazing in one spot for a while, one begins to get in a trance. With this trance and a bit of chance, you begin to see things.

With the wind in the leaves and a mystical eye, one can make out faces and images in the multidimensional illusion of a bush. This helps puts energy into your pineal gland, perceiving the reality that is overlooked and undermined. Inti saw many shapes and forms, like images in the sky appearing from clouds. This could actually be done with the clouds as well but took another approach to account for.

The higher you went the more languages there were to learn. It was like the difference in learning English and Japanese. They're both languages but completely different ways of perception and interpretation. So came the hard part in making sense of these images.

"It must be an intuitive feeling that radiates trust and confidence. The reasoning comes later."

Inti was taught to witness and aim his awareness to view life in all its aspects. The trees and bushes spoke about the balance of life, the cycle that was creation, preservation, and destruction.

Inti followed along with further teachings from breathing in the force of life, being Prana, to knowing the plants that could heal him. The sap or blood of specific trees could cure anything from snakebites to infections and wounds.

Curare wood was used for killing turkeys, pigs and monkeys while leaves, vines, and sticks were used for huts and snake traps. The Shaman was the flower, was the animal, he was the jungle itself.

"In a world full of knowledge, life is our college," the Elder began to sing with flute in hand.

The Shaman usually played a song or two when walking or resting. This flute was no ordinary flute. It was from the Brown Brothers of the North, handed down generation to generation. Made from the oak tree, its dark finish and well-kept glow remained a beauty to gaze upon. The feather of an eagle connected to the leather band above the keyholes.

It was a Thursday sunset with Venus and Jupiter playing about in the ultraviolet ocean of void. Our Shaman took the feather and pointed it against the westward wind. "Ah yes, just as I had felt," the boy did not understand. "What do you mean, what are you seeing," asks Inti.

The Elder hands Inti the feather while the boy takes position on the rock with sun-aligned eyes. The wind blew into the feather. Inti stared into its illusion of pulsating ripples. The listening method was applied and the message was received.

The micro-movements in the feather's texture were actually magnetic fields laced with microwave energy. The birds flew with these waves; to watch the birds was to know where Earth's magnetic flow was moving. The Native Americans knew this, so it was only natural that history was kept and handed down in the form of a feather, unlike the books we have today.

This feather was a pillar for telepathic communication. While tied to the Elder's head from time to time, few or no words were used in the decision of where to go. When Inti was on top of the rock facing westward wind, the transfer of methods was guided from humble teacher to observant student.

"Ah ha. I got it," says the boy, jumping off the rock in a rush of energy.

"Got what," laughs the Elder.

"The answer to your riddle."

"And!"

"It's patience."

"Two years no answer and you speak the truth," the Shaman's grateful smile was all that was needed. It was now time for Inti to work with the medicine. Mother Ayahuasca. The Grandmother. She has many names and heals in many ways.

A Shaman has many crafts and brewing a good batch of medicine is always in the arsenal of passionate hobbies. The Yaje root connecting to other Ayahuasca plants was personal choice. It gave stronger visions, dissolved boundaries and shattered the illusion of separateness.

The brew was thick, like mud after just raining. The smell was decent yet left an aftertaste punch to the throat. Inti already felt a bit wheezy.

"I will guide you while the Mother guides us," says the Shaman.

"What is this going to do to me?" asks the boy.

"Heal and awaken." So the Elder opened space with sage and a speech.

"We call now to the Eagle of the North, may you watch over us from above with love. To the Snake of Kundalini, may your power be a pillar that shines bright in the East. To the Panther of the Southern hills, may your courage be ever unbeaten and ever present. To the Whales of the West, may your songs of ancestry be forever admired."

The Elder poured one shot's worth of the red medicine, dipped finger in cup then tasted it... reading the brew. Having a cautious look upon face, our Shaman was being told what to do. So he filled up the wooden cup a bit more, handing it to the boy.

Inti slammed the shot if done a hundred times before. Not so surprising but a bit shocking. There's something about the youth that brings out the joy in everything. The Elder found this funny... he knew Inti had no idea what was in store for him.

You see taking the medicine isn't necessarily looked upon as a fun adventure as much as it's known for being a spiritual journey. This stuff is no drug. It's not something you take, feel great then have a comedown. It's quite the opposite in fact.

It came on slow for Inti. And then it kicked in... the stomach noises, the light-headedness, the feeling of nausea to be followed by purging of mental and emotional sicknesses. It's in those times of throwing up that some of the best realizations come, and when the Shaman can see clearly into our bodies.

When the Elder looked at Inti, he saw this boy had already done much cleansing. Perhaps a karmic debt! There was however some emotional dharmas that surfaced when looking with the trained eye.

Inti journeyed within his own consciousness many times, making many friends, waking and sleeping, physical and non. His closest astral friend was the Greek messenger Hermes, whose wings weren't only on his feet but on his back. Hermes' cloth looked like a cloak of a god once praised and worshiped rather than fellow messenger. Inti had many races with Hermes and lost every time, but it wasn't the end Inti always pointed out, it's just the beginning.

Around and around they spin through the jungle. Cutting through trees and brush. This was how Inti ran into the cricket's kingdom; which wasn't a place but a specific time of night. They are the true shepherds of the forest, maintaining equilibrium and order.

Inti's love grew strong... for the land, his ancestors, and for Stella. Now Stella Stone was no ordinary girl. At age ten she was leading chess champion in her county and by age thirteen she was already graduating high school. She joined along with her philanthropist/botanist father into the jungles of South America for the cure to death.

Stella's father, James Stone, was a single parent whose battle with cancer left his wife long since past. Stella matured at a supersonic rate. Her favorite pastime was proving her father wrong with math equations and philosophical reason. She was a smart cookie to say the least.

James spun a deal with the American government, locating and tagging plants that held specific chemical compounds and proteins. In return, James would have funds and means to study further into his more private work. Of course Stella came along and remained at her father's side, most of the time; however this all changed when Stella met Inti. Sparks flew with the months passing while young adults danced in infatuation.

James worked with the local Shamans, locating plants and learning their properties and effects. This gave much room for Inti and Stella to pick each other's minds, to share a first kiss, a first sexual climax... a first love.

Stella taught him about the intellectual sciences while Inti taught her the intuitive nature in life. It was the innocence of love. The first kind of love we come to know that's held in a long list of emotions stretching throughout our lives... leaving breadcrumbs to keep track of our journey. More events took place that made love stick... clouding everything.

It was summer and hot as usual. The leaves' edges were turning inward. Green to yellow then brown with an aftertaste of a flakey crunch. The sun ruled most days as people kept to the shade and water sources. Inti's mother took care of the house.

Inti's mother was born in Peru yet never officially recognized as born. Going through the business of proving you're alive, getting a birth certificate, that was too much for her. She was simply known as Mama, the village caretaker and most of the time, local therapist.

Mama's encounters with the Elder Shaman left a list of crafts she could put to command. Local plants and animals were Mama's specialty. It wasn't long until Mama invited the Stones to live at her house.

James was there much longer than planned. The Americans kept changing their points of interest, always moving James from one project to a new one. The government, in search of various interests, started moving in by force. This angered the people and drove local hillside villagers off of their land and onto others.

Most of the scientists began motion to have the plants patented and controlled, so only the U.S government had authority to use such plants. Justified by the War on Drugs, some plants such as Ayahuasca and the chemical compounds that inhabited these plants were being abused, bringing great concern upon the village and more specifically the Elder.

"We must go now Inti."

The boy's saddening heart grasped hard onto Stella and his mother. Too much time out of the jungle had effects in the stability of emotions. Inti wanted more time with Stella but understood he must leave with the Shaman.

"It's hard leaving those you love or have fallen into love with. Emotions cloud intentions, you must let go my friend. Purpose comes before emotion."

Mostly the boy asked few questions, however it had been almost a year since they last drank. Ayahuasca wasn't a thing to be done habitually, like say tobacco. There is a time and place to do such things for healing, awakening, and in this case, council.

"We need to speak with the Elemental council clearly. It will be four days until we reach space. How long we are staying for, I do not know. My wish is for you to come with me. But you must do this from your own free will… not because I have asked this of you."

"I will follow you Master."

"I've told you, do not call me that. You are my student as much as I am yours."

"But what am I suppose to call you when you don't care about names?"

"I am master of myself. Nothing more, nothing less."

"I believe names are more powerful than you think!"

"My friend, I believe you could be on to something."

The Shaman entered the jungle first. Stillness was all that was felt. The wilderness remained untouched, the birds and creatures alike knew our Shaman to be of their own. Inti followed. The birds began to chirp while the locust relayed the message. The forest recognized him, remembered him, but still a tint of distance was picked up. Inti still had time until the jungle and his heart were one in the same. Only then would Inti be able to understand what was needed for a boy to choose his own destiny.

Two days past, slowly they reached Mulu; beginning to set up camp the boy looks towards the Elder as older brother.

"Do you ever think you could marry someone?"

The Elder's expression was one of curiosity when he replied, " I haven't given it much thought."

"What do you mean haven't thought about it? I thought all guys eventually get married?"

"Not all, and besides, there is much more than just girls to keep a person occupied."

"Ya but her hair smells so nice and the way she kisses me… and other things of that nature. I mean that's got to mean something right?"

"It means she kissed you and you had sex. You got what you wanted."

"I always get what I want."

"Don't get ahead of yourself now Inti. Just because you get what you want, doesn't always mean it's what you need. One day you won't get everything you want. Even if you did get everything you wanted, you would always have to be careful of what you wished for, yes?"

Inti didn't understand. O wait, correction, he did not want to understand. There is a difference, you see, in not understanding and not wanting to understand.

"I am a warrior, I've stood ground against the mighty Panther, raced the legendary Hermes. Saved the fairies from the dark gnomes. I always win, it's a hero's quest!"

"Hero are you? A warrior?"

"Yes, and that's just the beginning. I will show everybody what I can do. I will save the village. No more big trucks and loud machines destroying our land. No more foreigners. No more oppression."

Inti stands high, pointing stick in air like if political realists at prep rally.

"A hero is not a warrior as one would think. A hero is one who comes to resolve through peaceful means," the Elder speaks, knowing the passion that flared in Inti. His heart was in the right place but his head was a bit twisted from all the stories Stella would ramble about.

"Now the true meaning of a warrior is not so black and white as you paint it. It does not have to deal with fighting against something or someone. Being a warrior means not being afraid to stand up for what you believe in. It's not about forcing that belief onto others. There's a fine line between the two."

"This is what makes a warrior?"

"The path of the warrior is painted with betrayal, loss of faith... suffering. This is why they are warriors, because they must endure these times of doubt and pain without losing the hope to improve."

"So what do we do about these Americans that are abusing our land? We must force them to leave or our culture will fade away. Our ancestry will be lost."

"It's not the people exactly who are abusing the land, it's the idea behind their actions that I'm more interested in." Inti's face looked blank as usual when diving deep into the Elder's reasons of action.

"If we can understand why someone would want to control plants, why people take orders to do things that go against the natural way, then we can look at them as an individual and treat them as such. The idea has the power, not them."

That night Inti had many visions. He was able to lucid dream quite frequently. The only visions he was not in control of were dreams of events yet to pass. Inti dreamt of pain and suffering. Voices throughout the flames of burning tribes fell upon the boy's imagination. He had this vision before; it came once or twice a year. Recently these glimpses became somewhat troublesome. Mostly Inti kept to himself about these matters. However, every time these night terrors happened, the Elder would comment,
"I heard your dreams last night!"
"It's ok, I'm fine."

They journey deeper into the jungle. Thick humidity stuck to smoke then skin... someone was here already. The breeze blew a fresh fire, and in these parts of the jungle, only the fittest survive.

Curious was the Elder and even more so with the boy. They investigate a path that the new comers left. Inti pushes forward with the tracks of boot in mud. The Shaman stops, urging to continue in his direction.

"We have our own reason to be here, let us accomplish one task at a time."

The Elder knew what lay before them if they followed the boot prints. The birds were more than active that day and when high activity occurs, it meant a lot to talk about.
"Many people have traveled on this path, too few we are."

"What about mind over matter, out thinking them, out talking them."

"What are you planning to do? Why are you thinking this? You understand where your actions will lead you? Mindfulness brother." Deep breaths inhaled then exhaled; Inti calms the quickness that emotion gives.

"Your time will come. But now we must push forward," the Shaman urges.

To come and understand the Elemental council is to come and understand any type of gathering among people. Usually a gathering is for one reason, and that is to accomplish a goal. Inspired by the nature of light and dark, balance was the key. Service to humanity was the overall intention and sole purpose of the Elementals.

There are five positions being: Fire, Earth, Water, Air and Aether. In reflection it can be viewed as The Warrior, The Healer, The Scholar, The Sage and The Lover. A role is recognized then acted out in an Elder's life, however these roles can be switched instantaneously through free will and reincarnation. They embody all roles while usually reflecting just one archetype in a lifetime.

Each person carried an instrument or tattoo in representing the element from which they fully embodied. Our Shaman, one of four who still had physicality, resembled Earth (the Healer). His ways were just that... to purify in the most creative of ways.

Nala, the daughter of an African witchdoctor, was the Scholar. Her knowledge surpassed all in the matters of metaphysics to anthropology. She played the drum in reflection of our heartbeat.

Veena accepted the role of our Lover long ago. Playing the Rudra Vinya is his craft. The preservation of life is an offering from the Element of Aether. Due to this role, Veena acquires great longevity from lifetime to lifetime... all a part of being in resonance with Vishnu.

The Sage of this council was a mysterious one in nature. Her rule was to have no rules. Living in constant paradox. Soka always shifted and adapted to serve the needs of the people at large. Soka has an unusual pattern of shifting that which needs changed, in all its magnitude.

As for the Elemental of Fire, his heart was young and courage strong. Inti had vision and trust yet lacked experience... we shall soon see how this story plays out...

Soon came reason for the council to unite and purify once again. When the council was formed they had their first meeting. Not only in physical space but in all realms.

They connect on higher planes of thought, on Earth and off it. So when Inti and the Elder arrived at space, it only meant conditions were now favorable for communication.

"Why no people? Who are we meeting?" The Shaman explains and still the boy finds it difficult to understand.

"You mean I am allowed into the council if I can see the council?"

With a nod of his head, the Elder whispers, "Exactly."

Inti never worried before... and this time was no exception. Sun fades west like a coin sinking towards Earth's enchanting game.

Inti made himself up a nice brew to help his meeting with the Council. The boy refused to throw up this time. Usually this was ok, but not tonight. Tonight Inti wished to hold everything in. Why? Well, the inner working of a teenager is a complex design to understand.

The mixture of excitement and curiosity fueled Inti's actions. He drank and waited with crossed legs and a straight spine; eyes opened then closed like jars of honey. The medicine was strong and working Inti like a slave.

"Good. A boy needs a beating every now and then to show him his place."

The voices of many became clear as glass. A gathering of the ancestors was made aware. This had not only to do with humans but with every life form in the jungle.

The omnipresence of subjectivity was now the vantage point. To the boys right sat the Elder of the Earth. His simple attire left only loose clothes over our Shaman. Next came Veena, the last Rudra Vinya player. The lover's song could be heard in the subtle background while sounds of rejoice echoed the halls of Akasha.

After Veena came Nala. She wore long black dreads with feathers stuck in between. A third of her locks had razor sharp blades at the end. One space was left open then came Inti.

"You have found your place young man, amongst the weight of service," words spoke through the minds of our Elder's towards Inti.

These words were heard from within and from without, like a radio blasting straight out of a chest. The pulsating vibrations sprouted goose bumps along the arms.

"We now answer the call of Gaia. What is our role in the great waves of change?" Nala exhales.

Visions grew from white to color. The Grandmother was with them and foretold the events to come ...

Volcanic eruptions gasped liquid magma... scratching the sky. The ground shook; ash clouds dragged the heat down. Villages turned aflame, only to become embers in the memories of glowing souls. Animals ran in terror while trees torched away.

These visions had been the same Inti dreamt about, just dosed with a larger scope in the situation. When Inti thought this, so everyone reacted. They all shared the same existence. The collective unconscious was made conscious as awareness pulled towards Inti. The boy's rage shined, his fear of losing everything was building in the psyche.

"Fear not. Love all," calming voices respond to Inti's impulses.

"He will endure much. You will endure much," Veena leans over while speaking more to our Shaman.

"What if he is not ready? I'm a lover, not a fighter... can only train the boy so far, he must choose his own path," Veena explains in a concerned manner as Inti only catches glimpses of the conversation.

The Shaman held no reaction. Once he made up his mind, it was done. However Veena's input was always noted. Inti remained a bit lost, unaware the full extent of these circumstances. Inti felt this for an instant, and then all was released. Nala came closer to Inti; she scoped his body. Calculating probabilities.

"Why do you choose to fight young one?" Nala's voice extends towards Inti's ears.

"Because they are ruining everything I love. I'm tired of not making a difference. We can do this. We must do this," Inti's voice rises.

"The boy lacks control of emotion," Nala reasoned.

"Were we not any different?" our Shaman replies.

"There is no stopping what must come to pass. The waves of change are near!" Veena explains.

"I intend to stop nothing, only to push it in the right direction," our Shaman concurs. Quickly and gently came the wind and with it flew Hermes. He brought message from the air.

"In the recent knowing of what most likely will come to pass, Soka has entrusted me with a message for the council's ears," Hermes continued.

My brothers, my sister, I have chosen a road less traveled thus it is time for the physical to take form again. It will not be hard to find me yet requires no lack of effort. I miss you all greatly and will see you on the other side. My friends, my family... Be here... Be now... Be one...

Tears of joy swept the council. Even Inti poured liquid from eyes with no reason; his heart leads the way. Hermes rolls up the message and throws it in the Akasha flame that burned sky blue within the Aether of the nether force. The boy was still a bit confused yet the pieces were falling together. The council bowed towards each other, Inti being the last, following the Shaman's lead. Hermes extended his gesture of respect.

"Do you know why I always beat you when we race?" Hermes whispers to Inti.

"It's because I know I'm going to win. You only think you will. Ambition can be somewhat blinding. Automatically thinking you must prove some worth of value. Jumping at the first chance you get to prove yourself. Passionate yes, but foolish if done with wrong intentions. Remember my words and know your intentions young friend," and away Hermes sped off into the distant background.

Inti had questions the Shaman needed to answer. The Shaman needed to know what Inti was trying to understand.

"Soka, the Air Elemental… that was your friend who died the day with Mulu and the panther."

"Again your insides serve you well Inti."

"How did Soka die?"

"An incubus by the name of Krill ended the physical." The Shaman lowers his head.

"Why did Krill want to kill Soka?" Inti's investigation continued.

"There are some souls out there who wish to do harm in their twisted search for power."

"Is he connected with the council, with the fires?"

Again our Shaman lowered his head. "Your visions are no coincidence. You play a bigger role in this than you realize. You have a gift Inti." Stillness took the boy.

"Are we to stop the fires of death then?"

Elder bends down to eye level, his warmth encompassed Inti.

"Cultivate detachment. There is still unraveling to be done. I think your role in all of this goes far beyond any burning villages. You will understand more. We have time to prepare."

"Prepare for what? You mean the villages really are going to burn?

"I said no such thing. However, if it does, you are not so mighty as to stop it from happening. I am referring to the preparation within. These visions are just high probabilities of events to occur. We can choose to live in a different vibration if we will it so!"

"Yes but if we stop the Americans then they won't hurt our Mother and then there won't need to be pain," the boy's fire ignited as he stood up, breathing fast.

"Inti relax, you do not listen. They do not speak for America; they are a few key members of a company that uses fear to control actions in their favor. Be smart. Know your role. Be mindful! I assure you, a village will not burn any time in the near future."

Inti listened, nodding his head, beginning to walk back home. The Elder remained still. The boy stopped, "What are you doing, this way right?"

"Don't know. Do you know how to get home?" The Shaman sat himself in a tree above the brush, unfolding his flute.

"Of course you know, and yes I do... maybe."

Inti's mind franticly races through his memory, connecting the dots of how to get back home. Problem was, it was night. Of all the things Inti learned with the jungle, he forgot to memorize the map of the stars.

The first storytellers of ancient days, the stars have foretold countless sagas, guiding those who have strayed too far. In Inti's case he was in luck, for the Elder knew the ways of the stars and was more than generous to teach the boy. It would take time, so Inti played it safe... voting on patience.

"The brightest light in the night is our Moon...something I will discuss further in time. The second brightest light is Venus, which just fell past the horizon. The third is our friend Jupiter just above us."

"How do I know where north is?"

"The planets and Moon follow the Sun east to west. This should give you a rough start to distinguish true north. Of course you can look for the North Star, but if you can't find it, revert back to your planets."

"In the morning the Sun will tell us which way is east anyhow," Inti added.

"Correctly so. Best not to travel at night anyways. Let's get some rest."

"That's it, no more teachings?"

The Elder begins playing his flute. Soothing tones guided the Jungle to rest, lighting the road for nocturnal life. The Shaman spoke at the end with Inti lying under pondering stars.

> Moves to the future,
> Recalls all past.
> Living present moment,
> Hardly seems to last.
>
> Knowledge is its thirst.
> Concepts it will grasp.
> Willing is its essence.
> Applying is the task.

Mornings heat baked the boy like a pig without the blanket. The locusts were screaming in frenzy. The Shaman was nowhere to be found. Inti panicked for a moment until he realized the directions, then headed home.

"The Elder must be playing games with me. He did say that riddle," Inti talked to himself out loud. Finally he came to a large hill with a tall cliff. Something he remembered nothing about.

Inti sat down catching his breath, weighing the options of what to do next. Top of the cliff might provide good opportunity in finding water sources and paths, but who knew how long it would take to get there.

The farther Inti looked up, the higher the cliff got. Towering trees covered everything. It was still early and for now, Inti focused on keeping his energy. Food enough for one and a half days, three if he stretched it out. That left a day or two worth of food that needed to be gathered.

Midday approached, Inti kept thinking about getting home while sharpening a spear out of wood. He came upon honey in a nearby bees' nest. Inti used smoke from dry tree leaves to get closer and cut off a slice of the hive. He was stung four times while moving along quickly. The poison spread through his arm. Inti scanned the ground, looking for jiva. Well that's what his mom would call it.

"The stems of that amazing flower. The red and purple one," his mother's voice comes to memory.

Finally the flower is found. Snapping the stem, he oozed the white nectar onto the bites. The jungle was ruthless, but for Inti's sake, he had grown much here. Only the fittest survived.

The bites slowed things down a bit, although Inti recovered quickly. All he wanted to do was leave the jungle and now he found himself four days in, by himself and lost. Fear kicked in and this time it didn't leave.

Inti dwelled on what the council said. It tightened the skull until falling asleep. Inti sharply woke to the traps he set around the camp. One goes off and then another. Multiple catches he thought. This was not so, Inti realized it was something much bigger than small game.

There was no moon in sight. No fire ember to faintly glow in the twilight. Only darkness crept towards the boy. He grabbed the spear and took stance. A slow growl begins to emerge from his left while the presence grows closer. His breath paused. His focus narrowed. The eye before the storm was calm. Eerie. Inti was being hunted.

The boy sure could use Mulu at his back again. The growls grew louder with terror stepping forward. Inti forced a mighty roar of his own in defense while jabbing the spear into darkness. He felt a swing hit the stick and deflect.

Another growl emerged. Inti stepped back a few paces. Pure instinct remains with another thrust of the spear. Strike two, a miss and even worse, no swing back. With instant reaction the boy ducked down, dodging the cougar's strike as the beast jumped over him.

The heart beats fast in these situations. Inti now saw the cougar with smell and sound giving light to sight. "I am not your enemy," Inti says honorably. Man and beast stare off into the void of one another. Both on guard yet somehow entranced by it all.

Off in the faint distance comes a melody of interest. The male cougar's attention is drawn towards music and away the feline went. The tune caught Inti's interest as well. He knew that melody. It was the Elder.

How far away was the question and how to get there was another. Inti wouldn't be able to get there if he wanted to. Too dark... Too tired. It brought comfort to know the Elder was not far, and so sleep won the battle of rest once again.

Rising dawn, rising legs, the goal was meeting the Elder. Inti finishes the dried up honey while pushing forward, licking fingertips and all. The jungle had fewer trees gathered in certain spots, naturally clearing a path rather than cutting one. Then came the stretch. Twenty-five feet would be a fair judgment in measuring the rocky cliff that reached the top.

Inti walked upward for almost an hour. To turn back now would be a hard thing to live with. On the other hand, climbing that steep cliff was a daredevil's adventure in itself.

"One slip and it could mean trouble," the Elder's voice bounces down.

"If you can do it, so can I," Inti screams.

Bare feet, bare hands, Inti scaled the wall like a spider fleeing water. The boy could climb, no doubt. The jungle gave him that. The jungle also gave him a situation that tested limits. Gravity and stamina took the boy by his arms. His muscles burned, the breath becomes short and many.

"Focus. Visualize," the Elder encourages from above.

Arm reaches rock, then root. The boy made it to a safe spot, dangling for a moment. Regaining his composure Inti rushed quickly upward.

Trees' spreading like grass was the sight within poetry. Smells of fresh mountainside engulfed the two. The view was timeless. A hint of adventure sparked... freedom was near. Inti saw most of the forest but was unfamiliar with the dark patch of trees towards the west.

"It leads to a cave that few have passed," Elder speaks, reading Inti's mind.

It is never known completely how a medicine man works. They can understand the mind, body, and soul as one living being. After fifty odd years of invested time and energy, reading someone's thoughts becomes easily attainable.

"Let's go. It's the only place I haven't been and it feels right," Inti says.

"The path is not straight. The jungle is thick. It is beyond a gorge that pities no man. You go there because you feel like it?" The Elder's voice showed interest.

"Yes," Inti speaks simply.

"You know you must have the utmost serious commitment, the strongest determination. This is not just going to a cave. This is training. This is trial. When you return you will not be the same."

The boys heart drops. Body tingles. Smile grows, and the Shaman knows a boy is to become a man. A few days past, finally coming to the deep gorge of running rapids that sliced bone like bread.

"Had you given any thought of what you were going to do when you came to this?" our Elder asks.
"A solution will present itself," Inti confidently responds.

The Elder would always say this, so Inti applied reason into action and marched towards the unknown. The path grew hard to navigate at any constant speed. Trees upon trees lived everywhere. Spider webs cross in between the leaves and branches.

Arachnids the size of Inti's chest sat still with silent speech. The sun glides towards the dirt below, blending with the silk webbing. This was where quantum leaping occurred.

"We camp here for tonight, the trees provide safe rest. At night it's best to be off the ground in these parts of the jungle," the Elder advises.

Quickly Inti climbed a large tree while the Shaman took position a bit away from the youthful Fire Elemental. They overlooked the gorge. Large grey clouds in the north were brewing. Thunder and mist came ever closer, finally pouring upon land in a much-needed shower after a hot day's journey.

The lightning strikes shine synchronicity in every direction, until finally a bolt hits a nearby tree. The two watch, as it snaps and breaks downward into the rapid abyss. But wait, it doesn't happen like one would assume. The huge trunk becomes lodged in between the edges of the gorge. All Inti sees is a new path to the other side. "Solution presented!"

The newly made bridge seemed dodgy at best. They crossed fast just after the rain ceased and the sun's rays rose above the horizon. Light, soft, quick, agile, they move with purpose and skill. Like monkeys they are, jumping over rocks and branches.

"The force moves you. The earth guides you," Elder expels while continuing towards the distant cave.

Days passed with a number of bonuses. Inti's understanding grew, allowing intuition to fully direct him. Inti finally saw results. His reflexes were beyond his reasoning; like some distant skill that broke free. Funny thing about teaching yourself; you never know until it finally happens, sprouting curiosity and excitement.

The air grew still. Spine vibrated chill. When they crossed the hill, Inti's eyes began to fill. Terror with doubt crept up with a shout. His wits crunched to a doubt, while his mind wonders about.

What lies inside this void of darkness? Place reeks of molding dead carcass! The ego plays tricks when thoughts become thoughtless. White becomes black as spots melt into spotless.
The Elder sits outside the cave, waiting for his brother.

The cave was wet. Damp. Moldy. Only vermin survived in these parts. Urban myth and folktale were born in places like these. Tiny echoes bounce along the narrowing walls. How deep must one go until self is revealed?

Frustration consumed Inti. Everything was going wrong. His torch had gone out. The path leading outside was far gone for any light to make presence. A few hours pass, each moment lasting forever. His blank stare into darkness was the only approach. What else to do in pitch black?

"Will you show me what I must know already, I don't have all week," says Inti in a humble forceful manner.

It is spoken thus it is so. Color creaked thru the fabric of reality as the astral world became viewed within physicality. And so the show began...

The Condor and Eagle, what best of friends they are. They play like brothers of the global tree. Many forms these relationships take. For the Red Road comes to us all as fate.

The Eagle flies away, being drawn to material in the north, while the Condor remains in the Americas of the south... the heart. Brother Eagle used his mind in many ways. Thus sprung technology and ignorance. Not enough heart to spiritually mature. Condor had trouble expressing intellectually what the heart felt. The mind in the heart, the heart in the mind, they must remain as such.

With this stretching of symbolic birds comes a bridge that connects them. The Red Road is born as a journey, a quest, and a pilgrimage that spans lifetimes into karma itself. Its goal... to once again unite the two birds so all shall blossom together once again.

The story changes tides when Inti begins to feel sad. Hurt. Loss. The mind swelled up. Migraines slammed the boy to the ground. Visions of Mulu, the Elder, Stella had come to pass. Fear traps the hurt of death. Inti lays on wet rock in vanquishing darkness.
But just as darkness will rise, so it shall fall.

"Wait a minute," Inti thinks. This cannot be, no. My brother is not lost or dead I feel him so. What game has this dungeon placed before my eyes? What magic has been cast that makes hurt rise? This is not his fate, not hers, nor mine. This is a mirror of masks through space and time.

Inti assures himself from third point of view. He shines up the darkness, what else is light to do? The building of courage is within the mastering of situations. For living present moment is the father of all meditations. So Inti sat very quietly, still as a bat. Legs folded tightly, back straight and flat. Beginning to listen from the air to the ground, his mind was lost and needed to be found.

Time passes while the Elder shows no worry. His daily activates consist nothing more than gathering and simply being. Sleeping and eating come when seated. The body provides energy with yoga when needed.

The dawn had just risen and with it Inti from his three-day hibernation. The boy was weak yet fully refreshed.

"I must stay in the jungle longer. I wish to control this emotion… this energy in motion."

"And how best will you do this Inti?"

"You will teach me. The Red Road has shown me many things," Inti replies with confidence.

"And what makes you think I can teach you such things?"

"Because I know the answer to your riddle."

"Which is?"

"The mind."

"Then the mind is where we will begin!"

Vengeance

Our Elemental sits comfortably alongside the crisp Himalayan air. Tibetan flags move gently, overlooking the land of the Thunder Dragon... Bhutan in common tongue. This mountaintop sanctuary was home to the prayers and songs of the Rudra Vinya and its master.

A thousand unlit candles rest within the shrine, perfectly balanced by reflection and speculation. The melting snow races then drips on stone and dirt. Winter was ending. Solar rays grace the eyes, recharging the spiritual machine that is the soul. Time is not only linear but also happening instantaneously in a variety of ways, but this does not change the simple fact that the will of the wicked always find a way.

This last thought entered without permission, not being our Elder's in origin. A laugh that twisted fear found its way to the silent Elemental.

"Veena..." Krill makes his presence fully known walking towards the entrance with distaste and envy.

"Where have you been hiding him?"
Veena sits silently with instrument in hands.
"Speak you fool!"
Stillness. Silence. Our Elder remains unaffected.
"Good... I will enjoy your suffering."

Krill reveals Japanese Steel but is quickly stripped of weapon by a forceful pick of Veena and his Rudra... and so the playing begun, knocking Krill out through the surrounding mountainside.

Our villain comes back for blade but is again thrown away by the pulsing scales, now growing faster. The symphony of destruction was well matched by the timeless glow of the Vinya in full power. The unstoppable force of Krill met the immovable grace of Veena.

They danced this dance for some time, however Veena had the upper hand with cosmic law in order. Neither one could win therefore neither one would fall. Equally matched, equally measured, Krill stops in exhaustion from the show of electricity bouncing off sound waves.

"This isn't you, fight back Kaiden."

"Kaiden is nothing but a vessel. He will never have his body back. Now tell me, where is the Shaman?"
"You think I would tell you?"

"I will have my vengeance with or without your compliance."
"Vengeance?"

"It is only with vengeance that I will have power enough to watch this world burn."
"You will never win."

"You have your seers, I have my spies... in the end I will take this planet and its decaying race into darkness. Taking with me all life and light."
"That's not going to happen."

"I don't know Veena... is it?"

Krill's blade returns in hand, rushing towards Veena. In a defensive move, the two are teleported instantly. Out into the stratosphere they appear... both drift towards the great vacuum. Krill's grip clenched the Elder's throat.

Where Krill went, Veena followed. The two slowly freeze; spinning around the blue diamond we call home. In that beauty of spaciousness and expansion, it's almost hard to forget the grave danger with such courage.

Giving in, Veena teleports farther down the troposphere with Krill tagging a ride. The two fell extremely fast. The sword flies from Krill's fingers with Veena fighting off every strike.

The sandy sea was an oasis of brutality and endurance. The Sahara lays witness to a fallen angel's savagery. Grounds tremble. Skies are momentarily scared. Villain and Elder crash with pain and sinew. The grim found Veena then embraced Krill. Effortlessly Japanese Steel falls from sky near its well-acquainted master, whose bones were now healed from devastating descent.

"Ready to die." Krill extends sword, sending it into the throat of Veena... only to be diluted by the unshakable force of Aether. Over and again Krill stabs in a tireless effort to overcome Veena. With each blow the blade tastes nothing but air, slicing straight through our Elemental now in a mixture of fog and smoke.
"Coward."

"To kill is the true act of a coward. No amount of clarity will fully convey the mistakes of your life. You are nothing but tragedy."

"And you are nothing but fading stardust. It is your compassion for life that makes you weak, makes you act from a sense of honor."
"You know nothing of honor."
"Honor is ego's most admired mask. A tool, that is all."
"Your cruelty is your weakness."
"Your faith is yours."
"The time for worshiping yourself will soon end."

"By whose hand... yours? As long as people desire and love, they will always have something to lose. You know this yet choose not to act upon it. You hide

behind your values and nobility. You are but reflected hypocrite and I your mirror... look upon yourself."

Krill walks towards Veena.

"You know what he did to me, you know his fate. Tell me where you're hiding him."

The incubus draws near. Veena looks downward pondering words spoken.

"This is true justice Veena. Hanuman would have agreed."

"He would have never agreed. You know nothing other than what's in front of you. You think the physical is some kind of finality? You truly believe in death that much you would let the darkness take over every action?"

"It is, not as they say... option."

"What do you mean... what have you done?"

"I have seen the world you hide from humanity. Your precious Elementals are but shattered glass. Soon I will drink their insides as wine from severed skull. At last I shall have victory."

"There is no victory in slaughter."

"Wrong. Only through victory are my chains broken. Only then do I have power. I am their beginning and your end."

"You are a slave to power and always will be. Your reckoning will be your own."

" Only through conflict can we better ourselves."

"Your passion for strength does not guarantee perfection."

Krill snaps back, sending Veena into a delicate dance of danger and doom. Our Elder flips beast over shoulders then forces a high kick to the arm, sending Japanese Steel into the air. Veena steps back, gaining energy for his jump in hyperspace.

"You can't hide him forever!"

"..."

"It is inevitable Veena... you are only a delay."

"And you but an illusion!"

With these words spoken, our Elemental turns into fading smoke; drifting towards the multi-dimensional prisms teleportation creates. Krill retrieves blade, standing alongside dry heat and a fist full of anger. Flames and devastation sweep the coarse halls of the monsters mind. With patience lost, there remains one path... murder. Nor the cruel or diligent claim these savage images their own, that undoing belongs to the sun, the moon and beyond.

Red Road

The jungle was noisy. Humid. Life thrived… and so did Inti. With the passing of years and the coming of age, our Elder exchanged the knowledge of life… and the history of it.

With this came investigation into the nature of things, bringing forth events that ripple throughout the lives of many.

The history of our moon has been passed down as an oral tradition from ancient lands. Having roots in Africa, the village and the tribe shall go unnamed for there is no translation. The story is fairly simple yet spins a web of cause and effect.

"Long ago in the time where speech was flourishing and writing was an understanding beyond many, laid a civilization that spoke with the stars. Mostly these people listened while there observations taught them the rhythms and cycles of the cosmos.

Eventually one man and his ambition for truth decided to send a message. Of course this was done in fire circles of many with ritualistic chanting on the equinoxes and solstices, however there was no answer. Time kept on spinning. But it was not without notice.

Legend foretells of an unknown traveler in the sky with a peculiar orbit, as it had none. It was heading straight for Earth and the people knew this. Twenty-nine months pass with the object becoming increasingly bigger, and then it stopped. So the moon was revealed with its milky surface reflecting the sun. It never spun around like Earth or other planets. It remained fixed on one side, forever showering its tides, crescent-to-crescent, full to new moon.

The seas roared, whales and dolphins screamed… the planet reacted with violent force. Eventually the seas died down, only getting stressed when moon is fullest. This was seen as a sign in the eyes of many, but what kind of sign?

People started idolizing the moon, worshiping its phases and cycles. Thus an entire age was thrown away from the sun and into a reflection of it. The moon brought with it a type of heightened receptivity. So the occult and secret societies were born for the good and the bad.

The moon casted a shadow of light towards the astrologers; they no longer saw the night as it once was. Blinded by this new object began the process of generations living without seeing what their forefathers had seen. The way was lost... the world had changed.

Females became affected most noticeably. Moon cycles brought troubles with absorbing blood. Those kinds of practices had been lost with the heaviness of procrastination and leisure. The moon had many avenues of persuasion.

Men also became affected but in a much more internal way. Closed and cut off from emotions they became, just the polar opposite from the outwardly expressive females.

So began argument and war overriding reason and logic. Fear spread as the selfish used what they knew to gain what they could. Thus rose sages and wizards of folklore to polarize the dark magic that foolish men had thought they mastered.

King Arthur and the Knights of the Round Table was just one story that surfaced in the ever-changing battle between light and dark. So the world divides itself and pushes further from source. But there is always a slingshot effect, for all paths lead to the one way.

Soon came the naming and individualizing of energy and events. Spirituality, religion, science, consumerism, capitalism, all brought forth to be enhanced and suppressed by the moon. Of course this is a certain point of view, however the origin remains the same. The moon is beyond this solar system. I tell you this Inti because one day you too will have to tell this story."

The young man was now eighteen and had matured much. Inti's questions were not as impulsive or emotionally attached like before.

"When I feel the moon, it tells me that it too has felt suppression, only to be forced to shine this upon our world. If I am to assume correctly, then it would appear some one was controlling the moon!"

"You would be more correct than not in this assumption Inti. It is a channel that is being broadcasted... hijacking our minds."

"Then the question remains, who and why?"

"This my brother leads us to another story that I have not spoke about for some time," our Shaman expresses.

"You would do me an honor brother by telling such a story... I feel it is leading me down a path I must understand."

"And what path is this Inti?"

"A path to help change that which binds us!"

The story was told in parts, after supper, for a few hours. Conditions had to be just right. It's not an easy story to be told. The weight of the words alone can burden a mind.

At the time of this story our Elder was young, still adhering to what his guru asked of him. It was some time in the early nineteen-forties when Veena and our Shaman became friends. Veena was far older yet time weaved a brotherhood that stood beyond physical conditionings.

Veena talked with Hanuman behind closed doors. Pressing matters fell upon the Sage. Finally Hanuman walked out, looked towards the young Shaman saying, "Pack your bags. We leave for America."

"Is Veena coming?"

"He has already left and is contacting the others."

"Who else is coming?"

"A gathering is happening of all orders."

"Why?"

"To answer a call that should have never taken place."

What did Hanuman mean by this? Well, just as men long ago tried to call towards the stars, so did men of our civilization... and they got a response. It was called Project Sigma and was spoken about only to those who needed to know.

A meeting was to take place. When the United States received a message back from the stars, they called out to the nations of the world to send representatives in every branch of humanity to establish a fundamental means of interaction and procedures.

Hanuman was not pleased with the way things felt. It was rushed, urgent and held some type of presence that overwhelmed the bodymind. Two weeks later Hanuman and our young Shaman found themselves among eight hundred or so fellow humanitarians, anthropologists, scientists, and philanthropists arguing about what to do and how. When it came for Hanuman to speak, he spoke with force.

"Let it be known, that this night holds with it the opportunity for change. What direction shall a select few choose that the majority will be forced to follow? Are we willing to accept that life outside this planet is just like our own, that with this leap brings with it uncertainty and dare I say... death! Are we prepared to shake the foundations our civilizations are built upon?

There is something very alarming about those who wish to meet in private. What are their motives, why did we send a message and will ambition weigh more than wisdom.

I have been summoned here today for my opinion, so I will keep it simple. We must treat this with the utmost respect and caution. Any mistake on our part will lead towards separation. Mindfulness above all else! We have no idea what these beings are capable of. We have no idea what we are capable of.

I do not mean to strike fear into the hearts of those listening. I only mean to reveal the nature of the situation. With this I send hope and courage to do what is right for the world at large. Thank you."

People began to clap... speak... then argue. Those who agreed and disagreed both shared their input. Among those who disagreed strongest was Kaiden Rothschild. Few knew Kaiden's intentions... among these few were Hanuman.

Childhood friends, apprentices to the same teacher, they were more than brothers... they were bonded by blood and bone. Kaiden had reasonable points, but played the card that few knew how to play... inspiration. His words fell upon many, driving people from the present to future visions of the world in a greater sense. It would be the end of war... of disease... a step closer to God... the Christ consciousness. All in the hopes that technology would drive us further into a better life.

Hanuman of course knew Kaiden's intentions just by reading his aura, being clouded in emotion. Unclear was the future of Kaiden, and by the looks of it so the rest of the world.

That night Kaiden had capitalized on the hopes of others in an attempt to negotiate a trade. This was alarming. Trading with intergalactic beings was not a regular field one gains much knowledge in. With the passing of time came the future in present form... And the trade was simple.

The Greys or EBE (extraterrestrial biological entity) had met at an air force base just eight days after the gathering of cultures. Sixteen humans would leave while sixteen Greys would stay on Earth. These sixteen were known as the first ambassadors of Earth. There was a handing down of technology and knowledge in the specified fields of time travel, quantum mechanics and weaponry. In exchange for this all the Greys wanted was to study humans and animals. Certain abductions would take place and a list would be given on such individuals.

The American government and its allies sold the people of Earth for technology and knowledge. This broke the heart of the Elementals. Our Sages and young Elder stayed at the base for many months, interacting with the

Greys. Hanuman and Veena were well diverse in telepathy, and the Greys being telepaths, communication was easiest when they had time alone.

The first Grey to give clear their name was Azual. Veena and Hanuman showed the most compassion and integrity among the translators so Azual opened up in an attempt to reveal true motives.

The story Azual painted was one all too familiar to the intuition of our Sages. Azual's race came from the Orion constellation. The constellation was a type two planetary civilization, meaning its reach covered all the stars and planets within the star constellation.

The Grey race began cloning the perfect body in their ideal vision for the Divine vehicle and immortality. Along this process they became copies of each other, losing the very essence that made them unique in the first place. They began to devolve.

More of a synthetic robot than anything else, the Greys became fearful of their own demise. They began searching through the cosmos for beings with genetic structures undamaged and ready for extraction. Humanity being a hybrid of the same genetic stock, the Greys valued our DNA, among other agendas.

A civil war had begun in the colonies of Orion. The rebellion was against what the IKAR or government was doing to other races. The Greys are one of the few races that can come down to such a biodiverse ecological environment and stay for an extended period of time. Most species out in the cosmos view our Earth as a precious gem, yet highly hazardous... that being said, there were also other factors beneath the surface holding persuasion and influence over the Greys' arrival.

Most of the Greys were taking orders from another race much darker and powerful. When asked about this other race, Azual became a bit tense, looking around like being watched or listened upon. All Azual replied was,

"They prefer to be called Alpha Draconians and it's better to never cross paths with one."

This was most curious in the eyes of our Sages. They glance towards one another. It was the nineteenth sitting with Azual when the alarms started to ring. Tapped in, Veena, Hanuman and Azual instantly knew that fighting was taking place with the Greys and Kaiden.

There was blood. There was agony. There was death all around. Guards rushed in, leaping towards Azual. Within a flash Azual vanished into thin air. Teleportation was based on light and electromagnetic energy fields. Veena and Hanuman rushed outside to catch up with Azual. He might have been a teleporter, but it was much easier to outrun a telepath than to hide from one.

Eighty-seven humans died, along with five Greys. There stood Veena with Hanuman across smoke and fire where Azual and the other Greys stood their ground.

Kaiden came up behind the Sages in a rage of fury. His face was covered in blood and ash from burnt chemicals of an exploded bunker. Kaiden's voice grew louder. Veena instantly tapped into his mind, seeing what had happened.

"Get out of my head Veena!"

"Kaiden, I can help you."

"Then help me," Kaiden says, revealing Desert Eagle in hand.

Four Greys teleport around Kaiden instantly as the Eagle tasted flesh and bone. The extraterrestrials underestimated the will of men. Kaiden had anticipated the movement of two Greys, fluidly stepping side to side, dodging the Greys' two strikes. Kaiden's offense was his defense. His defense was his offense. Azual appeared, breaking the battle apart. The Greys' voice screamed a high pitch, bringing all to the ground except Veena.

Veena was master of sound and therefore was not governed by it. This showed Veena as equal in Azual's eyes. Being able to withstand such a pitch requires the greatest degree in control of one's senses.

Kaiden threw a bullet towards Azual… STRIKE! Straight through the chest, a little to the right, the hole dripped black blood upon red soil. Our young Shaman screams, rushing towards Kaiden from the shadows. Picking up a 9mm pistol from an officer gasping for life, a young boy becomes a man as trigger meets metal, sending three bullets into chest… a little to the right… red blood dripped upon burnt soil.

Kaiden was stunned, as was Veena and Hanuman. The Greys instantly pulled the bullet out of Azual while healing hands glowed white light in the repairing of tissue… there was much more than meets the eye with these creatures.

Kaiden ran towards our Shaman with a look of vengeance, but was stopped just as quickly with a rush of wind knocking him down. Hanuman's skill in the empty force was strong to say the least.

Tanks, jeeps and four hundred armed personnel surround the three Greys and our fellow Elementals. Aim; locked on target, fire was taken. And within a blink of an eye, Azual and his kind vanished.

The guns fired. Two bullets struck Hanuman in the back with one hitting the leg of Veena. With a flash of light appears another Grey, grabbing the two Sages and our young Shaman. Space-time becomes separated and stretched into stillness… teleportation is one spectacular experience.

Veena, Hanuman, Azual, the two Greys and our Shaman now found themselves in a safe haven; they now resided in the space of Mulu. Still weak himself, Azual rushed towards the wounded, beginning to heal Hanuman.

Azual's wound was beginning to show again. The life stream from one being transferred to another, Hanuman's wounds quickly healed. Azual began to have trouble standing, eventually falling to the ground.

The other Greys were far too weak to heal another so quickly. It seems even spiritual powers have their limits. The Greys' skin was like a horse without hair. They derived somewhat from plants, with photosynthesis being their best friend. Luck it seems was not in their favor. The sun being far from sight left little ability in recharging and healing.

A leg wound was far from Veena's worries. Limping and circling the dying extraterrestrial, all communication was of the mind and our young Shaman was far from translation of such a subtle language. However in the eyes of our Sages, the conversation was as so…

"Azual, you risked your life to save mine. I owe you my breath, yet am unable to give you yours."
"Think it not as saving or losing… only preserving life."

And like that, physicality was lost with a final gasp into the afterlife. A fairly simple conversation yet holds so much depth. They built a fire, sending the body into the torus field of our Earth. Azual now resided in the Bardo, the in-between that would see his reincarnation as human if chosen so.

"Everything happens for a reason," Hanuman explains to the young Shaman.
"His soul will find the hall of our ancestors."

"There are still two survivors being held captive," a voice appears in the Sage's awareness… the other Greys.
"If we can be of help in any way possible…"

"This is not needed, you have sacrificed much. This is not your mission. We must leave now. Thank you for your sacrifice and understanding."

The Greys looked the three Earthlings in their pupils. Lowering heads while keeping eye contact, they vanished into darkness.

"You killed a man?" Inti replies with a stunned voice, returning back to the present moment.
"Yes and no!"
"Then Kaiden is still alive?"

"Your assumption is correct, however only a part of him is still alive. That night Kaiden fell ill, this much is known, however something else now walks this planet. His body was injected with nanotechnology, leaving a gateway for the hive mind complex known as Krill to enter."
"Krill! The one who killed Soka?"
"Correct."

"Why did you shoot him, I thought violence solves nothing!"

"I was young, emotional and did what I had to when the moment arose. I chose the lesser of two evils in my narrow perspective."

"Krill killed Soka to find you! That means he will come here!" Inti connects the dots.

"Krill has gone great lengths in keeping hidden from us, as we have from him. He is more machine now than man. Twisted by greed and power, his blood runs with the technology of beings from distant stars. He is a puppet."

"How can this be… the moon, the Greys, Draconians, why doesn't anybody know about this?"

"Because there is tremendous power in knowledge… and the secrecy of that knowledge. They have infiltrated the minds of the masses. Television, the news, music, symbols, thought spheres, it's just the beginning in an arsenal of methods used for control."

"I don't believe this…"

"It's not a matter of believing in it or not. It just is."

"It's just what?"

"Inti, try not to think in such ways of true or false. In time you will see for yourself what is real and what is fiction. All you need is a willing heart and no small amount of will."

"What are you trying to say?"

"I'm saying that a day will come when you must carve your own path. Make your own choices… you have learned much from me, yet you still have much to learn of the greater community we inhabit."

"You speak of inner knowledge and the thread that connects us?"

"Precisely," The Shaman says with a smile.

"So we are made of the light and the dark."

"Indeed we are."

In all cultures there are certain milestones that are recognized as tests or trials that turn men and women into the person they will become their entire lives!

Our story shifts towards the Elemental council. Inti had recognized his place as Fire, yet had not fully accepted the hardships and burdens that come with such title.

Inti, now a young man, pondered this for some time. The passing of seasons marked a new transition into the collective soul. Inti decided to blend the ego with the heart… not such an easy task as one might think. But with any task that is dealt with inside the body, so it is equally matched from the elements of the outer world.

Inti thought of Stella for some time. Hermes taught Inti the arts of astral travel, eventually visiting Stella in her dreams. It is not as farfetched as one might think.

Before you go to sleep, focus upon the third eye. Keep this focus laying in corpse pose and remain conscious. Of course there requires a specific diet, sleeping pattern, yogic practices such as Shambhavi Mudra, Rajakapotasana, Shirshasana and of course meditation if you really want to push the limits.

Once Brahmacharya (withholding of the sexual energies) was cultivated, Inti was able to become aware of his physical, vital, astral, and mind bodies. Eventually his Anandamayakosa (causal body) was realized for a moment.

The stages of sleep come fourfold. Jargut – the waking tired state, is the first recognized. Listening to our body this will easily be brought into awareness. The second was Svana, light sleep dream state; this is where Inti flourished and became stuck in the so-called "astral trekking" experience. He found Stella, made love, played music, bounced together in a haze of infatuation… he even protected Stella from a few astral vampires.

In time Inti found Hermes within the astral and began the intense training into the third stage of sleep… Shashupti. Now this R.E.M. dream sleep is beyond any normal dream. It's knocking at the doorstep of the fourth stage, Turiya.

Inti was far too young to push his way into Turiya on a mere conscious level, however he boarded the Turiya train every night, as we all do. It is the deepest state, going beyond what we call duality. It is a state of Samsara. Sublime at its finest.

O yes, we all go into a state of complete nirvana every night, recharge our battery and wake up refreshed, anew to live another day. Breathe another breath. Love another lover. The highest form of self-realization is with us every night. This comforted Inti yet filled his glass just a bit more.

Diving into these realms had its influences to say the least. The young man was creating karma. Something that had not been fully comprehended until words fell from mouth upon listening ears. However this time the lesson was equally shared. The Shaman had taught Inti more than realized.

"Whenever an idea becomes so widespread within the world's consciousness, the original meaning changes. The more an idea gains acceptance, the more distant from its original intent it becomes. Such is the case of karma, which is not only an idea, concept or thought but rather a cosmic law.

As more people accept the fact that this law exists, there is greater tendency for the law itself to become twisted as each person interprets it through their own level of understanding. Thousands of people have tremendous arrays of answers to what karma is."

Inti picks up where our Shaman pauses.

"In order to clearly understand what karma is, we must trace its meaning from basic sources and synthesize these into the most meaningful brew of what actually is the essence of this universal law. As Buddha taught, you are what you think, having become what you thought; mankind is always trying to question what we are. The fact is from moment to moment, what we are changes."

"Very much so Inti, it is in these changes that make us wonder if there is anything constant about us at all. We are what we think and the moment we stop thinking is the moment we are no longer a product of that thought. Thus a fundamental principle in karma is based in thought."

Inti pushes forward with more conversation.

"Now if karma is based on the effects of what we think in the past, then in order to overcome outmoded thought patterns an individual must consider the effects he has caused in other people's lives by trying to impress his own past thoughts upon others. Because of this it is mathematically impossible for any individual to rise above their karma until every other individual whose life they have touched has risen above their own karma."

"Unique insight Inti. As Newton's laws of physics puts it, for every action there must be an equal and opposite reaction. Everything is in relation to everything else. We are the doer and the creator of our life. We are receptive and susceptible to the effects of all we have created. Now half of the time we are an actor, the other half a reactor... Still, we are very much a part of cause and effect."

The Elder continues onward with further education.

"When this happens, we are truly meeting self. I am referring to a mirror through which individuals use their life experiences to see themselves. The best way to know what being human is all about is to look at the way we look at our self. Although this is not our absolute reality it is a powerful enough reflection of our current reality for us to believe that it is all that exists."

"So man constantly seeks to see himself through the eyes of others!" Inti inquires.

"Interestingly enough, the more we do this, the less we are truly our self. But through habits of generations it seems to be the most natural way for mankind to learn.

Even in the most normal, mundane, everyday conversations people have with each other, it is so easy to notice how individuals are almost always talking to themselves while giving the appearance of talking to another. There is always this outward verbal conversation accompanied by the inner conversation one is having with oneself at the same time. The mind constantly questions what the other individual is giving to them or taking from them, what they themselves are giving or taking, and how much approval they are receiving for their efforts. If an individual operates in this manner then how difficult is it to know his karma?"

Inti pauses… beginning to speak at the pace of the Elder's intuitive flow.

"It is based on the fact that within each individual there are actions and reactions. Only when the two balance out will a person be able to come together in the center of their being. Only then do we truly meet ourselves. The mystery of the great pyramid is one of the oldest and most mystical known to man. The triangle having two points at the bottom and one at top reflects man having two legs with a single mind. If man is to be unified, he must rule the coordination of both.

In all the teachings of yoga there is always a reference made to recognize man in his lower self, divided by the yin and yang influences. Only through learning and training does he develop the third part of himself, the top of the triangle, which looks at the other two identities created through cosmic viewpoint."

Inti kept talking while our Shaman listened.

"The impersonal I, would be the top of the pyramid. It is only though the development of this impersonal I, in its oneness of mind, that man is able to finally know himself. And from this knowing eventually comes fullness, which is actually accepting oneself! This point at the top of the triangle cannot exist alone, it is the outpouring in years of struggle between the two opposing triangle points."

Inti's passion ignited standing proud and tall in a rush of energy. Lips spilled wisdom upon a brother in awe.

"As long as an individual preoccupies the mind with the problems of duality, they live in an oppressed consciousness. The world is not allowing them to be all that they feel they can be. As people keep switching identifications from this to that, they seek to find blame in all that oppose what they believe to be the path of fulfilling desire. They may blame their childhood, religion, sex, teachers, jobs, friends or society in which they live in, ironically keeping themselves within the restrictions of which they believe are the causes of the conflict. What they do not realize is that by viewing things this way, they are doing all they can to violate the basic principles within the law of karma."

Inti's emotions gathered in the breeze, turning distant leaves into passing travelers.

"It is at this point that we can begin to understand the real meaning of karma. The only thing truly in common with all of the events, circumstances and people in our life is ourselves."

The wind calmed. Leaves settled. The elements responded to the truth spoken. Brothers lowered heads. Inti now comprehended the hardship of being human. He understood what being an Elemental was all about. Our Shaman revealed flute, playing soothing songs with the majestic sunset.

Moves like the wind.
As warm as fire.
Hard as stone.
As emotional as water.

Drives you from
Point A to Z.
If you searched the world
You would not find me.

Its depths beyond
The infinite abyss.
Its actions evolve
From kindness to a fist.

Its reasons have
No logic that's sound.
The essence of action
Is where I am found.

The Elder's song lasted all night, the riddle only a moment as dawn steadily approached. The riddle was somewhat of a test; at least Inti saw it this way.

"Passion… the answer is passion!" Inti answers.

"You have achieved much brother. There is little I can offer you now!"

Chills vibrate down the spine. Again and again explosions go off in the distance. The rising sun was a red one. Blood had been spilt. Hermes comes in with a flash of wind, a speedy abrupt entrance to say the least. He brought with him news of various arrays.

"Hermes!"

"It's Krill. He is looking for you. Blackwater has a team of twelve ravaging through the villages."

Our Elder takes a moment and contemplates chess moves upon battle.

"What villages have they hit?" Inti asks, fearing his own was under siege.

"I have spread word to those aware that it is not safe. I am not sure about your mother Inti. What is your course of action? Krill is drawing near."

Attention shifts towards our Shaman. Krill was after him; therefore choice on his fate would be his own. Inti and Hermes knew this and were to help in any way possible.

"Hermes, tell Veena to make preparations."

Our messenger lowers head in respect.

"Hermes, where is Stella?" Inti asks.

"Last I saw she was with her father, a quarter days walk from Mulu."

This being said, there was no choice in the matter. They had to make way towards Mulu. A Shaman is no soldier and must pick his battles carefully when presented with such choice.

Our Elder did believe in protecting innocence from harm's way though. A non-violent approach required specific skill. Clever is the Elemental when forced into hostile situations, for they value life, not the absence of it.

With the power of Ajna, the third eye, our Shaman had the ability to manifest what his ego willed. Imagination into visualization upon realization of creation brought in manifestation.

Everything that's projected takes time to make reality. The Elder knows what to expect because it is all planned out. As his torus field becomes enlarged, our humble Shaman's imagination projects outward, becoming the village's reality. Blackwater mercenaries find themselves stopped by a young child no older than twelve, now caught within an illusion.

"How many times must I tell you beasts, this is not the time for madness," the small Indian boy rests basket on ground, while the men stop in their tracks.

"Would you like to see my magic trick?"

The mercenaries act accordingly with a gesture and words.

"Move aside boy, this is no place for kids. Go find your parents and leave."

"But you haven't seen my trick yet," the kid sarcastically responds, taking the lid off the hand woven basket. There inside lay rope galore. The child pulls it upward forever more.

Up up it goes the boy's rope continually grows. Higher and higher, the men with guns become a bit quieter. Amazed and consumed with a chill, the rope hangs from nothing… drifting it is still.

"What magic has this boy conceived… what power this is indeed."

All the soldiers take a step back; the leader one forward for his focus was intact.
"Show me more young child."

The boy laughs with a smile, running up the rope for what seemed a mile. The men insisted on leaving, some ran through the village screaming and weaving… through the huts then the trees until the mind races up to these impossible scenes.

The leader climbs up, then the boy falls with some luck. The leader's confidence was struck; the kid's leg a stick, the man's face a puck. The brute was in rage, pulling pistol from leather bound cage.

"I am sorry about that sir, but this is what you deserve. Now please leave while there's still time, no more violence or stepping out of line."

A screaming father comes from the streets, "O God don't shoot," these words he pleads.

"Your son has gone too far. Punishment is in order, one that burns flesh into scar."

The father yelled and roared, "You foolish kid, I will train you no more." Out came the sword, severing young spinal cord.
The rest of the men stand back, the leader still in his tracks.

"My God old man, you're most savage with sword in hand. This child was to be punished, not sent to hell."

"It's fine, don't worry. I will show you and I will tell. This kid is no kid, just a part of a spell."

The father takes his son's head and spins it back on tight, "TADA," our youngster says as his trick went just right. Villagers run… Mercenaries… there were none. All that stood left was a leader and his gun.

"What trouble you have begun, this day of our sun. If anger is what you keep then in blindness you are deep."

The boy, (a figment of our Shaman's imagination), stood in front of the leader. Broken in disbelief and stunned with miscalculations, a small hand blessed the man with a broken will. The solder saw life from the grace of God. All that was left was for the ego to judge.

Weapon falls from hand to dirt. The humble embrace of gratitude embellished his heart. Fears and desires all torn apart, with a new beginning and a fresh start.

Inti placed hand upon the Elder, giving energy and presence towards our mentally exhausted Shaman. It was a most extraordinary sight, watching mercenaries react to nothing, leaving the leader with opened eyes finding nobody in sight. Leave it to an Elder to turn hostile situations into lessons.

"We must make way to Mulu. I fear the worst has happened. They must not go any farther."

Inti pauses. Patience was a must in order to guarantee a solid mind.

"I will follow you brother… although I feel it is a trap."

"Of course it's a trap, but we have the element of surprise and the jungle as our ally… and a powerful ally this is!"

The brothers begin to run. So fast they are, like the wind they glide. Our Elder pulls flute from back. Holding one note the entire time, he gathers what beasts are able to meet. Music, the Shaman's most powerful tool, held value among most. Inti watched the jungle run with them!

"Can you use your mind trick again?"

"The Indian rope trick will not help us now. Sprung is the trap when we entered the village."

"So we are just going to walk up and do what exactly?"

"We must keep peace at all costs. This is not your fight Inti, this is my undoing... please save who you can from harm's way. Krill can be quite dangerous."
"Then who's going to save you?"

They continue to run. Black panther appears by Inti's side. A flash of webs filled the brother's eyes as intuition told the spider kingdom heard the call. Birds flew above with locusts echoing in the background. Trees moved with critters of many kinds, snakes, monkeys, and our two brothers of solid minds.

"Any chance of you teaching me that rope trick before we head in here with no plan."

"No plan you say... this outcome lays with our intentions and emotion, only then will solutions present themselves. Open we shall be in order to see clearly."
"...And the rope trick?"
"...Another life perhaps."

Kundalini rises with their feet moving the air beneath them. They arrived to Mulu half past midday. There stood James and Stella just about to leave with briefcase in hand and an ancestral tree robbed of its genetic knowledge.

"Stella..."
"Inti..."

The two run towards each other in hugging embrace with a kiss.

"It's not safe, why are you here?" Inti whole-heartedly asks.

Stella says nothing, remaining in warm arms growing tighter by the moment.

"James... You may not leave without giving back what you stole!" our Elder speaks.

"I do not need your permission to take that which is Earth."

James snaps back with aggression and protection, all a part of a father torn apart by loss of love, being replaced with vicious ambition.

"These plants could hold the elixir to life. Cure every illness. Cure death! Who are you to stop such a cause?"

"Everything is meant to pass. Destruction is a natural part of life. To hold someone within this body forever would be a prison. Widen your vision James!"

"Then why do you protect those you love? Why do you try to save them?"

"I preserve life as long as nature intends it to be, not by the selfish conquest of others. To aim for a cause that does not condone reentering the life stream is a vision for the blind."

"Your words fall short of impact. I have made my choice. What I'm doing is no more wrong than what you're doing. This knowledge is power and it is to be used for the world."

"I do not disagree with you on that James, only about whose hands it falls into."

A slow sinister laugh begins to creep from above. Wicked. Sinful. Our Elder knew this laugh... KRILL!

Dark clouds begin to form; the sky reacted to the cruelty of a man turned servant to darkness. Feet to head Krill floats down from the trees like a feather.

Krill's form outlined a skinny tall structure. Much like the tall Greys. The nanotechnology had morphed his body for agility and strength with photosynthesis as regeneration. Krill's albino skin bounced glowing red eyes with yellow scars running across the iris. The beast's armor was a black leathery exoskeleton, changing with the environment and fighting conditions.

James walks towards the beast, bowing head to dirt. In this moment everything was revealed. James stood behind Krill, commanding Stella to follow.

"You and I have unfinished business!"

"Krill... Stop this," Our Shaman replies.

Krill reveals Japanese steel, attacking the Earth Elemental without haste. So fast Krill moves, with purpose and power he strikes, but misses to the intuitive reflexes of our Elder. Again and again the two danced an elegant show of self-preservation and fury. Our Shaman knew his role.

Inti ran towards James, so James ran into the jungle. Stella followed quickly behind.

"I must admit you're pretty fast for an old man!"

"Hanuman would be disappointed in you Krill, seeking to oppress others rather than freeing them."

"Hanuman chose his path... and I shall send you to meet him in the afterlife!"

Anger sweeps the tyrant. Another round in moving the empty force was used to deflect every attack that drew from blade. A defensive offense was the Elder's game. Counterattacks here and there began to emerge. Their fighting expanded, destroying trees while bouncing off them. Krill received faithful cut towards our Shaman's upper ribcage.

The panther lunged from the trees in a surprise attack to Krill. The black claws rip flesh from face. The jaws lock onto Krill's shoulder. More laughter consumed the tyrant as he throws the black beast off.

"I underestimated you... there is still some fight left!"

Round three begins with Elder and panther facing off against the darkness. Krill's speed increased, bouncing off trees, flipping gravity up on itself. The sword was a new prototype. Electricity surged through our villain's energetical veins from the blade. Eyes widen as the harmful dance continues. With every missed strike, more rage rose in Krill.

Meanwhile Inti had caught up to James and tackled him to the ground. Wrestling one another, Stella jumped in between the two with intentions of peace, yet only found war. James reveals gun. Inti freezes to a trigger between the eyes.

"Not so tough now are you kid," James says with a loss of breath.

The panther lunged at Krill only to find steel striking through the jugular. Our Shaman screams in sadness.

"Finally you show some emotion... I want you to beg for mercy before you die!"

Round four begins. It never ends. Krill had already healed from the panther's slash to the face and shoulder. The empty force rushes the Elder. Wind blew furiously. Rain fell from observant sky to brutal battle in hopes of a cleansing release.

Like a record on repeat, so our Shaman spins Krill around. Nothing stood in his way of revenge. Our Elder quickly found himself in a troublesome situation.

Krill raised blade up high, lightning strikes from sword and flesh. Krill unleashes kinetic energy towards the Elder in a magical display of power and physics gone mad.

Strike two, Elder falls to his knees. His breath became heavy and deep. Stillness overcomes the Shaman. Krill ran for fatal kill, however an Elemental is not that easily disposed of. When Japanese Steel pushed straight for the chest, our Elder stops death with a flat palm grip of both hands around blade.

Blood leaked from flesh to dirt. Razor force gleamed its pointing tip towards certain fate. Our Elemental's body soaked in the electricity of the hybrid blade. Kinetic energy built up until finally a blast was released, leaving shockwaves dense enough to clear rain for a moment's time.

The two flew back instantly. Our Elder hit Mulu while Krill was sent off into the jungle. Water continued to fall hard. The flute is revealed. This time it was not played in songs or riddles... this grandfather flute held much more strength than meets the eye.

Inti's eyes on the other hand still found a gun pointing to his skull. When the blast from the battle with Krill echoed throughout the jungle, attention was broken and opportunity presented itself. Inti took the offensive like a flame ignited. Feet kicked gun from hand, fist to the throat came with speed. They exchanged blows, clip for clip, pound for pound. Stella grabbed the 9mm with nervous wits and a nervous hum.

In the heat of the moment the two men flew towards Stella. Her fear turned tense… trigger was pulled. Everything happens so fast. In one moment it was this, and in the next it will be that. Inti's intuition instinctively turned James around to receive bullet in upper spine, just a little to the left. Stella screams, dropping everything in a rush towards her father. Inti was speechless.

Round Five! Krill comes flying in from the brush towards prepared Elder. The flute provided some protection against the thrusting blade. So they raged on in a display of power and quickness, bouncing off one another. They danced this dance for a moment's time.

They were as two electrons around such nucleus of a ravage nature. The third strike came with a breaking of the Elder's flute. Japanese steal struck the chest. Down our Earth Elemental went with blood and bone hitting mud and rain.

Inti felt this. His heart burned. Stella's shouted at Inti with hatred and sadness. He grabbed the gun and briefcase. These last moments with father was best spent in solitude. Inti left with tears of a broken heart. Stella sat in a world torn apart.

Inti ran urgently, coming towards our now dying Shaman laying face down. Krill soaked in every moment. Victory was at last his. Inti fell into shock. Disbelief. Krill turned around with a grin. Inti raised the gun with anger.
"I'll be needing that briefcase now…"
"Can't do that," Inti quickly responds.

Krill's laugh brought terror… only igniting the flames within. Bullets flew like rapid streams of light. Japanese Steel caught every one of them with Krill pushing out his blue-hued sword of magnetic electricity. Bullets stuck to the blade… eventually falling to Earth.

Inti again fell speechless. This was a match he could not win. Beaten so quickly yet luck always remains, he could still make it out of this with his life. With deep regret and a sigh, the case was thrown towards Krill. The grin never left the face of our villain.

Krill put away his blade, grabbed the briefcase, choking Inti in the process. Krill stared into the eyes of the young man, looking through the images recorded. The dark incubus was searching for something.

The Fire Elemental was far too young to do anything. His feet dangled off the ground while hands desperately tried to free the death grip.

"When vengeance has overtaken you... I will be waiting!"

Our Villain throws Inti so fast against Mulu, the wind was knocked right out of his chest. And with that, Krill walked off, vanishing into the trees where he eventually came across James and Stella. Still crying over her father's last moments, Krill took the hands of Stella, now in a haze of anger.

"Don't let your father die in vain. Continue his work by my side!"

Grey clouds begin to clear. The vision fades in our Elder. Inti sits in morning of his brother. With the rain having stopped, Veena appeared out of thin air with Hermes and four monkeys carrying wood. They land into the mud, with the Rudra Vinya case following closely behind.

When Hermes was asked to tell Veena about preparations... he was talking about death. How could Inti be so blind? This was always meant to be. Inti locked eyes with his brother as last words were spoken.

> I know I'm here,
> And then I go.
> That's all I see.
> That's all I know.

The breath fades. The soul detaches. Veena reveals instrument for performance. The monkeys threw the wood towards Inti while a proper fire was constructed. Spiders all shapes and sizes came from everywhere, spinning gateways into the multi-dimensional afterlife.

"Why did Krill want to kill our brother so badly? Krill isn't dead. Why take a life that hasn't robbed you of your own?" Inti thinks out loud.

"Krill wanted revenge because anger and fear must latch onto something. It is the hive mind that works towards service to self."

Ambiance of the jungle set in heavy. Mourning is a delicate process.

"Krill won't be too happy when he opens that case," Inti says, wiping tears from his eyes.
"Why do you say this?" Veena leans closer.

"I knew Krill could read minds, so I hid three plant samples in various places and kept the last one. I couldn't let Mulu be robbed of his ancestry."

"How did you mask this when Krill pealed into your mind?"

"Well I didn't look at myself when I hid them, I just looked up in the trees. He seemed to be a two dimensional thinker, so I improvised."

"How did you know Krill reads minds from images they record?"

"Luck I guess. I didn't know what to do and there was so little time so I just acted."

"You are wiser than you give yourself credit for Inti. You know the strength of your own mind and trust this strength. But be aware, Krill is only trying to manipulate you by leaving you here."

Hermes comes into the conversation with a bit unfortunate news.

"Given the talk about Krill, it brings me great regret to inform you… that your mother was caught in the fire at your village. I'm afraid it was Krill."
"What do you mean caught?"
"I mean she has passed away."

The Fire Elemental's heart raged. Screams echoed through the jungle. Tears gushed from eyes. Fists tightened. The body's temperature heightens with steam rising from back and head. The taste of revenge overpowered emotions, but Inti was no fool. Now was not the time for such things. The young Elemental needed training if revenge is to come and pass.

Veena assures Inti everything will be ok. His mother's soul would find the halls of everlasting contentment alongside our Shaman.

"Inti please listen to me, revenge will not bring you peace. This is something our brother wished to express yet could not simply tell you in words. If you have revenge in your heart, Krill will have control over you. This is your path… you must choose alone."

Inti remained quiet for many hours, watching ash drift into the night. He had lost much this day. Mother. Lover. Brother. His world shattered.

"One stage of your journey has ended… and another has begun. The body will burn, float to the atmosphere above then fall upon soil. Seeds will sprout then fruit will bare life as it is eaten. The cycle always continues.

The individual particles that leave our Earth Elder will one day return to a loving mother who will grant child onto this Earth. This is why we burn him now, so he may have a fast cycle of rebirth. This is why I bring instrument in hand, to play the song of the quickening."
"The quickening?" Inti asks.

"Yes, it is a vibration that is earned through karmic debt of selfless deeds to others. It guarantees all souls traveling throughout the great illusion that time spent in spiritual pursuits will once again find the knowing memory of the present incarnation. It is a constant continuity in life, I am simply assisting in speeding things up a bit."

"So the universe then becomes a place where one can contribute towards intent. As we give to this reservoir of knowledge that is serving us, that nourishes us, it provides a direction we may choose to follow."

"You have realized much Inti. There is a presence with you that is unseen. We all have a greater plan. We cannot understand it. We can only participate within it. All beings living in separation have a choice whether to continue to live in separation or begin a pathway of return."

"So this must be your theology for life in the universe," Inti simply states.

"Correct. It is applicable to the larger scheme of things beyond our imagination and speaks to the intimate part of our existence. It is a theology that brings clarity and unity of purpose. We begin to serve with all beings guided by knowledge… how to express and understand this knowledge is your next step along the path."

"What must I do know?"

"You will learn to discern the difference between knowledge and the manifestations of the mind. You will be able to see this clearly. It will make all the difference in how you view yourself and those around you in an emerging world."

"Discern in an emerging world? You ask a hard task Veena."

"You must learn to look without preference. The more you value your strength and identify with it, the more you will build confidence in the face of uncertainty. At a deeper level you are beginning to understand that you were sent here on a mission, and nothing will satisfy that mission except the mission itself."

"Veena, brother… how will I know where to go, who to meet, how to respond to life and its great waves of change? How will I keep myself from losing heart or giving up?"

"You will have to leave part of your life open and mysterious. The sense of authority in your life must be established beyond your personality and ideas. It is like climbing a mountain; you must climb to gain perspective. If your service is pure, if it comes from love and compassion, then you give because you must give, not because you are assured of an outcome. This will guide you while you pay attention to the signs that are given. You are governing the mind instead of being governed by it, you see?"

"I am beginning to understand. Within the context of the world we are here to find out why we are alive. What our talents are. What the world needs from us. That which we are specifically equipped to provide."

"Indeed Inti! While the answer is within us, the calling is not. It is beyond us. It is out of this world. It is a great challenge to be awake while others still sleep. This is the time to see what others cannot see, to feel what others cannot feel and to do what others will not do. Your spirituality will be about feeding people, serving people and taking care of the world around you."

"So I guess the question is... what next?"

"We do not get to see the pathway and then decide to take the journey... you must take the journey in order to see where your path leads... follow your feet and you will know."

Veena sat on top of his case, the quickening was about to take place. Hermes sat in position forming a circle with Inti.

"The Red Road reveals itself as shamanic wound. The road connects dreamtime and waking life. The Vesica Piscis! These are the experiences that mold us... carving the path. Death is but transition on our journey."

"How long does it take for a soul to take form in another body?"

"Anywhere from eighty to three hundred Earth years incarnation usually occurs, all depends on their karma of course. However with this old soul... there are certain agreements. Time is very relative in nature."

"How do we recognize the other Elementals upon reincarnation?"

"By the name of their soul of course... how else do we distinguish one soul from another?"

Inti sadly chuckles while looking down. Again Inti laughs to himself like it was some kind of joke... life's final riddle.

"Why do you laugh?" Veena asks.

"I never knew our brother's real name. He said it was never a big deal when given so many."

"Yes, this does sound like something he would say."

Fingers pluck strings. The Rudra Vinya spills melodic tunes, paying homage to a fallen brother crossing the great bridge.

Take only pictures…
Steal only time…
Leave no footprints…

"In the days of his youth and the time that we shared… let him be remembered as MAHA!"

About the Author

Michael Bannister is an Astrologer who emphasizes the condition and quality of our experiences in life. Embracing the Hindu and Buddhist pathways, these teachings are synthesized with his approach in navigating the density that is consciousness.

Words from the Author

I hope this book helps connect the dots on how we can use astrology and mythology in our lives. It is a tremendous joy to share this perspective with all those who feel inspired by it.

If you want to learn more, contact me for a free consultation and reading, just mention my book and let me know what you think. Lets explore more on how to use the filters of astrology for self-transformation. From health, career, relationships, personal traumas to addictive habits, there is a way to gain insight and higher understanding in all of life's unfoldment.

Nativeeyesastrology.wordpress.com

Twitter.com/lastmanhattan88

Facebook.com/EdibleJazzMysticalJunkie

Edible Jazz Playlist

"Road To Zion"- Damien Marley
"Eternity"- Titan
"Euphoria"- Monty
"Haiti"- Arcade Fire
"Summertime Sadness"- Lana Del Rey
"Los Angeles Daze"- People Under The Stairs
"Acid Raindrops"- People Under The Stairs
"Soul"- Asheru
"Revolution"- Asheru
"Rolling in the Deep"- ADELE
"Knocked Up"- Lykke Li
"Dig"- Incubus
"Closer"- Kings of Leon
"Razorblade Kiss"- HIM
"Parachutes"- Coldplay
"Sparks"- Coldplay
"Love Music"- Jay Scarlett
"Animal"- Miike Snow
"Shiva Moon" [Moon Nectar Remix]- Prem Joshua
"Butterfly" (Bass Flo Remix)- Talvin Singh
"As the Rush Comes" (Gabriel Chillout Mix)- Motorcycle
"When The Levee Breaks"- Led Zeppelin
"No Quarter"- Led Zeppelin
"Come"- Buckethead
"Hayling"- FC Kahuna
"Spark"- Nitin Sawhney
"Building Steam With a Grain of Salt"- DJ Shadow
"Faultered Ego"- On! Air! Library!
"All These Things That I've Done"- The Killers
"Outro"- M83